Say My Name

ANGIE DANIELS

--THE DECADENT DELIGHT SERIES –

ISBN-13: 978-0615536798

For questions and comments about the book please contact angie@angiedaniels.com.

Caramel Kisses Publishing
PO Box 1773
Chesterfield, VA 23832
www.caramelkissespublishing.com

Cover design by HotDamnDesigns.com

Say My Name

ANGIE DANIELS

--THE DECADENT DELIGHT SERIES –

I want to thank Elizabeth Simons for editing this project. You rock!

This book is dedicated to all of the people who
helped make this dream possible.
You know who you are.

ONE

"Would you like some company?"

Would I? Goodness! For a second there I thought tall, dark and chocolate would never ask.

"Yes, if you'd like," I said, trying to sound like it was no big deal, when in reality spending the evening together could possibly become the most important moment of my entire life.

Logan smiled and kissed my lips, sending goose bumps down my arms as I watched him climb out of his fully loaded Range Rover. I sat back against the butter soft seat and ran my tongue along my painted lips while my stomach bubbled with excitement. The evening was going better than I had imagined. We'd had dinner at my favorite Italian Bistro, followed by a horse-drawn carriage ride through the cobblestone streets of downtown St. Louis. For a first date, what more could a sistah have asked for?

I tried to remain calm, but I was already planning the next six months of our relationship, all the way up to the very moment Logan would drop down on one knee and confess his undying love for me while holding a beautiful five-carat platinum diamond ring in his hand.

Giggling, I waited for him to come around to the passenger side and open the door for me, the way a gentlemen should. Yes, indeed. Logan was definitely everything a woman wanted in a man—money, looks, and charm. Did I mention he had money?

Last month, in Forbes Magazine, his father's software corporation was reported to be worth more than eighty million dollars. Carson Cambridge's health hadn't been the best, which meant Logan, who served as CEO, was next in line. Naturally, behind every successful man was a beautiful wife, and that's where I would come in. Before I let Logan leave, I planned to show him everything I had to offer.

I don't know how long I sat there daydreaming before I was startled by a knock on the glass. I jumped, then looked through the window to see Logan standing outside my door.

"Why aren't you getting out?" he asked.

Is he for real? Biting my tongue, it took everything I had not to comment as I reached for the door handle and opened it. So much for being a gentleman. I climbed out and convinced myself it wasn't important, then swayed my hips provocatively up the sidewalk towards my deluxe condo, my shoes clicking with every step.

There was nothing like looking fabulous, and I knew it, with a five-hundred-dollar weave that hung loosely around my shoulders. I was showcasing all my sweet curves in a black silhouetting dress that stopped mid-thigh and dipped daringly between my large breasts. On my feet were strappy high-heeled come-fuck-me shoes.

I sashayed to the door, stuck my key in the lock, then stepped aside so Logan could enter first. The look in his eyes told me he was impressed with everything he saw, mainly me.

"You've got a nice place," he replied after a quick sweep of the spacious room. Gleaming wood floors, a large spacious room and expensive contemporary furnishings.

"Thank you. I can—" Before I could answer, Logan snaked an arm around my waist and pulled me to him. I let myself go slack, unresisting, and moaned when he brought his lips down over mine. *Oh, my.* He would have been a fabulous kisser if it hadn't been for his tongue that was licking me like he was part man, part puppy dog. And then there were his teeth.

If he bites my tongue with those sharp fangs, I swear I'll bite his ass. "You got me so hard I can't wait to be inside of you." Moaning, he cupped my ass and pulled me against his arousal. "I'm planning to give all of this to you."

Lucky me. What I wanted to asked was, *all of what?* Because it didn't feel like he had more than four inches to work with. Logan started rubbing and touching and I reminded myself of his wealth and the fabulous life we'd have together. Within minutes I felt my body heat up and I was turned on. Money does that to me. Or maybe it was because I hadn't had sex in almost three months. I'd been waiting, saving myself for the perfect man.

Ever since we'd met at a fundraiser a week ago, I'd had a feeling Logan was that perfect somebody. I couldn't wait to show him off at my sister's wedding next weekend. Jeanna was going to be so proud of me.

His hands reached for the buttons on the front of my dress, and I didn't object as he released one right after the other. My eyes were glued to his, staring deep into their chocolate depths. The fabric dropped onto my carpet and I quickly kicked the dress away, not caring where it ended up, then stepped back and propped a hand to my slim waist so he could see everything I had to offer.

The hunger in his eyes was unmistakable. "Christina … you're beautiful."

I grinned. Not that he was telling me something I didn't already know. What woman wouldn't be gorgeous standing in a red satin bra and matching low-ride panties with a pair of red Manolos on her feet?

I sauntered toward him and he pulled me into his arms and swept his tongue across my lips, leaving them sopping wet. "So beautiful," he murmured. He slid a hand up to my breast and cupped it a little too eagerly. "Play your cards right and you won't ever want for anything ever again."

That was the plan.

He brushed a thumb across one hardened nipple and smiled triumphantly when I gasped. "That's it, baby. Give yourself to me." He massaged my breast slowly. "You want me?"

I pulled back slightly and stared up into his face. "Yes, Logan. I want you." *And everything you have to offer.*

Grinning eagerly, Logan reached for his belt buckle. Stepping back, I licked my lips thinking about the night I had in store for him. Trust and believe, before the night ended Logan was going to be mine. I had never been so aggressive with a man before, not that I was about to enlighten him of that tiny fact.

"You ready?" He exhaled a harsh, aroused breath.

"Absolutely," I answered in a low sultry voice. With a crook of my finger, I signaled for him to follow me up the stairs to my bedroom. My foot had barely touched the bottom step when I heard a knock at the door. Logan's brow rose and he looked clearly disappointed at the interruption. Well, he wasn't the only one. I was preparing to answer it when I heard loud pounding.

"What the hell?" I muttered under my breath. I padded to the door, looked through the peephole and spotted a woman standing there, balancing a small child on her hip.

"Who is it?" Logan hissed impatiently.

I looked over my shoulder and shrugged, "Some curly-headed chick holding a little girl." It was then I noticed his eyes grow round as saucers.

"What?" I asked, and suddenly I didn't want to know.

Before he could answer, the woman pounded her fist against the door again, but this time she screamed, "Logan … I know you're in there!"

Swinging around, I saw the fear on his face. "Who is that?" I whispered.

Logan was quiet for several seconds before he finally answered, "My wife."

"Your *what*?" I screamed. I don't remember him mentioning once in any of our conversations that he was married. How come that information wasn't available on the Internet?

"I want my daddy!" wailed the little girl at the top of her lungs while his wife continued to pound at my door.

In record speed, Logan zipped his pants and slipped his shoes back on. I was so shocked I didn't know what to say. I just stood there as he moved toward the door. "I'm sorry. I'll call you tomorrow," he said. Reaching up, he caressed the side of my face and then winked at me, like I was really that stupid and desperate. Logan had no idea. Unlike my mother, I wasn't interested in being someone's mistress. It was all or nothing with me. Being second was not an option.

Suddenly I found my voice and spat, "Do me a favor and lose my number."

I reached for the knob, swung open the door and stared at the woman with tear-stained cheeks holding the crying child in her arms. Logan looked from her to me, and when I refused to make eye contact he finally stepped out onto the porch and scooped the little girl into his arms. Mrs. Cambridge gave me a triumphant smile. I watched as she laced her fingers with her husband's, and the three of them moved out to the curb, climbed into their vehicles and pulled away, leaving me standing there with another disappointment and shattered dreams.

TWO

"I don't mean to laugh at you, but that's what your retarded behind gets!"

I shifted on the chair and fastened a brown-eyed glare in Tamara's direction. Ever since I'd made the mistake of telling her about my fiasco with Logan, Tamara had been falling out of her chair with laughter.

"What kind of cousin are you?"

"Your favorite cousin," she replied and blew a kiss in the air. "You know I love you, Christy, but I've told you time and time again, there's more to a man than his wallet."

Right. Try telling that to my mother.

Jeanna Jamison had allowed herself to love once, and that had been with my father. Their relationship had lasted two years—from the moment Carlos Holloway had walked into the expensive gift shop my mother once ran in the airport to buy something for his fiancée.

In less than twenty-four hours, Jeanna had become the mistress of Carlos Holloway, owner of one of the largest beer corporations in the country. It was his penthouse she had moved into, and his money she'd spent. She'd had it all but had wanted more, including his last name. After a year, Jeanna discovered she was pregnant and was certain Carlos would call off his engagement to a French fashion model and marry her instead. How wrong she had been. Shortly after I was born, he'd ended the relationship. Broken-hearted, Mother swore never to let her guard down again. At that point she'd put the shovel into gold-digging.

The moment I was old enough to understand, she had taught me to never settle for less than the best, and that a beautiful woman could have anything in the world she wanted if she played her cards right.

Well, so far her theory hadn't worked out too well for me. Jeanna said it was because I was trying to focus on way too much. I, on the other hand, disagreed. Nothing's wrong with a woman wanting a career and a little something she could call her own.

I spent years working at some of the finest restaurants in the city before finally training in culinary arts. As far as I was concerned, I was the best caterer this side of the Midwest. I was a mover and a shaker and a memory maker. And yes, Jeanna—who'd refused to let me call her mother until I was ten—was right. Why in the world would I want to settle for anything less than the best?

"I have standards."

Tamara's lips thinned with displeasure at my response. "So do I. I just think you need to lower yours a little. Or in your case, maybe a lot."

I turned up my nose. Tamara always did think that because she was a year older it made her wiser. She was an attorney with the largest law firm in the city. All her life she'd had men falling at her feet, yet she'd settled for a man who had just started his own landscaping business with two employees and one company vehicle.

Turning away from my cousin's assessing look, I surveyed the crowded room around us. My eyes traveled over to the table on my left where my younger sister Portia sat, wearing a Vera Wang gown. She and her new husband were sitting and eating wedding cake. I sighed. Their wedding had been absolutely beautiful and the reception at the Frontenac Hilton Hotel had had everything any bride could have possibly wanted for her special day: elegance, sophistication, and style. As far as Jeanna was concerned, she got the best that money could buy.

As I'd walked down the aisle in a mauve strapless gown, holding a small pink bouquet, I had asked myself if I was ever going to be anything other than a bridesmaid. Now, don't get it twisted. I've had offers and even several marriage proposals, but none of them or their money ever seemed to be quite right. One reason was because I refused to settle for less. The other was that Jeanna would have disowned me if I had. In my desperate search for Mr. Right, all I seemed to find was Mr. Right Now. Meanwhile, my younger sister Portia, had snagged herself a doctor. Can you believe it? A freaking pediatrician, to be exact. Why couldn't I have been so lucky?

As I sat there nursing my second glass of champagne, I watched the way Dr. Evan Smith gazed adoringly into her eyes. I couldn't help but feel a tinge of envy. I was truly happy for my little sister, but selfishly, I wanted the same.

At the far end of the table was Jeanna, with her hair pinned up in an elaborate coiffure, sitting with her third, wealthy, husband. Walter was on one side and her ex-husband—Portia's father—was on the other. Jeanna sat back in the chair, chin tilted upward. Her baby girl had married well and done her proud. I, on the other hand, hadn't even found a man worthy enough to bring to the wedding.

I shook my head. "Look at Jeanna. She's so happy for Portia. Why can't I find someone like Evan?"

Tamara waved her hand dismissively at my response. "That's why you don't have any luck with men. You're too worried about what your mother will think instead of allowing yourself to find someone you're attracted to. Face it, Christy, Aunt Jeanna is a gold-digger. This new guy, Walter? She'd known that old geezer, what, three months? The next thing we know they're flying off to Aruba and getting married. Now she's spending his money faster than he can make it."

I glanced over at the co-creator of *Extreme*, a popular energy drink. Walter was an elegantly dressed man. He was tall and graceful, but with a receding hairline and gapped teeth he was definitely not much to look at. But like all the others, he'd fallen for Jeanna and married her, thinking life would be so much sweeter with her warming his bed every night. I couldn't help but shake my head, because the dude had no idea what Jeanna had in store for him. Maybe I didn't agree with everything she'd done, but one thing I could say about my mother, she was smart.

"Tamara, now you and I both know Jeanna only wants the best for me. There's nothing wrong with wanting your children to marry well. And if she found out I was dating someone who couldn't bring more to that table than I already had, she'd have a fit."

Tamara gave me a shrewd look, then replied. "Aunt Jeanna doesn't have to live with the man. You do. You forgot my daddy had a fit when I first introduced him to Pierre, but after a while he got used to the idea, and now that I'm having his first grandson …" She was smiling and her voice trailed off as she sipped a cup of punch.

Tamara was right. Uncle Craig's attitude had taken a one-hundred-and-eighty-degree turn when he found out Tamara was expecting a grandchild, possibly a grandson. But even as I envied the smile on my cousin's round face, I remembered how Uncle Craig had reacted when he'd discovered she was no longer dating one of his investment partners and was instead seeing a man whose seasonal job left him unemployed during the winter months. My uncle had done everything short of disowning Tamara. However, my perky cousin had dug in her heels and had stood her ground and married Pierre despite her father's disapproval. The couple had flown to Jamaica and had a private ceremony. I'd gone along, even though at the time I wouldn't have dared admit it for fear Jeanna would have disowned me as well.

However, in the two years they'd been married, I had gotten a chance to really know Pierre, and had to admit I truly liked him. He had a fabulous sense of humor and catered to Tamara. There was no doubt in her mind he loved her. The couple was excited they were expecting their first child in four months. As Tamara had said, so what if she made more money than he did? Money couldn't buy her love.

However, regardless of how well things had worked out for Tamara, Jeanna was a different story altogether. She and Uncle Craig had grown up poor. Grandpa Calvin had lost his arm in a work-related accident and Grandma Celeste had to go to work to keep food on the table. She had worked for almost twenty-five years at a candy factory.

My mother had hated her life and had grown up wanting more than she had come from. After she left home she never looked back. All she'd talked about was what she'd never had, and she made sure Portia and I never went without. I admired my mother for being a survivor. Even though she could be a little money hungry and materialistic at times, she had always been a good mother.

"Our parents are two different people. You know my mother is way too damn stubborn."

Tamara shrugged a dainty shoulder. "Maybe, but it's your life, *not* Aunt Jeanna's, and you deserve to be happy."

My gaze swung to hers and I couldn't resist a smile. My cousin had always been her own person. Tall, shapely, with a strong dynamic presence, Tamara had never been one to care about what anyone else in the family thought of her or her decisions. There were many times I wished I could have been more like her. Instead, I'd spent my entire life trying to please my mother.

"Think about it, cousin," Tamara began as she rested her elbows on the tablecloth. "It's time for you to step out of your comfort zone and date someone different."

"Different, huh?" I replied while thinking about what she had suggested. A bank executive, maybe, instead of the president? It didn't sound too hard.

Tamara leaned in close "How about that sexy bartender over in the corner? He's been watching you ever since you returned from the ladies' room."

"A bartender?" I squealed. That wasn't at all what I had in mind, yet I followed the direction of her eyes. Sure enough, Dark and Sexy was staring. The second our eyes met, he held up a glass and smiled.

Frowning, I turned away. "He's too short for my taste."

Tamara clucked her tongue. "Sometimes I feel like I'm talking to a brick wall. What did I just say about lowering your standards?"

"Not *that* low. He looks like he barely comes to my shoulders. I'm five-eight. He looks five-three." Tamara stared giggling and I couldn't resist joining in. "Seriously, the man I date has to be at least six feet."

"Okay, maybe he *is* a little short." She gave me a long thoughtful look before suggesting, "But how about your gardener? Your mechanic?" Tamara wagged her brow suggestively. "At least they both know how to use their hands."

My eyes widened. "Tell me you're joking." I stared at her, expecting Tamara to tell me at any moment she was playing around, but the more I studied her expression the more I could tell she was dead serious. *A mechanic?* "You are really trying to get me disowned, aren't you?"

She shook her head. "Not at all. I just want you to learn how to enjoy life before it's too late. Come on," she urged.

"I *am* enjoying life … just on the high end of the scale," I muttered with a frown, and brought the champagne flute to my lips.

Leaning back in her chair, Tamara rested her hands on her protruding belly. "Okay, you know what? I'm going to do something I said I'd never do."

She had my attention now. "What?"

Her amber gaze locked with mine. "Give you Grandma Celeste's locket."

I'm sure my jaw dropped to the table. "You're kidding, right?" Especially since I'd been trying to get the locket from her ever since our grandmother had passed away four years ago. When we were kids, it was the one thing I had always admired. I would spend hours staring at the timeless photograph inside the locket of Grandma Celeste and Grandpa Calvin when they had first started dating. I had hoped she'd leave it for me in her will, but instead she had given it to Uncle Craig, who'd passed it on to Tamara.

Tamara shook her head. "No, I'm not joking. I'll give you the locket, but it's going to cost you."

Uh-oh. I was old enough to know that nothing worth having came free. "I'm afraid to ask."

The crooked smile on my cousin's coral painted lips were a clear indication she was enjoying having the upper hand. "You have to open your mind and date someone out of the ordinary."

Frowning, I downed the last sip from my flute and frowned, "What do you mean, *out of the ordinary*?"

"I don't know. Butcher, baker, candlestick maker. Hell, I don't know and I don't care, and neither should you." She paused for a long thoughtful moment. "In fact, don't even ask what he does for a living. Just try to learn everything else about him, because I'm going to call and ask questions. If you do as I suggest and the relationship lasts at least five dates, I'll give you the locket. No more CEOs, presidents, and rich boys with silver spoons in their mouths. I want you to find a man who works hard for a living. Someone with dirt under his nails, who makes you smile without pulling out a credit card to do it."

Dirt under his nails? Eeww. No gifts? Did Tamara forget I was a woman with acquired tastes? I gave her a strange look. "Couldn't I just babysit your first-born?"

"Nope. Because you're going to do that for me anyway," she said with animated humor. "Seriously, Christy, I love you but I want you to start exploring your options. You fall in love with the size of a man's bank account. For once I want you to open your mind and set your heart on marrying for love."

I held up my hands. "Okay, hold up a minute. Time out! I thought all I had to do was date some dude five times. You didn't mention anything at all about falling in love and getting married."

Tamara blew out a frustrated breath. "You're hopeless. You know that?"

I shrugged and crossed my legs. "Hey, I've been called a lot worse, but to finally get my hands on that locket I'm willing to do just about anything, including dating an average Joe for a few weeks. I mean, how hard could it actually be?"

As Tamara raised a glass of punch in salute, a wicked smile curved her mouth. "I guess you're about to find out."

THREE

"Leave all the worries to us … I promise you it will be an evening to remember … Of course … Thank you again, and we'll be in touch." As soon as I hung up the phone, I sprang from my chair. "*Whoo-hoo*!" The first Saturday in August was going to be another high profile event certain to draw *Cater to You* more business.

During the last two years I had achieved a number of goals. One was stepping out on pure faith, and with the help of my former college roommate, we started up our own company. Claudia was a confectionist, while I was responsible for putting together a fabulous menu of dishes all created by me.

It hadn't been easy, but ever since we'd catered an album release party for the rapper, Nelly, *Cater to You* had been in high demand. It had been an all-white party with a star-studded guest list. Word of mouth is such a beautiful thing. The party was the buzz on Access Hollywood and TMZ. Trust and believe. I made certain I landed fifteen seconds of the segment to market my company.

Since then I've received referrals from politicians, designers and even a couple of California rappers, which required my traveling to the coast, all expenses paid of course, to cater an event that had people talking for days. I myself would never listen to that gangster music, but as far as I was concerned their money was green just like everyone else's.

Lowering back in the chair, I allowed myself a moment to bask in my success. Not bad for a twenty-eight-year- old woman who had known since high school she would never work for anybody but herself. Or, like my mother, depend on a man for money. I had always been stubborn and determined to strike out on my own.

Cooking was my calling, which was ironic given how I'd grown up. Jeanna couldn't boil oatmeal or wash a single plate.

I circled the date on the calendar, then reached for my planner and jotted down a few notes from my phone conversation. The city wanted to honor local heroes for performing selfless acts of service and valor in the community. The event was to be held on the mayor's yacht, and *Cater to You* had been hired to provide the food.

"Christina, I'm leaving for lunch."

I glanced up at my partner, Claudia Winters. Standing in the doorway of my office she looked beautiful as ever in a mango-colored pantsuit with a wide belt tied at her dainty waist. Everyone thought she resembled Kimora Lee Simmons because of her height and grace, and also due to the fact that she was both Asian and African-American. Personally, I thought my best friend was prettier than the fashion mogul.

"So what did they say about our proposal?" Claudia asked as she strolled into my office, eyes wide with anticipation.

My lips curled upward. "They've chosen us to cater the event!" I was so excited I was bouncing in my seat as I told her about my phone conversation.

"Yeah, baby!" Claudia shouted with glee. "Christina, this is huge!"

"I know," I replied, beaming with pride.

Claudia tossed her honey brown hair away from her face. "We've gotta give this event our full attention. I can already visualize a midnight dinner cruise with blown sugar displays and sinfully rich dishes!" She clapped her hands excitedly "Everything has to be perfect!"

"I agree." Claudia was the most talented confectionist I knew. Her sugar designs were exquisite sculptures that resembled blown glass. I couldn't wait to see what she would come up with for the event. For the next few minutes we tossed around ideas for a few dishes that quickly popped in our heads, then giggled like two school girls. We truly loved what we did.

"Well, we'll have to talk about it some more this afternoon. I'm meeting with a client after lunch to plan a birthday party for a five-year-old."

"Fun," I replied with a hint of laughter in my voice. Even though we've been quite successful this past year, we still manage to do small events such as baby showers and birthday parties. It's the small events that have given us the success we have today, but the major events keep us in business, which is why the dinner cruise was going to be a very important and televised event.

We chatted a few minutes longer, then the champagne-eyed beauty rose and sashayed out the door.

I daydreamed a few minutes, then scribbled some notes. All kinds of appetizers were running through my head. I had created a new artichoke and cheese dip I was dying to share, and this would be the perfect event to show off my creative skills.

I don't know how long I sat there scribbling away before I finally rose from my chair and moved out into the reception area, then smiled as my eyes traveled around our storefront office with its mauve carpeting, vanilla damask patterned wallpaper and white leather furnishing. *Cater to You* was in gold lettering across the wall behind the reception desk.

We had started our business in Claudia's parents' basement before we were finally able to lease a place of our own. Carlos Holloway would have been more than happy to give us the money. A hefty allowance was his excuse for having been an absentee parent all those years. But Claudia and I refused to take money from our parents. Our business was something we wanted to do on our own. *Look how far we had come.* Success was ours. Jeanna didn't understand how a woman could put a career before marriage, but as she had taught me, a smart woman could have it all, and I intended to have just that.

I moved into the break room, removed a diet soda from the refrigerator and popped the tab. As I returned to the lobby, the bell over the door rang. I swung around, ready to put on my professional face and greet a potential customer. However, the second I spotted the man strolling through the door, I choked on my drink.

Oh.

My.

God.

He chuckled apologetically. "My bad. I didn't mean to startle you."

I opened my mouth, but words refused to come out. Standing before me was a chocolate dream. The man was the definition of sexy, and what every woman dreamed of having. Mahogany skin with a smooth bald head and beautiful big golden eyes surrounded by lashes so long I was certain they caressed his cheeks. When he smiled, deep dimples became prominent on both sides of his face. A pencil thin mustache darkened a thick, juicy, top lip. He could easily have doubled as Malcolm from *Single Ladies* on VH1.

"Are you okay?" he asked in a deep booming voice. Concern was apparent in his eyes.

Hell no, I'm not okay. It's not every day a sexy creature walks into my office. "Y-Yes, I'm fine." I blinked twice, then cleared my throat, relieved that my voice was back and I wasn't making a complete fool of myself. Thank goodness I hadn't spilled soda on my suit.

"Sorry about that." I watched as he stepped into the reception area, with a swagger that made my nipples pucker beneath my silk blouse. *Sweet Jesus!* Mr. Sexy stopped directly in front of me. He had to be at least six-five, but even in four-inch Jimmy Choos I had to tilt my head back to meet his intense stare.

"How … How may I help you?"

The grin he gave made my pulse race, and for a second I thought maybe he was going to suggest something almost as inappropriate as the explicit thoughts running through my head. "My parents will be celebrating fifty years in August and I need a caterer for their party."

It took everything I had to force my eyes away from his succulent lips, yet as he spoke I hung on to every word. "You've come to the right place. Follow me into my office." I swung around and took a deep breath, trying to pull myself together, even though I knew he was behind me. I could feel the heat of his eyes, and it didn't take a rocket scientist to tell me he was admiring the sway of my ass in my brown Donna Karan suit. I signaled for him to take the seat across from my desk and moved around and lowered into my chair. Thank goodness. I was glad to be off my feet. I wasn't sure how much longer before my legs gave out on me.

"By the way, I'm Dereon Sanders."

As fine as he was, I was tempted to ask if he was in any way related to Deion Sanders, the football player. But I decided to pass. The last thing I needed was for him to think I was flirting with him. "Sorry for my manners. I'm Christina Holloway." Rising, I reached across the desk, and the second his fingers closed around mine a jolt of pure sensation ran through me like a shot to the heart. I jerked back my hand, surprised by the intensity, flopped down onto the chair, and looked into his eyes. The twinkle in those sexy golden babies told me he had felt it too.

Reaching for a pen and paper, I decided it was time to get down to business. Crossing my legs, I leaned back in my chair. "Okay, so where are you having the party?" I said, clearing my throat twice.

He shrugged a broad shoulder. "I haven't figured that part out yet."

"Okay, well we might be able to help suggest a few places. What kind of event do you have in mind?"

Dereon grinned, dimples flashing in his cheeks. "Dinner, dancing, you name it. When it comes to my parents, money is no object."

He didn't look at all like a man with a bottomless checkbook. He was very relaxed and casually dressed, but extremely handsome nevertheless. For an instant our eyes met and I had the strangest feeling that I was drowning in those golden-brown depths. There's no telling how long I might have sat there staring at him before he glanced down at his watch and asked, "Have you eaten lunch?"

I was startled by the question. It was not at all what I was expecting. "What?"

"I said, have you eaten?" he repeated, his voice low and vibrant.

"No, but—"

"Good," he interrupted. "Me neither." With that he rose in one fluid motion and lowered his gaze to mine. "I saw a bar and grill on the corner. Let's eat. My treat."

For a few seconds I didn't know what to say. *Lunch with him?* Doing business with the handsome stranger was one thing. Sharing a meal was another. I knew almost nothing about him except how he made my belly quiver, as if I were riding a roller coaster. It was already clear that being around Dereon was going to be hard on the hormones. If I spent too much time with him there was no telling what other effects I might encounter. Smiling politely, I shook my head. "I'm really not that hungry."

"Fine. Don't eat. You can come and watch me. While we're there we can talk about my parents' party. I'm planning something off the chain. Something unforgettable, with plenty of good food. I was told you were the woman who could make that happen."

Off the chain? Unforgettable? Those two things meant sparing no expense. I grabbed my Chanel purse. Only a fool would turn down his offer of lunch. He may not have been my typical client, but Dereon's check would deposit the same as any of our other clients, or at least I hoped so. Besides, the lunch was strictly business. Right?

I locked the door to the office behind us and moved beside him. Mia, our part-time assistant, was vacationing with her cousin in Mexico and wouldn't be back until next week, so Claudia and I were trying to juggle the office the best we could. You never realize how much you value an employee until she's gone. I couldn't wait for her to get back on Monday.

As we headed toward the bar and grill on the corner, I tried not to brush against Dereon, which wasn't easy because he took up most of the width of the sidewalk. It was early June, sunny and warm outside, which was a good thing. Midwest weather could be so unpredictable, beautiful one day and raining the next.

"Have you lived in St. Louis all your life?" he asked, breaking the silence.

I nodded and was pleased he was trying to ease the moment, because I was truly nervous as hell. "Born and raised right in Ladue. What about you?"

His hands were buried deep in his front pockets. "I grew up in the heart of East St. Louis. I didn't move to this side of the river until I was twenty."

I figured as much. It was in the way he moved and the sexy yet cocky smile on his lips. I allowed my eyes to travel the length of him from the red Rocawear polo shirt down to his stonewashed loose-fitting jeans all the way down to the fresh white Air Force Ones on his feet. Even though he was dressed like a rapper, Dereon was definitely something to look at, but a man who looked that good definitely couldn't be single. Not that it mattered. I knew there was no way in the world he could afford me or my lifestyle. And it was probably a good thing. As handsome as he was, it would be hard as hell to say no.

We stepped inside the restaurant and were met by a gush of cool air. Dereon placed a hand at the small of my back and escorted me to a small table in back. I tried to ignore the heat seeping through my veins from his touch and took the seat facing the window.

"Have you eaten here before?" he asked as soon as he lowered in the chair across from me.

It was a narrow place crammed with tables and rickety chairs. I glanced around at the brown paneling and dim lights, turned up my nose and shook my head. "I've never been one for dark places. I thought it was a pool hall." Inside, the restaurant was nothing more than a hole-in-the-wall. Reaching inside my purse, I removed a small bottle of hand sanitizer and rubbed it all over my hands.

Dereon took one look at me and chuckled. I found the sound refreshing. "Yo, answer one question for me. Have you ever eaten a hamburger before?"

Okay, he was trying to be funny now. "Of course I have," I replied with a defiant tilt of the chin. "I'm just particular about where I eat. No offense, but what some restaurants consider beef isn't what I would call *meat*."

He glanced down at the menu, then back up at me. "It looks like they have half-pound Angus steak burgers here. No scrimping on that."

Why did I get the feeling he was making fun of me? Maybe it had something to do with the mocking note I heard in his voice. A rebuttal was on my tongue, but I reached for my menu instead. The waitress came carrying two glasses of water, ready to take our order. I wouldn't dare mention the only water I drank was out of a bottle. Instead, I politely asked for a diet cola, but that wasn't until after Dereon asked for lemonade. He ordered a burger and fries and I decided to order the same, just to prove to him I did eat hamburgers like any other red-blooded American.

After the waitress left with our order, I reached inside my purse for a notepad and pen. I was good at what I did and believed in never leaving home without them. Besides, with our knees touching under the small table it was starting to feel a little too intimate, and I needed to get this meeting on the right track so I could get back to the office and send his sexy behind down the road somewhere, anywhere, as long as it was far away from me. "Okay, let's get back to business. What type of dinner do you envision for your parents?"

Dereon leaned back in the chair, legs spread wide. I wasn't sure how many times my eyes strayed down to his crotch before I realized what I was doing. "I wanna formal sit-down dinner with ballroom dancing."

Ballroom dancing? He didn't seem the type. I guess the look on my face must have given me away.

Dereon chuckled. "What's wrong? You look surprised."

"I am," I heard myself admit. "I guess I didn't take you as the *formal* type."

He leaned forward, and for the first time I noticed the diamond stud in his left earlobe. "What type do you take me for?" he asked, as

I watched his tongue sweep across his top lip. *Goodness!* How could I be so captivated by a man's mouth? And then there was a roughness about him that I found so damned intriguing. Dereon oozed bad boy. The one thing I've always steered clear of.

"I figured you to be more of a … buffet man."

My answer brought a hearty laugh, dimples and all. "Actually, you hit it right on the name. I'll take a little ole school music and some collard greens and cornbread any day," he added with a slight smile.

"Just what I thought," I replied with a triumphant smirk. No matter how fine he was, it was clear he was way too urban for me and Jeanna's taste.

Dereon rested his elbow on the table and replied, "But the night isn't about me. It's about my parents, and I want to do something special for them."

"What type of people are your parents? I like to plan a meal that reflects the clients' personalities as much as possible."

A smile tipped his lips and pride glistened in his eyes as he spoke. "Well, I can tell you this, my parents are simple folks. My mother is a retired music teacher. She worked for the East St. Louis public school district for years."

The waitress returned with our drinks. I sipped the cola through my straw and was glad the carbonated drink burned at the back of my parched throat. "What instrument does she play?"

"The piano," he said, between sips. "As long as I could remember we had this old piano in our living room. Mama would play it every evening after dinner, and she made sure her kids could play as well."

"Are you any good?" I asked. I wasn't being nosy. For some reason I was actually curious to know how well this man could use his hands.

Grinning, Dereon took a drink from his glass before answering. "I have my moments. But playing the piano's like riding a bike. Some things you just never forget."

Ooh, I liked the way that sounded. My mind had just traveled off in some area it had no business going. "Let me guess. Chopsticks, right?"

An easy smile played at the corners of his delicious mouth. "No, Mozart."

"Mozart? I would have never guessed that."

His brow rose with amusement. “See, you were judging me. I can see it in your eyes.”

This time there was no way I was admitting what I was thinking. “No, I wasn't,” I countered.

Dereon crossed his arms against his hard chest. “Yes, you were. “

I found it impossible not to return his disarming smile. “Okay, so maybe I was.” *Goodness, what was it about this man I found so irresistible?*

The waitress returned with our food and we dug in, giving me a chance to think of a way to get the luncheon back to business. I hadn’t come here to judge him or try to get to know him as a person. I was a professional and it didn’t matter if we liked each other or not. All that mattered was that I provided him the services he requested.

I asked about his mother again, and while he focused on his food I managed to control the conversation, which wasn’t easy, considering how good Dereon looked gazing across the table at me. I swear if he licked his lips one more time, I was going to be tempted to kiss him. And being intimate with a client was a definite no-no.

“What about your father?” I asked.

“He managed a small corner store. Still does, when Mama lets him out of the house,” he added with a hearty chuckle.

“Really? Where at?”

“In East St. Louis, near the projects. Bought that storefront building back in the fifties and it’s been open ever since. For years he was the closest store in the area to buy milk and bread. Now he sells mostly candy, cigarettes, lottery tickets and forty-ounces.” I noticed the faraway look in his eyes, and as he continued I could tell he was lost in the memories. I nodded and clearly understood. I, too, remembered all the weekends we spent with our grandparents and Grandpa Calvin giving Portia and me each a dollar. We used to race to the store for ice cream and candy. “Did your father sell Lemon Heads?”

Dereon nodded. “Oh yeah! Lemon Heads, Boston Baked Beans … He even sold snow cones.”

I giggled, clearly enjoying the trip down memory lane. “I used to love snow cones.” Except when I spilled the syrup on my dress and Jeanna got mad.

“So did I. But Dad stopped selling them. About three years ago he decided it was time to enjoy retirement with Mom, so my cousin Jay now runs the store. Now my parents travel all over the place together. For their anniversary they're planning to take a cruise to the Grand Caymans."

He continued to talk about his parents while we ate, and just by listening I could tell he had a deep affection for them. I admired that. My father, who had just divorced his second wife, was too busy chasing his twenty-somethings to have time for me. Monetarily, I'd never wanted for anything, but love was something I just never managed to earn, no matter how hard I tried. I couldn't get his attention long enough for him to have ever really noticed me.

After we were done eating, Dereon insisted on paying for the meal. I could have written it off as a business expense, but since lunch was his idea I didn't argue. We walked back to the office side by side, arms brushing. This time I felt the attraction snap, crackle and pop. Stay focused, I kept chanting to myself as I tried to get my body to cooperate, but right now it was craving something it hadn't had in months. With someone as fine as Dereon in my company, it was only natural.

That's it!

What I was experiencing was a natural reaction to going for so long without sex, nothing more. It was lust, pure and simple, stoked by sharing a cozy lunch together. Knowing that's all it was allowed me to regain some control. I pushed my shoulders back and moved toward my building. However, some of my confidence slipped when I noticed Claudia hadn't returned yet. I unlocked the door and Dereon followed me inside and back toward my office.

"Have a seat," I said as I moved around my desk and lowered into my chair. "I have a list of locations you can look at and you can decide where the best place would be to hold the anniversary dinner. Most of the hotels are out because they don't allow outside catering, but there's the chateau and several banquet halls and nightclubs you can reserve for private parties." I reached inside my drawer, then glanced up at Dereon, wondering why he was still standing. "Unless of course you'd prefer a bar and grill? Or to have it at a familiar, uh … establishment on the East side?"

"Familiar establishment?" he repeated, eyes sparkling with amusement. "Familiar like what? A hip-hop club or some hole-in-the-wall?"

I shook my head. I guess I stuck my foot in my mouth with that one. This was clearly Claudia's area of expertise, not mine. "That's not what I meant."

"Okay, so what did you mean?" he asked as he continued to tower over me. I gazed up at him and forced myself to swallow.

"Well … I, uh, well, most of the locations where we've developed relationships are kind of upscale."

"And you don't think I can do upscale?"

From the look on his face I couldn't tell if he was upset or pulling my leg. I was leaning more towards the latter. "No, I mean, yes, I mean, I wasn't sure if you'd feel comfortable in some of the places I was getting ready to mention." *Goodness, just shut up, Christina.* All I was doing was making matters worse.

Dereon stood a few moments longer before he finally slid the upholstered chair over to the edge of my desk and straddled the seat. "Okay, it's my turn to judge you."

The look in his eyes told me I definitely didn't want to go there with him. "Dereon, really—"

He held up a hand, silencing me. "Uh-uh! It's only fair."

Oh, goodness. Lowering my gaze to my desk, I was certain my cheeks had just turned beet red.

"Christina, I see you as a sexy milk chocolate sistah who's doin' the damn thang. I ain't mad. You believe in having only the finer things in life. No exception … including men."

After a few seconds I leaned back in my chair with my arms folded. "There's nothing wrong with that," I replied with a note of annoyance I didn't even bother to mask.

"You're right. There ain't nothing wrong with it except that you're bougie as hell."

My eyes widened with alarm. *How dare he!* "I'm not bougie."

"I think you are."

"Well, you're wrong."

"Then prove it by having dinner with me tomorrow tonight."

What? As I nibbled on my bottom lip my eyes traveled lazily over his attire. Polo style shirt, gold chain, earring in his lobe and dark jeans hung low on his waist. There was no way I could date someone I couldn't take home to meet my mother. If he wasn't good enough for Jeanna then he wasn't good enough for me. Right?

"Sorry, but I already have plans."

"Then change them," he said with challenge gleaming in his golden brown gaze. "You know you want to. I can see it in your eyes."

Nothing made me madder than a man trying to read my mind. "Whatever," I mumbled.

"Are you trying to tell me you're not attracted to me?" he taunted.

"I'm saying that I've got other plans."

Determination was apparent when he rose from the chair. Suddenly I knew I was in trouble. "Tell you what … Three minutes from now, if you tell me you're still not attracted to me, then I won't ask again."

I wasn't following him. "Three minutes? What's going to happen in three minutes?"

"I'm going to kiss you." Dereon rounded the desk, took my hands and lifted me to my feet.

A warm shiver passed through me and my body responded on contact. Common sense was screaming at me to run as fast as I could so I shook my head. "Dereon, I don't think—"

"Don't think, just feel," he ordered, then pulled me snugly in his arms. He gazed at me a moment longer then slowly dipped his head.

Quick! Do something, my brain urged, and I did. I closed my eyes, tilted my chin upward and met him halfway. The moment our lips touched, I felt it. Fireworks as explosive as those down on the riverfront during the Fourth of July. My hands moved to his chest just as I felt his arms pulling me even closer to his amazing body. Dereon's mouth was soft and warm and I felt my body relax. When he finally pushed his tongue inside, a whisper of a sigh escaped my lips. Dammit, the man could kiss. It would have been so much easier to resist if he had been a slobberer, but instead he had mastered the craft. All through lunch I had been curious about how well he could use his hands, now I knew as I felt them glide down the small of my back, along my narrow hip, and rest on my voluptuous ass, where he squeezed and lifted me off my feet, bringing me closer to his hardening flesh. There was no doubt in my mind what he was working with. The size and length of his erection made it perfectly clear Dereon was blessed.

He groaned against my mouth, and all doubts vanished from my head. To hell with my firm rule about not mixing business with pleasure. I sighed, wrapped my arms around him and leaned closer, meeting each swirl of his tongue with one of my own. After all, I had no choice. The last thing I wanted was for him to think I was inexperience and lacked skill and finesse. I was a proud, confident black woman, and I wanted to make sure I left no doubt about that in his mind.

Dereon kissed my mouth with sweet passionate thrusts that were slow and controlled and downright confident. The way he kissed took skill. With each sweep of his sweet tongue I felt my control slip, and the moist intimate area between my thighs pulsed with need. Oh, it had been a long time since a man had made me feel this good. His mouth was sweet and delicious and I felt like a woman with a box of Godiva chocolates. One wasn't near enough.

I gulped greedily at his mouth. My nipples tightened and moisture settled between my thighs. I was floating towards heaven and couldn't believe I'd gotten there just from kissing Dereon. He was masculine and dominant and a damn powerful kisser.

I knew this was a big mistake. If I had any sense I would end the kiss now and get back to planning his parents' anniversary party, but for the life of me I couldn't think straight. For once I had lost control, and I didn't care about anything except the man holding me in his warm embrace as if I was the most precious thing in the world. It was crazy, yet I couldn't think, only feel. His hard body against mine had my own on fire, and I found my hands doing what they were itching to do. I allowed them to slide across his chest, over his broad shoulders and down his solid arms, stopping at his firm backside, then squeezed. Damn, his ass was perfect.

Dereon lifted his head slightly, then gazed down at me with heavy lids half covering those big beautiful golden eyes of his. Our hearts were thumping, our breathing ragged, and lips moist. Then he dipped his head and parted my lips, and once again we were kissing, hands caressing, tongues stroking in unison.

"Christina, I've got you a salad … Oh, shit!" I heard Claudia say.

I was flying high over the clouds and would have kept right on kissing if Dereon hadn't turned his head to stare at my startled partner. Smiling, he slowly released me. As soon as his warm hard body was no longer pressed against mine, the heavens evaporated instantly and I came crashing back down onto planet earth.

"Sorry, I didn't mean to walk in," Claudia said.

Yeah, right. She was loving every moment of it.

My breasts rose and fell heavily as I realized what had just happened, and before I had a chance to react Dereon walked over to Claudia and extended his hand. "Hey, whassup?"

Her hand was lost in his. “Hello, I'm Christina, Claudia’s partner. Oops! I mean Claudia, Christina’s partner.” Well, at least it was a relief to know I wasn’t the only one he had that effect on.

Dereon looked clearly amused. “Nice meeting you, Claudia,” he replied, then his heated gaze fell over me as he said, “Yo, Christina. I'll be by to pick you up tomorrow at eight. Be ready.” He winked and turned toward the door.

Heart pounding wildly, I pressed a hand to my moist swollen lips. “Y-You don't even know where I live,” I called after him.

He glanced over his shoulder without breaking his stride. “Don't worry. I'll call you.”

FOUR

"Who the hell was that?" my partner asked.

I walked around the desk, suddenly needing to sit down. My heart was pounding, my legs felt like rubber, and I was afraid I was going to pass out at any moment. "That was Dereon Sanders."

Her brow arched. "Any relation to—"

I shrugged a weary shoulder. "I have no idea."

"Oooh! A name like Sanders, he can't be anything but sexy." Claudia set my salad on the end of my desk, then dropped down into the chair and flipped her shoulder-length hair away from her face. "Where did he come from and how do I get one of my own?"

I cleared my throat for several seconds, trying to shake off the spell. What had just happened? I had forgotten who I was and what I wanted. All that had mattered was the gorgeous man whose lips had covered mine less than ten minutes ago. "He's … uh … our new client."

"New client? You were *kissing* a client?" Claudia squealed. Her champagne-colored eyes glistened with surprise and curiosity. "Whatever happened to your cardinal rule of never mixing business with pleasure? In fact, you had the bylaws plastered onto the refrigerator."

That rule had gone out the window the second I'd swung around and spotted Dereon coming through the door. "Well, it's … uhhh … kind of complicated."

A perfectly arched eyebrow rose. "Complicated how?"

"He called me bougie and when I—"

"Bougie?" she cackled. "I can't believe he said that." She was really laughing now.

I was glad someone agreed with me. "Neither can I, but he did. And when I denied it he—"

Claudia held up a hand. "Wait a minute. Christina, dear … You *are* kind of bougie."

I was appalled to think my partner thought that of me. "I am not! I just have standards."

"Yes," she hesitated. "But they are pretty high, don't you think?"

Why did this conversation feel like déjà vu? "And you're saying you're not? Come on, Claudia, your family has money," I retorted, then blinked, going for an innocent expression.

"Yes, but my father worked hard for everything he got, and unlike you I believe in bargain shopping. There's nothing wrong with shopping at a discount store."

I shuddered listening to her. "I believe in quality living, and I can only get that at quality stores."

She tossed a dismissive wave in my direction. "Trust me. Dereon was right about you. Sometimes I wish you would tone it down a notch."

I couldn't believe we were having this conversation. I was beginning to think Tamara had called and brainwashed her. "Anyway …" I began. "My preferences seem to be a topic of debate I'd rather not discuss. Dereon asked me out to dinner, and when I refused he challenged me. He said that if he kissed me and I didn't respond it would be strictly business between us, but if I did … then he was taking me out to dinner tomorrow."

Claudia's smile widened. "It looks like you'll be having dinner."

"Pretty much," I said, then groaned. "I don't know where my head went. The second he kissed me I sort of lost it."

"Well, I can definitely understand why. He's gorgeous." Smiling, she leaned back on the chair. "So what does he do for a living?"

My heart was still pounding from the kiss. My lips were tingling and felt raw and swollen. I wondered if Claudia noticed. "I don't know. He didn't tell me."

"Didn't or wouldn't? A man of mystery. I like him already."

She wasn't the only one. My pulse was racing just thinking about him. Never, and I mean never, had I ever been kissed like that. Sure I'd had my share of men, and even those I had fancied myself to be in love with, but none of them had come remotely close to making me feel the level of heat that man had brought my way. By the time he had stepped out that door, Dereon had my hormones boiling all over the stove.

"He seems to be a little rough around the edges. Kinda … What's the expression? Uh … kinda hood," she added in a far-off voice. "But he definitely has swag."

Yes, definitely. He was intriguingly delicious, to say the least. Dereon was a man who knew what he wanted and didn't allow anything or anyone standing in his way. He hadn't hesitated to kiss me with those urgent and succulent lips, and then his tongue had probed, teased and explored. I had enjoyed it so much I'd been seconds away from having sex on top of my desk. That was way too weird, because I almost never lose my head.

Claudia gave me a long, thoughtful look. "You said he's a client. What kind of event does he want us to cater?"

"A fiftieth wedding anniversary for his parents."

"Awww! A man who loves his parents. What more can a girl ask for?"

I could think of a couple of things, but I wasn't about to go there. "Anyway, he wants something nice for the weekend after the mayor's big shindig."

"Then he shall have it." Claudia named off a couple of possibilities. I frowned and shook my head.

"Nah, that's what I thought. No, he wants something really nice and classy for his parents. The entire evening is about taste."

"Okay. I can do classy and tasteful." I knew she would love hearing that. "I'll work on sweets while you focus on the menu and your sexy new man."

"He's *not* my man," I mumbled

"Oh, but he will be. I saw the way the two of you were looking at each other. I stepped in and this room was on fire!"

I laughed, trying to brush her words aside, although my insides were exactly that—on fire.

"Trust me," Claudia said with a decidedly mischievous grin. "That man wants a lot more from you than just an anniversary party. And I got a strong feeling that what Dereon Sanders wants … he gets. And what he wants … is you."

There was no way I was going to admit it, but Claudia was right. What I couldn't understand was how could a man, a man I didn't even want, affect me so completely?

FIVE

I left the office shortly after six. The afternoon had been a total disaster. I had been so distracted I couldn't think straight. All because of Dereon.

The audacity of that man! How dare he just assume I would go out with him just because he challenged me? Okay, so maybe he was one hell of a kisser, and maybe I was a little curious, but that was beside the point. I had never met such a cocky man in my life and was ashamed to admit I was actually intrigued by him. However, that was neither here nor there. I knew going out with him wasn't a good idea, and I would be going against everything I'd built my career on, which is why first thing tomorrow I planned on calling Dereon and letting him know going out was a bad idea.

Nevertheless, on my way home I decided that maybe I needed to go shopping for a new outfit, just in case. Nothing worse than having a date and nothing to wear. Not that I was planning to go out with him, mind you, but you never know. I might not have anything to do tomorrow night, and decide by default that going out was better than sitting around the house on a Friday night. And there was always the chance that Dereon would refuse to take no for an answer. Besides, I loved to shop, and right now any excuse would do.

After an evening shopping spree I pulled into my driveway shortly after eight. My back seat was filled with bags. I had gone out to buy a dress but decided, what's a new dress without new shoes? And then there were the accessories to go with it. Of course, who wanted a new dress without brand-new undergarments? I couldn't dare let Dereon see me in anything I already had, not that I was planning to take my clothes off, but you just never knew. It would be like forgetting to shave and then arriving at work and remembering you had an appointment that afternoon with your gynecologist.

I lugged all the bags inside, then spent the next half hour trying everything on again. I'd even bought a brand new bottle of Chanel Mademoiselle. If I was going to look new, I wanted to smell new as well. I posed in front of the mirror and smiled, pleased at how well the dress hugged my generous hips. I was twirling around in my new shoes when the phone rang. I raced around the bed and grabbed the receiver on the second ring. "Hello?"

"You sound out of breath. What are you doing? Or should I ask?" Tamara giggled.

I lowered onto the bed and smiled. "I was trying on a new outfit I bought."

"Ooh, you went shopping and didn't tell me?" She had the nerve to sound insulted.

"Sorry, cuz. This was a last-minute sort of thing. I might have a date I don't want and I needed to have something to wear just in case."

"Uh-uh. Hold up a minute! I need to hear more about this. A date you don't want? What's up with that?"

What's up with that? Goodness, Tamara had been hanging with her teenage sister a bit too much. "Well, I got a new client today. He wants to plan a fiftieth anniversary party for his parents."

"A *he,* huh? What's *he* look like?"

I had to swallow and take a couple of deep breaths, otherwise Tamara would know before I even got the words out. "He's okay. Tall, dark, bald-headed, um, mustache."

"Ooh, Mami! He sounds gorgeous. And he asked you out?" she shrieked.

"Yes."

"What's he do for a living?"

Reaching down, I unstrapped my shoes before saying, "I don't know."

Tamara sighed heavily into the receiver. "Well, what does he look like he does?"

I frowned at that thought. "He's a little too rough for my taste. Looks like one of those rappers. Sneakers, loose-fitting Rocawear gear."

"Oh my goodness! A thug is perfect."

"Perfect?" *Was I missing something?*

"How quickly we forget. Portia's wedding two weeks ago … Grandma Celeste's locket … Opening your heart … do I need to go on?"

The locket! How in the world could I have forgotten? Especially since I wanted it so badly. Tamara kept it in her jewelry box, but I planned to wear it around my neck every day. But Dereon … There was absolutely no way I was dating him. "I don't think so."

"Why not? He sounds exactly like what we were looking for."

"We?" I repeated with laughter in my voice.

"Okay, you, but he does sound perfect. Goodness, it's been two weeks and he's the first candidate you've mentioned."

I huffed. "Because he's the *only* candidate." Since Logan had put a bad taste in my mouth I'd been so busy at work I'd decided to put sex and romance on the back burner for a little while and just buy a monthly supply of batteries instead. I would have to make a mental note to check with my broker, because there had to be stock in batteries with all the lonely women in the world. "Dereon is a client, which means I can't date him."

"Who says?"

I chuckled. "I say. He really isn't my type. And after his kiss, I—" I had to jerk the phone away from my ear at the sound of Tamara's high-pitched scream. She was so loud you would have thought she'd gone into labor.

"Oh, my goodness! Did you just say he kissed you?"

Me and my big mouth. "Yeah, I guess I did."

"When did this happen? I thought he was a client. And what was the kiss like?"

"Is there anything else you want to know while I'm at it?" I asked with a huff.

"Yeah, I want to hear every detail, starting from the moment you first laid eyes on him."

From the beginning. I had to swallow because my body started to overheat just thinking about Dereon Sanders stepping into my office. I curled up comfortably on the bed and did exactly as my cousin asked. I started from the beginning and ended at the point Claudia had walked in on the two of us kissing. By the time I got done Tamara was screaming in my ear again.

"This is absolutely too much! Okay, okay, now tell me … How was the kiss?"

Unforgettable. His was one kiss I was certain never to forget. My lips were still tingling from the firm pressure of his mouth against mine. Even now my body shook just remembering the way he parted my lips and slipped his tongue inside. He'd had me so hot there was no telling what might have happened if Claudia hadn't walked in when she had. I might have knocked everything off my desk onto the floor and had him lay me down on my back. Goodness! Even now I could feel my body responding to what had transpired, and what could have transpired. "It was good."

"Good?" she squawked with disbelief. Damn, I could never get anything past her.

"Okay, it was better than good," I admitted around a deep breath.

"Now that's what I'm talking about! Handsome and a wonderful kisser. Christina, it sounds to me like you found the one. It won't be long before he has you calling out his name! Say my name, Christina … Say my name."

I couldn't help but giggle. My cousin can be a fool at times. However, her comment had me fantasizing about Dereon and me making love. Me at the center of the bed with Dereon lying between my legs, stroking deeply inside my welcoming body until he'd brought us both to orgasmic bliss. Goodness! Heat shot straight down to my toes. Uh-uh, that was one fantasy I needed to stay away from.

"Christina!"

"Yeah," I replied, pushing away those dangerous thoughts as I tried to focus on my cousin again, but I'll have to admit it wasn't easy.

Tamara snorted. "I asked you a question, but obviously you've got something more important on your mind. Please do tell."

I frowned. This conversation was getting to be a bit much. I rose from the bed, slid into my slippers and padded across the thick tan carpeting into the other room. "Nothing worth repeating. How's the baby doing?"

"She's doing fabulous."

"Oh my goodness! You're having a girl?" I shouted. What fun I was going to have dressing my little cousin in designer clothes.

Tamara sighed. "I still don't know what I'm having but it doesn't hurt to hope." She wanted a little girl as much as I did.

"You're too much," I said with a giggle as I walked down the stairs onto the oak wood flooring of the foyer.

"And you're hopeless. Now getting back to Dereon …"

As I headed toward the kitchen I released a heavy sigh. I might as well get comfortable, because as far as Tamara was concerned I was in for a long night.

SIX

"Okay, so I was thinking about smoked salmon bruschetta, melon wrapped in prosciutto, crab-stuffed mushrooms, and maybe scallops for hors d'oeuvres."

Claudia gave me a long thoughtful look. "What kind of budget are we working with?"

I glanced down at my notes. "More than enough to feed two hundred people."

She nodded. "Maybe even my Virginia Ham biscuits?"

"Mmmm, sounds delicious." I never could eat just one.

Sighing, Claudia slumped back in her seat. "It must be nice to have the money to buy a yacht. Some of us never get to find out what that type of life is like." Claudia's father was a family practice physician who'd worked his way through medical school. Her mother was a lawyer. With a younger brother and two sisters, I always joked that they were the modern-day Huxtables.

"I'm surprised you've never been aboard one."

"I have, just not a luxury yacht." My brow rose. "Why does that come as a surprise?"

"Because you've always managed to be in the right place at the right time. You grew up with a nanny and had a car by the time you turned sixteen, whereas my parents made me save up for a used car."

When I listened to Claudia talk about growing up, it was easy for anyone to see why she was so humble. Even though her parents were well off, they wanted their children to understand what hard work was and made sure they earned every penny. Jeanna was the complete opposite. She'd made sure her daughters always had the best of the best and no exceptions. Just thinking about it, I released a long hot breath. In a way, it wasn't my fault I behaved the way I did. I was a product of my environment. I had grown up with a mother who believed in competing with the Joneses. When I turned four she'd met Portia's father, a restaurant owner who'd had a motorcycle accident and was later awarded thirteen million dollars. He had lost the use of one arm and suffered with migraine headaches and short-term memory loss, but he was a good man and had always treated me like his own.

It was amazing how I'd listened to other people dream about things I had taken for granted. I never realized how good I really had it until I went off to college and met so many students who'd gone without just to have an education, while I had a hefty monthly allowance and pulled up in front of my dorm in a brand-new Mercedes. Even my assistant, Mia, had come from a meager background. Her parents had divorced and her mother, an LPN, had worked extra shifts just to support a family of three, while my mother juggled a social calendar and spent Mondays with the cook planning meals for the week.

"I'm thinking plenty of rolls, a bite-size assortment of cheesecakes and truffles. Oh yeah! We're going to make this the social event of the year," Claudia announced with a determined glint in her eyes.

I smiled. "I agree." First Nelly, now the city. We were definitely making a statement in St. Louis. I stretched my arms high over my head. Claudia and I had spent the better part of the morning planning the festivities. As soon as we had a menu together I would fax it over to the Mayor's office for review and approval. Claudia had already spoken to the Mayor's assistant, Susan, and we were scheduled to tour the yacht next week in order to get a better idea of the layout.

My office phone rang, and instead of reaching for the receiver I pushed the speaker phone. "*Cater to You,* can I help you?"

"Good afternoon, Christina."

As soon as I heard that deep baritone voice I felt my lips tremble and my kitty-cat clench. Goodness, he was sexy!

Claudia mouthed, "Who is that?"

I frowned and tried to fake indifference. "Hello, Dereon. How are you today?"

"Better now that I'm listening to your sexy voice. Did you sleep well?"

I tried to ignore Claudia, who was fanning herself.

"Wonderful. Thanks for asking. What can I do for you?" I asked as I reached for his file ready to take notes.

"What you can do for me is give me your address so I can pick you up at eight," he said smoothly.

I dropped the pen and met the smile on Claudia's face. She was definitely impressed. Quickly, I took the phone off speaker and brought it to my ear, then signaled for my partner to leave my office. Of course she ignored me. I swung around on my chair. "Dereon, I know we had a deal, but I don't make it a habit of going out with clients."

"Good. Then there's a first time for everything. We had a deal, and you strike me as a woman of her word. Am I right?"

I groaned inwardly at the position he had put me in.

"Christina, I think he's waiting for an answer," Claudia whispered. I glanced over my shoulder at her and cut my eyes. She had the nerve to be ear hustling.

"Sorry, sexy, but we had a deal."

"All right, all right. I'll go out with you." I told myself I didn't have much of a choice. Either go or offend a client and lose his business. Then he would badmouth me to all his friends. And before long I would lose all my referrals and have to close my business altogether. I scowled. The only reason I was going out with him was to save my company from bankruptcy. I had no choice but to rattle off my address and cell phone number.

"Excellent. I'll see you around eight. Make sure you dress sexy."

"She'll be ready!" Claudia cried. I tried to shush her, but not soon enough.

Dereon chuckled. "Hello, Claudia. Christina, I'll holla at you later," he said, ending the call.

With a groan I hung up the receiver, then leaned back in the chair. "What in the world did I get myself into?"

"Oooh, Christina, he is so freaking sexy! I'd go out with him in a heartbeat."

I glared at her. "Then *you* go out with him."

Claudia shook her head with a ridiculous look. "Uh-uh, girlfriend. That man has the hots for you," she giggled. "What are you wearing tonight?"

"I guess the red number I bought yesterday."

"Yesterday?" she repeated.

I just seemed to be digging a deeper hole every time I opened my big mouth. "I went shopping after work and bought a slinky red dress."

She wagged her brow suggestively. "Sounds sexy."

Yep, it definitely was that. "I want to portray a you-can-look-but-can't-touch persona."

I didn't miss her piercing stare. "So in other words you already planned to go out with him."

I really needed to remember to think before I spoke. "No . . but I wanted to be prepared … just in case."

"You're bad," she giggled.

"I know," I replied with a coy smile. "I'm sure my entire outfit cost more than he probably earns in a week. I think that alone will change his mind about me."

She didn't look too convinced. "This I've gotta see."

After Claudia left my office I tried to get back to work, but it was useless. I ought to have my head examined. Seriously. Ever since I'd gotten got off the phone with Tamara last night, that persistent man had been consuming my thoughts. I'd tossed and turned, and when I had finally fallen asleep, I'd awakened a few hours later in a sweat. My nipples were hard and my female center yearned for something I was certain Dereon could give me.

And that was the problem.

I didn't want to want him. I didn't want to wonder what he could do to me. It was crazy enough I was imagining what he looked liked with his clothes off. Which was why I knew I had no choice but to go out with him. If nothing else, I hoped that by going out with him I would be able to prove once and for all he was all wrong for me. That's why I was determined for him to see I had class and style and expensive taste and was way out of his league.

Since I was seriously distracted and couldn't give my work a hundred percent of my focus, I decided it would probably be a good thing for me to take the rest of the day off. Of course, Claudia made a big deal about me leaving, and even had the nerve to laugh. I barely got out the door when she came rushing after me.

"Christina, wait!"

I swung around and watched her hurrying across the parking lot looking like a wild woman. "Here, take these," she said and smacked a small manila envelope into my hand.

I glanced down, then back at her. "What is this?"

"Condoms."

"What in the world do I need with those?" I replied with a giggle.

She gave me a knowing look. "What do you think? There's no telling what might happen tonight. You might as well be prepared."

I shook my head and tried to fight a smile. "Dereon and I are having dinner tonight, nothing more … But I guess I'd better hold onto these, just in case."

We giggled like two teenagers going on their first date, then she went back inside while I headed toward my black Jaguar.

As I was driving home I was still smiling. Claudia could be so crazy. There was no way I was sleeping with Dereon. The only reason I was even going out with him was because I was a woman of her word. *Yeah, right.* I thought about him all the way home.

I moved into the condo and slipped off my heels. My dogs were screaming. A bath was definitely in order. Nothing was better than a bubble bath and scented candles. As soon as the tub was filled I stripped off my clothes and climbed into the large garden tub, turned on the jets, leaned back, and relaxed. I tried to think about my itinerary for next week, but for some reason my mind kept traveling back to Dereon. Why, I didn't know. It wasn't like I was attracted to him. Okay, I was lying. Maybe I was attracted to him, but that didn't mean anything. I'd met men before and been attracted.

I closed my eyes and the kiss we had shared moved front and center. The feel of his mouth against mine and the way he slipped his tongue inside was enough to make my nipples hard underneath the water. I started having second thoughts again. There was still the dilemma of being sex-deprived, and going out with a gorgeous man with my hormones raging was a recipe for trouble.

I sat there and convinced myself I was a big girl who could handle him. I hadn't met a man yet who'd manipulated me into doing what my body wanted instead of what was best for me. Of course, right now sex was number one on my agenda, but I was confident I could put my hormones aside for one night and stay focused.

Thirty minutes later I was under the sheets. I'd decided a short nap was in order. After all, I needed to look my best, and bags under my eyes just wouldn't do.

SEVEN

Not only did Dereon show up on time, he had the nerve to look more handsome than before. The guys I typically dated wore khaki slacks and loafers. Dereon was wearing stonewashed jeans, a crisp blue and white pin-striped button-down shirt that hung half open, revealing a clean wifebeater, and on his feet were baby blue Timberland boots. The outfit may have been casual and thuggish on anyone else, but on Dereon it made him look sexy as hell. I don't know how long I stood there with my mouth open, staring.

"Whassup, beautiful? You ready to go?"

Standing across from him caused my body to remember what it had been like to be held in his arms. I blinked once, twice, three times, while trying to come out of that ridiculous trance. *He's just a man! He's just a man!* If I kept chanting that, then I just might be able to keep my head on straight tonight. "Sure, I'm ready. Let me just grab my purse." Quickly, I turned away and left him standing on the porch. No way was I inviting him in. Too many crazies out there. How was I supposed to know he wasn't one of them? Deep down I had a good feeling about Dereon, but I figured as long as I considered him a possible stalker, the better chance I had of maintaining control tonight.

I grabbed my small clutch purse, took a deep breath and stepped out onto the porch where Dereon was waiting patiently. I shut the door behind me, locked it, and swung around to meet his irresistible smile. I felt my body tremble with longing. *Jesus, give me strength.* Otherwise, I was in for a long night.

He took a few moments to take in my outfit, and there was no doubt in his eyes that he liked what he saw. "I'm glad you followed my advice. You look like a million dollars."

More like eight hundred dollars. "Thank you."

"You're welcome." Dereon then moved in closer and I felt my pulse begin to speed up a notch. *Oh my goodness*, he was getting ready to kiss me again.

His sexy lips settled over mine, and as soon as he applied gentle pressure I exhaled and rested my hands against his chest. Part of me was hoping the first kiss had just been too good to be true and the second would fail in comparison. Only, it was better than good. It was sensational, wicked and a bit wild.

There were no words needed to describe what he was doing. All that mattered was how good he made me feel. My entire body radiated with desire and I craved him more than I craved shopping for designer shoes. Kissing was by far so much better. Dereon adjusted the angle and I opened wider, tangling my tongue with his. Within seconds my nipples tightened and moisture gathered at my core. The longer we kissed, the less the idea of leaving my house and going to dinner appealed to me. What I wanted was right there on the porch, grinding against me. And since I was being controlled by hormones, if he had suggested skipping dinner I probably would have agreed. Thank goodness he stopped and rested his forehead against mine. We stood there, holding each other until our breathing slowed.

"You ready to get this date started?" he finally asked.

Taking a deep breath, I nodded. If that kiss was any indication, I was in for a night I wouldn't soon forget.

Holding hands, I followed him off the porch over to a black Infiniti QX56. I was clearly impressed, although I could have done without the twenty-six inch chrome rims. "Nice ride."

"Thanks. This here is Nikki, my baby." Dereon hit the button and unlocked the doors, then held the passenger door open for me. "I got you," he said, and before I could protest, he lifted me off my feet. Oh my! He smelled delicious. It took everything I had not to lean forward, press my nose against his neck, and inhale. As he lowered me onto the black leather seat I felt the muscles in his forearms flex. Nothing was more attractive than a man who worked out and maintained a hard physique. Dereon winked, then shut the door. While he walked around the SUV, I took a moment to get my breathing under control and try to cool off, because the second he'd touched me my body felt like it was on fire.

As soon as he climbed in and stuck the key in the ignition, a gush of cold air came through the vents. I was grateful for the blast against my heated body. I leaned back against the seat, secured my seatbelt, and forced myself to relax. I couldn't understand why my body wasn't cooperating. It wasn't as if tonight really meant anything, or like I was ever going to go out with him again. The only reason I had agreed was because we'd had a deal. *Keep telling yourself that and you just might start believing it.*

"You didn't tell me what you did for a living," I said. I wasn't nosy, just curious. How else was I going to know what kind of man I was spending time with? I also needed another reason why he was all wrong for me.

"I dibble and dabble in a few things. Why? Does it matter?" he asked with a twinkle in his golden eyes.

Dibble and dabble? "Uhhh, no, it doesn't really matter. Just trying to make casual conversation. You know what I do for a living, so it's only fair I know what you do."

He cleared his throat, and I didn't miss his eyes shifting to the left, then right. "Let's just say … it's nothing illegal, but I think I'd rather you got to know me a little first."

I swung around on the seat and faced him. "Okay, hold up, buster! My cousin Tamara put you up to this, didn't she?"

"Tamara … Who's Tamara?" he looked genuinely confused.

Okay, maybe I'm being ridiculous. "Never mind. If you want to keep your secrets, then fine. Just don't ask anything else about me!"

He chuckled. "How about this? I'll tell you when I think the time is right. In the meantime, I'll give you a hint … I'm not rich."

I pretty much figured that part out on my own. Fine. He could keep his little secret for now. I could tell he was trying to be mysterious. It should have turned me off, but instead it turned me on even more. Brushing the attraction aside, I leaned back on the leather seat and enjoyed the sounds of Sade coming through the speakers. At least he had good taste in music.

"Where are we going?" I asked as he drove through downtown. I was so hoping he would take me to this quaint little French restaurant on Market Street I'd been hearing about.

Dereon took his eyes off the interstate long enough to grin, and replied, "A place that has the best food on the other side of the river."

"Really?" He had my full attention now. I shifted on the seat and turned. "Whereat?" There weren't too many places I hadn't heard of.

"*Michelle's.*"

EIGHT

"*Michelle's*?" I repeated, then twisted my mouth as I tried to remember if I had ever heard of the restaurant before. "I don't think I've ever heard of it."

He grinned knowingly. "You probably haven't, but I guarantee you won't be disappointed."

Let me be the judge of that. I ate out enough to know which restaurants were good and which ones to steer clear of. As I watched him cross the bridge going over into East St. Louis, I had an uneasy feeling that increased as he got off the interstate and drove through a neighborhood I wouldn't dream of being caught in during the day, let alone after dark. I glanced over at the liquor store on the corner and the men standing in front laughing, like they had something to be happy about. Quickly, I checked the door to make sure it was locked. I then slid down on the seat just in case any bullets decided to fly through the glass.

"What're you doing?"

"Huh?" I had been so engrossed with watching my surroundings I had almost forgotten he was there.

"Why are you sitting low in the seat?"

There was no way in hell I was admitting to him I was afraid of being gunned down in the hood. What would Jeanna say? Especially after my photograph was flashed all across the six o'clock news. Goodness, I would never be able to live it down.

"Uh … I have a cramp in my side and was just trying to find a comfortable spot, that's all."

I figured Dereon had a hard time believing me, because he started laughing.

He traveled a few more blocks, then pulled into a parking lot behind a brick building and turned off the engine. I glanced out the window looking for a restaurant lit up with bright lights and saw nothing but a big ugly building and an empty lot across the street. "Is this some kind of joke?" *Please tell me this was an episode of Punk'd.*

"Trust me. You'll like it," he said with a confident smile before he reached for the door and stepped out of the SUV. I wished I could have believed him, but instead I was starting to have second thoughts about why I had even gone out with him in the first place. I mean, really. What did I know about Dereon Sanders except that he was gorgeous as hell and had swagger out of this world? Speaking of swagger, I watched as he walked around the vehicle, and I found myself licking my lips. He had a confidence that exuded all over the place, and that's what scared me. He was too sure of himself and our date. Little did he know that so far I was giving our evening two thumbs down.

I waited until he opened the door for me before I stepped down from the vehicle and stood beside him.

"You ready for dinner?" he asked. Even under the streetlights I saw the devilish sparkle in his eyes.

I swallowed. "Yes."

Leaning forward, he lowered his lips to mine in a kiss that was so gentle and soft, I immediately regretted thinking negatively about him. Dereon might not be rich, but he was definitely a gentleman. He pulled back, winked, then reached down for my hand and led me around the building.

My eyes traveled from left to right. Faint music could be heard in the background. Cars filled the vacant lot across the street and were parked along the street. As we rounded the building, I saw tinted windows and light beaming from inside.

Dereon opened the door and stepped aside so I could enter first. That's when the smell hit me. Fried chicken. *Yummy*. There were several other smells that made my mouth water. The lobby was filled with people sitting and waiting. Dereon brought a hand to my waist and guided me up to a short voluptuous woman with a cute tapered haircut, smiling behind the podium.

"Hey, Dereon," she said with a twinkle in her eyes that was clearly interest. Usually, I felt too sexy and cute to be intimidated, but for some reason I found myself leaning in close to Dereon's side.

"Hi, Alexia. I've got reservations at eight."

"Yes, you do. Give me a moment." She walked off to the dining area on the left.

As soon as she was gone I moved closer and whispered. "You must eat here often, because you and the hostess seem quite chummy." I hoped I hadn't sounded jealous, because I wasn't, really. I was just being nosy.

"I eat here quite a bit, but Alexia happens to be one of my tenants."

Oh, my goodness! A bell was ringing frantically in my head. "You own real estate?" *Okay, that sounded just a little too eager.*

He nodded. "Yeah." And then he turned his head toward the door, putting an end to the conversation. Damn that man! He wasn't going to make this easy for me. How was I supposed to cater an event if I had no idea what kind of budget he was working with? Okay, maybe that wasn't the real reason. Although I don't think there was anything wrong with wanting to know what type of a man I was spending the evening with. Was Dereon Sanders chopped liver or prime rib?

Several other couples walked through the door, and there were quite a few people sitting on a long bench. Some were even standing in the corner.

"What are all those people doing here?"

He tilted his head and gave me a humored look. "Waiting for a table."

My brow rose. Could the food really be that good? No, it couldn't be. I knew of every five star restaurant in the area and *Michelle's* wasn't even on the list.

Alexia returned, reached for two menus and signaled for us to follow her into the dining room. The place was dark and the low light came from candles at the center of each table. Jazz music was playing softly in the background. We were escorted to an intimate table at the corner of the room. It wasn't until I sat down that I realized the tablecloth was made of paper, and so were the napkins. I tried to discretely examine the silverware to insure it was clean. But out of the corner of my eyes I saw the humor burning in Dereon's eyes.

"What?" I said trying to sound innocent, even though I knew I had been busted.

"They're clean. No dishwasher here. Everything is hand washed."

I shrugged as if it were no big deal, when in actuality I was relieved by the information. Dishwashers did have a tendency to leave food particles behind.

I reached for a laminated menu and studied it. I had to admit that despite the abundance of fat and calories, everything sounded quite appetizing. "What do you recommend?"

His lips curved. "Fried chicken, collard greens and baked macaroni and cheese."

My stomach growled, sounding like a dog discovering an intruder on his front porch. Thank goodness Dereon pretended not to notice. "Hmmm. I haven't had baked macaroni since my grandmother was alive. And I love good fried chicken."

"Then you're in for a treat," he replied with a wink.

A young waitress with Chelsea on her name tag came over and took our drink orders. I browsed the menu a little longer, and by the time she'd returned with two waters and took our orders I had taken Dereon's suggestion. He ordered the same.

Within minutes Chelsea returned with a bottle of white wine and two flutes. We were quiet while she poured us both a glass. I smiled and thanked her and watched as Dereon held up his flute, allowing the golden liquid to gleam above the candlelight.

"Here's to making new friends," he toasted.

"Friends." I raised my flute and tapped it lightly against his. As we sipped we gazed at each other. My belly did a nervous roll. *God help me.*

Diverting my attention, I looked around at all the casually dressed couples and felt completely out of place. I was dressed like I thought I was *all that.* Well, in actuality I was, but that didn't mean everybody needed to know that, especially not in unfamiliar terrain. I leaned across the table. "Why did you tell me to dress up?"

"I said to wear something sexy."

I tossed my hair away from my face and smiled. Men can be such silly creatures. "Isn't that the same thing?"

"Yes and no," he replied with a smile and a shrug. "I wanted to see you look good, although I doubt you ever look any less." His eyes swept the restaurant. "You're the prettiest woman in this place, and you gotta helluva walk that had everybody turning and looking at you."

Everybody. My lips curled upward. Nothing wrong with being noticed. Smiling, I gazed up at Dereon and our eyes locked for so long I felt a responding tug of arousal between my thighs before I finally cleared my throat and leaned back against the chair. "Are we going to discuss your parent's menu now or after dinner?"

He studied me, soft candlelight flickering across his strong face. "Later. Right now I wanna talk about you."

My brow rose. "Me?"

"Yeah. Tell me who you are and where you're from. You got brothers or sisters?"

I took a sip, then crossed my legs under the table. "I have a younger sister Portia who got married two weeks ago to a pediatrician."

"So she snagged herself a doctor." He looked clearly impressed.

"Yes, she did," I replied, and couldn't disguise the envy from my voice. "Portia's a pharmaceutical rep. She met Evan when she was delivering samples to the clinic where he practices. That was nine months ago."

He smiled, leaned back and studied my expression. "I can tell you're proud of her."

"I am. Jealous, too. My sister has accomplished the one thing I still have not been able to manage." Marry and marry well.

"Why's that? As sexy as you are, I'm sure there're dudes falling at your feet."

I smiled and tried to play it off. If he only knew how many times I'd been proposed to and how many times something about them was all wrong. "I haven't met anyone yet that made me want to say I do. But I'm only twenty-eight. I've still got plenty of time." *Yeah right, tell my mother that.*

"So what do your parents do?" he asked.

I rolled my eyes. "My mother is a socialite and my father is the CEO of Boone Beer."

He let out a long whistle. "Wow! That's your father?"

"Yes, that's him. You know him?"

"No, but I drink Boone Beer. Yo, his Super Bowl commercials are hilarious."

Great. Another fan. "I wouldn't know."

Dereon looked at me and his eyes darkened with concern. "You sound almost embarrassed talking about your father," he commented between sips.

I toyed with my glass. "Because I don't really know my father. He and my mother were never married and they split up shortly after I was born. Over the years he'd come to see me, but as I got older it seems he figured the more money he gave me the less time he needed to spend with me. I would have given anything to have had a father like my Uncle Craig." I stopped, took a sip then shrugged. I don't know why I was telling him all of my personal business, but for some reason he made me feel comfortable.

Nodding, he replied. "I feel you. One thing I can say. We may not have had a lot of money, but my parents were always there, especially my father. I think every black man needs a strong male role model."

"I think the same goes for women. I would love to have had a father. Instead, I always felt like I was missing something."

"It's his loss."

I smiled at the compliment. "Thanks. I just learned how to fill the void with shopping."

He chuckled and I loved the deep, throaty sound.

"Hey, I'm spoiled. What can I say?" I wasn't going to apologize for that.

His brow rose. "Yeah, I figured that out."

I shifted on the chair and took a deep breath. "I've been rich all my life. You, my partner and my assistant all joke that I'm bougie, but I don't know how to be anything else. You know what I mean?"

He nodded. "I'm starting to understand."

"When I was thirteen my father sat me down and told me to marry and to marry well. Every marriage should add more wealth, not accumulate debt."

"Your father's a wise man."

Wise wasn't necessarily the word I would have used. "I wouldn't know, since I really don't know anything about him. All he and my mother did was give me material things, and I've grown accustomed to that way of life."

"Well, I wanna welcome you to my world," Dereon replied, holding up his flute in a salute. "Down home cooking, some classic old school at its best. No Grey Poupon here."

I fluffed my hair and chuckled just as our waitress arrived with our food. I glanced down at my plate and my stomach growled on cue. Everything looked wonderful. I got ready to dig in, but Dereon reached across the table and took my hand in his. I looked up at him in surprise, then watched as he bowed his head. It took me a moment to realize he was getting ready to say grace. I was embarrassed as I lowered my eyes lids and listened as he gave thanks for both of us.

" … Amen."

He released my hand and I opened my eyes and gazed over at him. "Sorry, the only time we ever said grace was when we went to my grandparents' house. That habit died with her."

"That's a shame," he said and almost looked sorry for me.

The last thing I needed was someone's pity. I cleared my throat and reached for my fork and brought the macaroni to my lips. As soon as I tasted it, I moaned appreciatively. Dereon had been right. "Oooh, that's good."

He sent a grin in my direction. "Told you."

Yes, he had, but words didn't begin to describe how wonderful the macaroni tasted.

I talked about my ideas for his parents' dinner, but I was so busy savoring the food that conversation wasn't necessary. I gave up trying to use a knife and fork to eat my fried chicken and settled for using my hands. Twice I found myself licking my fingers, something I never do. When Dereon caught me I started laughing. "Hey, that's a sign that the food is good," I said in my defense.

"True," he replied with a nod. "I take it you don't eat much soul food."

"No. My mom was always into us watching our figures, and now I'm so busy catering events for everyone else I rarely have time to prepare anything for me. The only time I have anything like this is when I visit my cousin Tamara. Before that it was my grandmother's specialty." I bit into my chicken because it was so wonderful. Then I continued. "She was raised in Sylvania, Georgia, and every now and then she'd prepare something she wasn't supposed to be eating." I paused and giggled, remembering the way she used to make me promise not to tell Jeanna. "Grandma Celeste was diabetic and on a strict diet, but there were days she'd get rid of her nurse long enough to cook in her own kitchen."

"She sounds like my kind of woman."

"She meant the world to me." I felt my throat catch. "Anyway, she used to make sweet potatoes, mac and cheese and the best fried chicken."

"I guess there's no chitlins on your Thanksgiving table."

I gave him a weird look. "What's that?"

Dereon grinned. "Pig intestines."

Was he serious? "Eeww, no."

He wasted no time tossing his head back with a chuckle, and despite the fact that he was laughing at me, I joined in. "Sorry, but unless you're asking about turkey with apple stuffing, I can't help you."

"Stuffing?" he shook his head. "Hell, no! My mama makes the best cornbread dressing in East St. Louis."

I reached for my flute. "Hmmm. That sounds good."

"Yo, for someone who caters food, you sure are missing out on a lot."

I stopped chewing momentarily and thought about what he'd said. "You may be right, but I try to promote healthy eating. Soul food is high in saturated fats."

"I agree, and that's what makes it so good, like that chicken you're killing over there." He chuckled and I joined in.

The rest of the meal we talked sports and music. I tried to steer the conversation to the anniversary party again, but every time I did Dereon managed to change the subject.

"How about a slice of sweet potato pie?" he suggested.

"Oh, no way," I replied rubbing my belly. "I couldn't eat another bite."

"Then let's dance." He pushed his chair away from the table and rose. I glanced around and noticed the small dance floor at the end of the dining room. Two other couples were dancing close and tight. The tempo had changed to a slow, pulsing beat that trembled through my limbs.

Quickly I shook my head. "I don't dance."

"C'mon. I'll teach you." Dereon reached for my hand, and before I could protest further he drew me to my feet. I found myself following him as if in a daze. It couldn't have been more perfect. Good food, soft music. The mood was set, calling to my soul with a power too strong to ignore. I told myself it was the wine making my blood hum, not the touch of Dereon's fingers laced through mine.

When we reached the dance floor he turned and drew me into the circle of his arms. Oh, did his chest feel good. Too good. So good in fact, I felt a gut-wrenching ache growing deep down in my belly. I moved to the beat of the music, stiffly at first, but then as I followed, our movements eventually became more coordinated. Within seconds I began to relax, and was no longer worried about following his lead. Closing my eyes, I rested my cheek against his shoulder, breathing in the masculine scent of his cologne while we swayed together. Dereon moved with such style and confidence I didn't want the moment to end. What in the world was wrong with me? Because for some crazy reason, as we rocked to the beat of the music, I started thinking about another dance, a sensual dance with our clothes off. This was absolutely nuts! One moment I was refusing to have dinner with him and the next I was ready to go somewhere private and get naked. Dereon pulled back and gave me a weird look, and for a second I thought he had read my mind.

"I thought you said you didn't dance." His breath was cool and sweet against my cheek.

Shrugging a shoulder, I replied, "I don't … not really. Well, maybe a little tap dancing growing up, but I've always had two left feet, and after I ruined a dance recital when I stumbled over a prop and brought the house down, my dance teacher advised my parents to find something else for me to do and not bring me back."

Dereon's chuckles were warm and infectious and I giggled just as he tightened his arms around me. "Yo, just follow my lead and you'll do fine." A deep breath escaped my lips as Dereon reached down and cupped my butt, pulling me closer to his hard form. "Sorry, I've been dying to touch that phat ass all evening."

I guess I should have felt insulted and walked away, but I didn't. Instead I slid my arms around his waist and leaned in close, absorbing the heat of him through my clothes. Dereon dropped his head and claimed the side of my neck with his lips and tongue. With every warm caress I couldn't think, only feel him. The heat and strength of his body surrounded me like a warm cocoon. It was as if no one else was there.

"I wanted you the second I set eyes on you," Dereon whispered and his breath tickled my ear.

The words should have sent warning bells going off in my head. *Danger Will Robinson!* Dereon was so wrong for me, but right now, this very moment, I didn't care. I stared up at him and whispered, "We're worlds apart."

"We're a lot more alike than you think. If you give a brotha a chance you might find that out." Lifting his hand, he trailed his fingers lightly down along my cheek. "I plan on breaking down that wall you got around your heart, then show you how much fun life can really be, for a fraction of the cost," he added with that damn cocky grin of his. "I know inside there's a woman just waiting to let her hair down. I know I'm right. I can see it in your eyes."

My heart was pounding like crazy against my chest. Nobody had ever spoken to me like that before. I wanted to shove him away, deny what he was saying. "I really don't want to waste your time," I replied, shaking my head. "It would never work."

"Christina … just let it do what it do. You can't say this don't feel right." His lips skimmed my collarbone and went up to my jaw, and then I was staring into eyes that had darkened to a golden brown. They were filled with desire and searching for what I was thinking, even feeling.

"It will be so good between us," he replied in a lazy murmur and I felt my control slipping away. Rocking his hips, Dereon tempted me to sway along with him in an erotic dance that had me creaming in my panties.

Good Lord, I wanted him. It was that simple. Cradled in his arms, heart pounding wildly with yearning, I wanted this man like I had never wanted any of the others I had dated. And that said a lot, because normally I was guided by dollar signs. But how much Dereon was worth wasn't even a factor. My desire was solely based on physical attraction. And when I felt his arousal hardening against my stomach, my vagina clenched and I felt moistness slide between my thighs.

I searched desperately for a rational thought. Maybe my behavior was a result of going longer than any beautiful woman should ever have to go without getting any. I'd even blamed it on a hormonal imbalance. All I knew was I wanted Dereon sliding deep inside my body, making love to me until the wee hours. Driven by a need I couldn't even begin to understand, I arched against him and stroked my hands along his back.

"Christina, if you keep grinding against me there's gonna be consequences," he warned in a voice raw with need. "Yo, you just don't know how badly I wanna fuck you."

"Oh yes, I do," I moaned, then gasped when I realized I had said the words aloud. Dereon studied me almost as if he was trying to read my mind and confirm that that was what I truly wanted. Good Lord, I didn't know when I had ever wanted anything or anyone as much.

My heart beat heavily beneath my breasts and I had less than a minute to change my mind before Dereon practically dragged me off the dance floor. Common sense screamed at me to say no, but my body shouted, "Hell yes!" *Damn traitor.* I had no choice but to follow. I mean, it wasn't my fault that my body had a mind of its own.

While Dereon took care of the bill, his eyes stayed locked to mine, causing my blood to stir, then heat up. As soon as he tossed a hefty tip on the table, Dereon rose, took my hand again and led me out of the restaurant and back to the parking lot. My body pulsed with anticipation as I quickened my step to keep up with his long strides. This whole thing was crazy, exciting and so damn spontaneous.

He helped me onto the seat, then shut the door. As soon as he came around and climbed into his SUV, he reached over and lifted me over onto his lap. "C'mere." I positioned my legs so I was straddling his waist.

"I've wanted to do this since the moment I met you." With his hands at my waist, he leaned in close, his warm breath fanning my nose and lips. Dipping his head, Dereon grazed my neck and shoulder with his mouth as he whispered, "You got my dick so hard … I feel like I'm losing my damn mind."

He wasn't the only one feeling seconds away from insanity. Desire coursed through my veins as his tantalizing words played havoc on my mind and body. *This was crazy!* Common sense was screaming at me to resist, yet I couldn't get my body to listen to reason. Tonight was supposed to be about me showing Dereon how wrong we were for each other. But for the life of me nothing had ever felt so right.

"I want you," he said as his teeth nipped my earlobe, traveling downward.

"I—" His lips silenced me, making my head spin and my body overheat with need. I knew this was something I just might regret—although I seriously doubt that—so I made another weak attempt at resisting. "Dereon, I'm sorry but I … I really think this is a mistake."

"You think?" he chuckled. "I don't think. I *know*. I know I want you. It's as simple as that. No games. No promises. Just you … me … and this." With that, Dereon dropped his mouth to mine, his tongue sliding between my lips. I exhaled and realized I'd been holding my breath. My tongue met his confident strokes while my hands caressed his smooth bald head. What was it about this man I couldn't resist? I didn't have much time to consider that question before a moan slipped from my throat. Dereon explored, deepening my already stirred passion, and when he finally pulled away there was desire blazing in the depths of his eyes. "Tell me you don't want me," he demanded.

Nervously, I dropped my gaze so he wouldn't see the tattletale lust I was certain was burning in my own eyes. "I barely know you."

"I *know* enough to *know* I like what I see."

Dammit, there was that word again. He was so cocky and confident that if I'd had any sense left I would have moved over onto the passenger's side, but staring at his supple, moist lips, made that almost impossible. Dereon was sexy, and dangerous, and … Did I mention how wonderfully he kissed? Instead of demanding he take me home, I tilted my head and leaned forward, silently begging for more.

Those golden eyes darkened as his lips moved downward and met my waiting mouth. "You're so beautiful," he breathed.

I swallowed heavily. "Thank you."

Dereon kissed me gently at first, then quickly increased the pressure. I closed my eyes and allowed my body to relax as I enjoyed how good he was making me feel.

One hand slid up to cup my breast. Exhaling, I leaned into his touch, my nipples brushing against the silky fabric. When he slipped a hand inside my dress and captured a nipple between his thumb and index finger and fondled lightly, I gasped. *Oh, was I in trouble!* Within seconds my nipples were tight and erect. I opened my eyes and our gazes locked, and with the intensity I released another traitorous moan. Tearing my eyes away, I looked down and watched as he gently massaged my breasts. I sighed and lowered my eyelids again.

"Let me touch you … taste you," he whispered.

Nodding, I gave in to the overwhelming emotion. Dereon unbuttoned my dress, then dipped his tongue to taste me. I cried out and grabbed onto his shoulders, digging my nails into his flesh. "Oh … Dereon …" My head fell back, and my breath caught as I arched closer toward his mouth.

"You like me sucking your nipples?"

Like was an understatement. I couldn't ever remember feeling this aroused simply from foreplay. I loved the way Dereon nibbled gently with his teeth before closing his lips around my swollen nipple and suckling. At the same time, his fingers fondled the other breast.

My breathing was ragged as I rocked my clit along his length. My body was burning up. Somebody, anybody, quick, bring me a thermometer and take my temperature, because I was beyond delirious! I wanted Dereon right then and there.

Well, that was before I heard laughter and the clicking of high heels coming across the parking lot. Startled, I pulled back and met the satisfied grin on Dereon's lips.

"Unless we want an audience," he replied, "we better take this back to your place."

"I agree," I said and a soft wistful sigh escaped my lips. Dereon lifted me back over onto the passenger's seat and started the engine.

I was quiet on the drive home. With the smooth sounds of Marsha Ambrosius filling the air, talking wasn't necessary. We were on the highway heading back into St. Louis when Dereon reached across the seat and rested a hand on my thigh, eliciting a shiver from me.

I rested my head against the seat and stared up at the dark, star-studded sky. I couldn't believe we almost made out in his vehicle. Was I that desperate that I was willing to let a man take me wherever? No. I shook my head. It's just I was attracted to him like I've never been attracted to a man before.

So this is what it's like to be with a thug.

I had heard the rumors … had seen the movies … even read a few books, but nothing had prepared me for Dereon Sanders. My first bad boy. With my eyes closed, I fantasized about lying beneath him while he made love to me the way I was sure only he knew how, and that vision heated my body, causing me to fidget on the seat. It was lust, pure and simple, but regardless of what it was, I wanted Dereon, and I had every intention of sharing my bed with him tonight.

NINE

When we reached my condo, words weren't needed. As soon as I shut the door, Dereon swooped in and kissed me. Kissing led to heavy foreplay. Need and desire swelled and the fire between us began to burn out of control.

The kiss went on and on, and only a few feet away was a fabulous couch I'd recently had Scotch guarded, but I had other plans that included a queen-sized bed and six-hundred-thread-count sheets. One more sweep of my tongue, and I pulled back.

"Is something wrong?" Dereon asked.

I stared up into those beautiful eyes of his and shook my head. "Not anymore." Reaching for his hand, I led him up to my bedroom. As soon as we were there we started stripping each other of our clothes.

"This is so unlike me," I said as he tugged the dress over my head and tossed it onto the floor. The last thing I wanted was for him to think I did this sort of thing all the time.

"You wanna stop? All you gotta do is say the word and—"

I pressed a finger to his warm lips. "No, not at all. I'm just saying … that's all."

Grinning, he raised his arms over his head while I pulled off his shirt and tossed it. Who cared where it landed? Goodness, his body was a masterpiece! My gaze dropped and followed the narrow trail of dark hair over the ripples in his stomach to the point it disappeared underneath jeans that hung low on his lean hips.

"You sure?"

I nodded, laughing. "Yes, now take those jeans off."

Dereon blew out a low breath and reached for his belt buckle. "Thank goodness. I hated to have to go home to another cold shower."

"Another?"

He nodded. "I took one last night. I was so damn hard when I left your office. All I could think about was you."

My breath hitched just thinking about what he had done to relieve the tension. "No cold showers tonight," I cooed.

He dropped his jeans to the floor and stepped forward. "Why's that?"

"Because I want you inside of me."

"Tell me again."

"Dereon, I want you inside of me." He lifted my chin with two fingers and I witnessed the desire flashing in his golden eyes.

His erection thrust against my belly and my feminine womb responded to the thoughts of him filling me completely.

I reached behind and unclasped my bra and allowed it to fall to the floor, then slid my black satin panties over my hips and down toward my ankle. Standing in front of him, I watched his eyes travel over my naked body.

"Yo … you're sexy as hell."

I grinned. "Thank you."

He snaked a hand around my waist, drawing me closer, then dipped his tongue along my neck and trailed a path up to my ear. "Damn, I want you."

"I want you, too," I somehow managed to say before my hand began a dangerous descent.

Dereon's mouth suckled the tips of my breasts while I cupped his erection, stroking its length. He had definitely been blessed with plenty and had more girth than I could wrap my entire hand around. I took a second to think about all of *that* buried deep inside of me, and a shiver of anticipation zipped across my spine. I was definitely in for a satisfying treat. I caressed the tips with my thumb and Dereon sucked in a hiss. One of his hands rounded my hips and palmed my ass, as the other eased my hand from around his length.

"Christina … don't."

"Why not?" I asked with a hint of humor.

"You know why."Dereon lifted me into his arms and carried me over to the bed and sat me gently on top of the sheets. "Lie down."

He didn't have to tell me twice. I slid up on the bed, then sighed when his warm, hard body covered mine. Dereon looked down at me, his lids heavy over his beautiful eyes. "Damn, baby," he uttered. His fingers moved across my breasts, down my belly, and through the patch of dark brown hair at my apex before stopping where I was dying for him to touch. Skillfully, he slid two fingers across my folds, then slipped them inside. I moaned and arched off the bed. Dereon pulled his fingers out to the fingertip and then pushed again, touching me deep. I was wet and so incredibly aroused that I was spiraling toward orgasm. I started rocking my hips, meeting each delicious stroke, and was seconds away from exploding when Dereon stopped and removed his fingers. *Are you serious?* My eyelids flew up and I groaned in disappointment.

"Hold up. I don't want you to come just yet," he chuckled. "We've got all night."

Speak for yourself. I lay there pouting, ready to give him a piece of my mind. Was this some kind of sick joke? I was starting to think that maybe it was all a game when Dereon slid down on the bed and positioned his head between my thighs. He sent me a wicked grin that made my knees knock. "I'm gonna take my time … show you what it's like to be with a real man," he explained, and I felt his warm breath on my clit. With a need of its own, my hips rocked forward, desperate to feel his tongue on my most sensitive area. What the hell was taking him so long? I was ready to place my hand at the back of his neck and lower those juicy lips of his where I needed a more intimate kiss, when Dereon finally did me the honors.

Dereon pressed his mouth to my kitty, who, by the way, was meowing with need. The first stroke of his tongue on my clit drew a cry of pleasure from me. *Goodness, the man was going to be the death of me.*

It seemed as though he spent hours between my thighs, getting acquainted, licking and suckling until I thought I'd go out of my mind. I clasped my hands lightly behind his head, pushing him closer. My fingers brushed the softness of his smooth bald skin and followed the movement of his head as he tasted me.

I'm gonna … show you what it's like to be with a real man.

Dereon was clearly as real as it got—sexy, confident, and so damn skillful. He seemed to know what it would take to send me sailing into the heavens, yet he kept each swipe frustratingly light. Damn that man! He was trying to prove who was in control. He played around my most sensitive area but held out on giving me what I so desperately wanted—*a freaking orgasm* that he kept dangling out of my reach. I wanted to kick and scream but Dereon was holding my thighs firmly in place while he licked every inch of my kitty as if he had all the time in the world. He stroked up, down and around, using his tongue and teeth to add to the sweet torture, yet he never stayed in one spot long enough for the flood gates to open. Instead, it built and built until I thought I was going to lose my mind, and still he refused to give me what he knew I frantically wanted. "Dereon … please!" I cried. I mean … a girl can only take so much.

"Hold tight, baby. I'm not finished with you yet." He grabbed my hips, drawing me closer to his mouth, then swirled his tongue in tiny circles over the engorged nub. The man was driving me insane. But as incredible as it felt, I needed him inside me, buried deep in my feminine core.

I groaned, mindless with desire and frustration, my head thrashing on the pillow. "Please," I gasped, panting for air. It was more than I could bear. Grabbing onto his shoulders, I tried to draw his face away from my clit but he was too strong for me. "Please … fuck me!" By now I was squirming on the bed and moaning hysterically. I felt like my mind had shut down and all that was left was this throbbing need.

Dereon ignored my request, continuing to stroke and play with kitty until I was moaning and begging at the same time. "Please … I can't take anymore. Please … fuck me!" My hips were rocking frantically, yearning for his penis to be buried inside of me and for the orgasm that was dangling right out of my reach.

Please," I whimpered. I grabbed his arms and pulled, trying again to drag him up on top of me. Damn, he was strong, and no matter how hard I tugged, it was useless. That stubborn mule wasn't giving me what I wanted until he was damn good and ready.

Okay, enough is enough. I screamed in frustration, "Dammit, Dereon!" That got his attention. He finally lifted his face and gazed up at me with this savage look in his eyes. *Lord, help me.* He slid off the bed and moved over to his jeans, removed a condom from his wallet and stood over near the bed staring down at me as he lowered his boxers and slowly rolled it on. Thank goodness someone was thinking about protection, because it sure in the hell wasn't me. I was too busy staring at his magnificent length, wondering if I could accommodate all of that. I didn't have much time to think before he moved back onto to the bed and parted my thighs wide and position himself between them.

"You want me inside of you?" he asked. "Tell me."

"Yes," I panted. My body was weak with need. "I want you inside of me."

"You? Who's you?" he asked. "Say my name, Christina."

"Dereon … Dereon," I repeated his name over and over, and felt like I was losing my mind. "Dereon … please … fuck me."

Without hesitation he reached down, parted my folds and nudged at my opening. I pushed up to meet him as he finally drove inside, and I cried out in shock. Oh, he was big! Rocking my hips forward, I drew him even deeper.

"Christina," he groaned.

Dereon didn't stop, didn't give me time to adjust, and I wouldn't have had it any other way, because if he'd stopped even for a brief second I might have flipped him over onto his back and rode him like a horny lunatic. He began thrusting, pounding his length into me. I cried out, spreading my legs wider, wanting to feel all of him and more. Each deep thrust didn't seem to be enough until the pent-up frustration that had been building for the last several hours burst free.

"Dereon! Yesss … *yesss,*" I cried out with incredible force and the room seemed to shift as if something beneath the earth had erupted.

"That's it, baby … come all over this dick," Dereon groaned as I clenched kitty tightly around his penis, but he didn't slow his pace. He continued stroking me long and fast, drawing out my orgasm. I was seconds away from losing my mind. One, two, it had been three months since I'd last had sex and Dereon had definitely been worth the wait.

As he continued to stroke, Dereon whispered terms of endearment close to my ear. There was no mistaking the passion in his voice as he continued to drive inside of me. I pressed my lips into his neck, loving the taste of his smooth skin, savoring the way our bodies connected intimately. Then he began to move faster. I heard a strangled groan building in his throat as he tried to hold on a tad longer.

"Baby … I'm about to come," he growled.

As soon as I began gyrating my hips, he lost the battle. The muscles along his back tensed and Dereon cried out with pleasure as he came. The friction of his penis felt so good my body heated again and exploded.

TEN

Sunlight poured through the wide windows of my bedroom. I rolled over onto my back, and for a brief moment thought it had been one long delicious dream. But the throbbing between my thighs and the impression on the pillow beside me proved otherwise. Dereon Sanders was as real as it got.

Last night was like nothing I'd ever experienced in my twenty-eight years, and believe me, I've tried a lot of things in my quest to hook a rich man. But that insatiable man had a way of making a woman forget her first name, while I would never forget his.

Say my name, Christina.

I let out a slow shaky breath but still hadn't bothered to get up and start my Saturday morning. Not yet. I still had some things to sort out first. Dereon, for instance. There was something about that man. The way he smelled, his cocky attitude. Maybe it was his laugh. I wasn't sure. All I knew was there was something I was drawn to, and when Dereon pulled me into his arms and kissed me with those succulent lips of his I felt as if I had sprouted wings and gone to heaven. He was passionate and gentle, yet he was a man who knew how to take control. Last night, when we'd made love, I'd forgotten all about mixing business with pleasure and questioning if what was happening between us was a mistake I'd wake up regretting. Because regret was the furthest thing from my mind. The only thing that mattered was Dereon lying on top of me, sliding inside my body, and the time he had spent making love to me all through the night. Even now I could still feel his soft lips and tongue on my kitty as he guided me toward the verge of insanity.

Rolling over onto his pillow, I snuggled close and inhaled his masculine scent lingering in the fabric. "Dereon … Dereon …

Dereon," I sighed. He had skills others had yet to perfect. And what separated him from all the others was his confidence.

A smile curled my lips as I remembered waking up to go into the master bathroom. When I'd returned, I laid awake staring at his hard muscular body, all the way down to his beautiful penis. The shape and form were perfect. When I reached over and stroked him I felt the blood flowing and his flesh hardening. Groaning, Dereon flipped me onto my back, where I lay, legs spread invitingly for round three. When he pushed inside I cried out his name and closed my eyes, enjoying the ride as he stroked long and deep, until I thought I would die. No matter how hard I rocked my hips I couldn't get close enough. Every time I reached an orgasm I wanted more. When Dereon told me to look at him, I stared up into his eyes, holding the moment in my memory just as my muscles began to contract around his penis and a scream ripped from between my lips. Dereon watched the entire time and continued plunging deep inside my body until he could no longer hold on and finally cried out with pleasure.

Smiling, I lay there basking in the images of the entire night when I realized I smelled coffee. I slid out from under the cover and slipped my feet into the house slippers I kept underneath my bed. Grabbing a pink silk robe from the chair, I slipped my arms inside and tied the belt firmly around my waist. I padded down the stairs, smiling with every step. I'd never had a man make breakfast for me before. I was giggling to myself as I walked down the hall. I knew it sounded crazy, but I was glad he had stayed, and I had every intention of inviting Dereon to spend Saturday with me. My body hummed with excitement at the thought.

I stepped into the kitchen and frowned when I found it empty. Sure, there was coffee in the pot, but no food on the stove or on the table. I felt my face redden with embarrassment. I couldn't believe I'd thought he was cooking.

Or that he was still here.

"Dereon!" I called out, and called again as I moved through the condo. I got mad when I found it empty, and madder still when I saw his SUV was no longer parked in my driveway. I stepped back into the kitchen, dragged my feet over to the cabinets and grabbed a mug. As I reached for the coffee I spotted a handwritten note on the refrigerator.

Thanks for a lovely evening.

I guess I should have felt relieved that he had left without the awkwardness of the morning after sex. Instead, I felt like a hooker he'd forgotten to tip. He had left without even a good-bye after what I had thought to be an unforgettable night of sex. Suddenly I was embarrassed at everything I had said and done with a man who had clearly been out for one thing.

I stormed upstairs to my bedroom and groaned when I looked over at my bed and the tangled sheets. How could I have been so stupid as to sleep with a man whom I barely knew? Last night had been wonderful and invigorating, but it would never happen again.

It was well after twelve before I felt like I had my head back on straight. I was eating a salad and still feeling like a fool when I heard my cell phone. I tapped my blue tooth.

"Hey, sexy."

Dereon had a lot of balls calling me, and my body had even more nerve responding. "Good afternoon."

"Sorry, I had to leave. I had an emergency."

I waited for him to elaborate, and when he didn't I got angry because I was too stubborn to ask. "Actually, it was a good thing you were gone. I don't make it a habit of sleeping with men on the first date. It saved us from an uncomfortable morning."

"There was nothing uncomfortable about what happened last night. We're feeling each other."

Goodness! Even now I could still *feel* him all right. Immediately I pushed away the traitorous thought. "Yes, but even with that being said, I appreciate last night, but … Well, I think it's better if we keep things strictly professional from this point on. Sex was definitely a mistake."

"There was no mistake. I don't regret a thing."

Neither do I, but I'll be damned before I admitted that. "Listen, Dereon," I began as I played with my salad. "The only reason I went out with you was because we had an agreement, but I really don't think there's any point in making it more than it was—a one-night stand." Even saying the words made my stomach turn.

"Yo … Call it what you want, but I know what happened between us was more than that. I could tell by the way you were holding on to me. I heard it every time you called out my name. I felt it when the muscles of your wet pussy tightened around my dick each and every time I stroked deep inside your body. You can deny what you feel if you want, but I know what happened last night."

I was shocked and turned on by his words. I felt a shiver pass through me. Quickly, I cleared my throat. "W-Whatever you may think, it can never happen again," I said in a rush of words. I tapped my earpiece and ended the call, wishing I had gained back some control of the situation. Instead, I felt like an even bigger fool for giving in to desire and going against something I had felt so strongly about. It would never happen again. Of that much I was certain.

I spent the rest of the day cleaning house and trying to push Dereon from my mind, but it was hard to do, especially when I moved to my bedroom and stripped the sheets from my bed. I couldn't resist bringing the sateen material to my nose and taking a deep breath. The sheets smelled just like him. As I closed my eyes I found myself reliving the events of last night. Of his gently passionate kisses that ran down the length of my body before returning to my mouth again, and his plunging deeper and harder, again and again. A shudder traveled through me as my body began to respond to the memories.

Snap out of it!

My head flew upward and I pulled my shoulders back and carried the sheets down to the laundry room behind my kitchen. The sooner I removed all memories of him from my bedroom, the better. I started the wash cycle and was heading back through the kitchen when my doorbell rang. Curious who could be at my door without calling first, I looked through the peephole and groaned.

Jeanna.

Self-consciously, I combed my fingers through my tracks, trying to fix my hair as best I could. It was embarrassing enough to be wearing cut-off shorts, a faded t-shirt and flip-flops on my feet. Taking a deep breath, I put a smile on my face and swung the door open.

"Hello, Christina. For a moment there I thought maybe you were taking a nap." She blew me a kiss and stepped into the foyer, looking as fabulous as ever.

"No, I've been cleaning."

Frowning, Jeanna allowed her eyes to peruse the length of me down to my toes. I felt self-conscious, which wasn't hard to do standing beside my mother. "I see. I don't know why you won't hire a maid. Cleaning house is bad for your hands."

Trying to tell my mother I actually enjoyed housework was a waste of time. She felt there were better things to do with one's time than taking care of a house. In her case I could understand. She had an eight-thousand-square-foot home, while I barely had two thousand to maintain. "It's my condo. The last thing I want is some stranger going through my things."

Ignoring me, Jeanna sauntered into the living room and took a seat on my couch. At fifty-three, Jeanna had long black hair that was a result of weekly hair appointments. It hung loosely around her shoulders, framing an oval café latte face. I had inherited her large brown eyes that were surrounded by thick, long lashes. They were one of her most prominent features and Jeanna believed in showing off what the Good Lord gave her. She was wearing a beautiful two-toned brown Armani suit, and I can spot Armani anywhere. On her feet were rust-colored snakeskin heels that showed off long legs, proving that even at her age she still had it going on. "I was on my way to meet some friends for dinner and thought I'd stop by and see how you were doing."

I took a seat on the matching chaise lounge across from her. "I'm fine. Business is good. In fact, Claudia and I are catering a lavish affair for the city of St. Charles that's being held onboard the mayor's yacht."

"Really," she replied. Her eyes lit up with pleasure. I knew she would be impressed. It was rare when she thought there was anything appealing at all about cooking food for others, but catering a function for the mayor was altogether different. "That's wonderful. Wait until I tell the girls at dinner," she replied, then glanced down impatiently at her watch. "I spoke to Portia this morning. She and Evan are having a magnificent time in Morocco."

"That's wonderful," I replied, and prepared myself for what always came next.

"I'm so proud of her," Jeanna said mildly. "All those years I spent trying to raise my daughters to marry well, I'm glad at least *one* of you was listening." She gave a dramatic sigh and looked over at me with that sympathetic look I hated so much. "I really wish you would stop working so hard and focus on finding yourself a nice man."

"Jeanna, I have no problem meeting men," I replied and felt the nerve at my jaw begin to tick. My mother always knew how to rub me the wrong way. "I just think there are some things that are more important, and my career is one of them."

"You know it upsets me when you call me by my given name. I *am* your mother, after all."

How soon we forget. "*Mother*, I have plenty of time for romance."

She thinned her lips disapprovingly and I waited for her to continue. Because there was definitely more.

"I was talking to Kathy and she mentioned that Harold would be home next weekend."

Oh, brother. Kathy was one of my mother's phony rich friends. Harold, her son, was an attorney. It had been ten years since I'd last seen him. Back then he had asked me out, but unfortunately I couldn't get past his bad breath.

"She was planning a small get-together and was hoping you'd come by."

"Mother," I warned.

"Christina, I think it would be a wonderful idea. Harold *is* single."

I wonder why? Probably had something to do with the smell of halitosis.

"Kathy hinted that he just made partner at his firm and he's ready to settle down and have a family."

I forced a smile. "That's nice. I'm sure there's some woman out there dying to marry a lawyer."

"I wish that person was you. I don't know why you can't be more like Portia. After all, she landed herself a doctor. Can you believe it?" She paused and smiled with this far-off look in her eyes. I could tell she was already fantasizing about the house she was going to convince the couple to buy and the furniture she was sure to pick out as well. She'd tried that stunt with me but I'd refused. My condo is a presentation of who I am. The last thing I wanted to do was come home and have to think about my mother.

After several minutes of listening to her go on and on about Portia's wedding, I finally cut her off. "Mother, I'm only twenty-eight. I have plenty of time to fall in love and get married."

She frowned. "What about children? You'll be too old."

I groaned and prayed the Lord would give me the strength to get through this visit. "Mother, I still have plenty of years left before my biological clock stops ticking. Trust me."

"Well, at least give it some thought. After all, Harold is quite fond of you. He's forever asking Kathy about your welfare."

It was bad enough he had bad breath, but what was worse was the fact that his mother had given him a name like Harold. Who does that to her child? I rose from the chair, hoping to bring an end to our conversation. "Mother, you'd better hurry or you'll be late for your dinner."

Nodding, she rose. "Yes, you're right, although a woman should always show up a few fashionable minutes later." She frowned as she raised a hand to my hair. "I really wish you'd go see my beautician."

"I just got my hair done two weeks ago."

She shook her head. "That's the problem. You should go every week. A woman has to always look her best if she's going to find a husband."

Oh, enough already! I moved toward the door, urging my mother to follow. She hadn't even been at my house thirty minutes and already I was exhausted.

"I'll tell Kathy you'll think about attending her luncheon, and in the meantime, give our conversation some serious thought."

What conversation? All she'd done was given me that same song and dance about trading in my career for a husband.

"Sure Jean—oops—I mean Mother. You have a wonderful time." I swung the door open, and before she could step out onto the porch a delivery truck pulled in behind her chauffeured Maybach.

"Are you expecting something?" Jeanna asked with a curious glint in her eyes.

I shook my head as I watched the young lanky man move up the sidewalk carrying a huge bouquet of yellow roses. "Are either of you Christina Holloway?"

My brow rose. "That would be me."

He held out a clipboard. "These are for you."

"Oh, my!" my mother gasped, and placed a dramatic hand to her breasts.

I ignored her and scribbled my signature on the piece of paper. "Wait … let me go get my wallet."

"The tip's already been taking care of. Here you go, and enjoy." He handed me the large glass vase and bid good-bye.

I shut the door and stared dumbfounded at the flowers. I hadn't a clue who they could be from.

"Well, don't just stand there. Read the card," Jeanna insisted.

I carried the vase over to the side table at the end of the small foyer, set them down, then reached for the card. "I look forward to seeing you again," I said aloud, because Mother would have had a fit if I hadn't. I stared down at the inscription and couldn't resist a smile. The flowers were from Dereon.

"Well, well, young lady you've been keeping secrets from me. Who's your mystery date?"

"A guy I met a couple of days ago," I said in a far-off voice. I was too busy remembering the dimpled smile on his face, and for a second I forgot all about him sneaking out like a thief.

"A guy? And here you were letting me try and fix you up with Harold! Tell me about your date," Jeanna insisted with a hand propped at her hip. He was absolutely nothing she would approve of, but if I didn't answer she would never go away. On the other hand, if I told her the truth she would spend the next half hour lecturing me on why it was important to marry a man with money.

"He's a new client who's planning an anniversary party for his parents. He asked me out to dinner."

"Really?" her eyes sparkled with delight. "What does he do for a living?"

"He's a real estate broker." Okay, it wasn't a complete lie. He did own rental property.

Jeanna placed a finger to her lips and gave me a long thoughtful look. "Not bad, but you need to find out how big his portfolio is. If it isn't in the high six figures you need to ditch that one before you waste too much of your time."

Oh brother. "Mother, you're going to be more than fashionably late."

She gazed down at the slender gold watch on her arm. "Yes, I guess you're right, but we're not done with this conversation, young lady." Glancing over at the roses again, she smiled. "Maybe there's hope for you yet." She gave me a two-finger wave, flashing the five carat diamond on her left hand. I waited until she had climbed into the back seat of the Maybach before I shut the door and leaned my forehead against the cool steel.

Were things ever going to change? Probably not, and maybe I would never stop trying to make my mother happy. It was no easy task. Portia had always been her favorite, and nothing I did could compare, I think partially because Portia spent her entire life trying to please my mother. She had been the ballerina and the straight-A student. She shopped as much as Mother did and had gone to college with the same agenda—finding a husband—while I had done everything I could to be independent. Portia had given up her career and was looking forward to being nothing more than the wife of Dr. Evan Smith. I didn't get it. What man doesn't want a woman by his side who's his equal? At least that's the way I thought about it. I wanted a man who was proud of me and my accomplishments and enjoyed listening to me talk about the work I was passionate about.

One thing I'd liked right off the bat about Dereon was that he was interested in my job. While I'd talked he had really listened to what I had to say. I couldn't say that about some of the other guys I had dated.

Frowning, I moved away from the door and reminded myself that Dereon and I were not dating. What we'd had was a business agreement. I had allowed my guard down once and had given in to lust, but despite the beautiful floral arrangement and the ache in my chest, I wouldn't make that mistake again. I went into the kitchen and reached for the cleaning spray beneath the sink. The last thing I was going to do was waste any more energy thinking about him. Mother was right. I needed to keep my head on and stick to my agenda. Mr. Right was out there somewhere, and as long as I stayed away from Dereon I had a chance of finding him.

I guess, in a way, me and Portia weren't that different, because with every man I'd dated I'd always tried to make sure he was someone Jeanna would approve of, which was another reason Dereon was all wrong. Yet just thinking about him caused my nipples to harden. Why in the world did my body refuse to listen?

ELEVEN

"I tried calling you yesterday."

I know. I just pretended I wasn't at home.

"So … how was your date?"

I tried to slip into the office, hoping it would take a while before Claudia noticed. So much for wishful thinking. If I didn't say something she would never leave me alone. "It was nice." I brushed passed her and moved into my office and switched on the light. Of course, she followed, carrying a cup of that foo-foo coffee she insisted on drinking every morning. Just give me mine black.

"Nice? Is that all you're going to tell me? That it was nice? I want details, chica." And to make sure I knew she wasn't going anywhere until I did, she flopped down into a chair and crossed her long slender legs that looked fabulous in a conservative burgundy skirt.

I moved around my desk and put my purse in the lower drawer before finally making eye contact. "We went to a small restaurant over in East St. Louis."

"Really? You … in East St. Louis?" Her brow rose with intrigue. I don't know why she found that so surprising. I do try to be open to new things … most of the time.

"Yes, East St. Louis. *Michele's,* it was actually kind of, uh …" I paused trying to think of the right word. "… quaint. The food was good, which means I'll be on my treadmill for the rest of the week."

Claudia looked clearly impressed. "There's nothing wrong with good food. Speaking of food, can you bake a carrot cake for Nana's birthday this weekend? You know she loves your cake."

I smiled. "Sure, I'd love to make her a cake." Her grandmother was eighty-six and still walked a mile every morning. I had spent many afternoons at her home having tea and scones while listening to amazing stories of her life growing up in Baton Rouge.

Claudia took a sip, then leaned in close. "Okay, so what happened after dinner?"

She was staring at me, eyes wide with anticipation. I dropped my head and pretended I was logging onto my computer. "Nothing, really. We danced a little and then he took me home."

"Dancing? Ooh, that sounds wonderful!" she exclaimed, and then her expression changed. "Wait a minute. You can't dance."

I gave a small shrug. I don't know why the people closest to me think they know me. Jeanna used to say I was as complex as it got. "I didn't have to. All I had to do was simply follow his lead."

"So, in other words, you were *slow* dancing. Oooh! I can only imagine what it felt like being held in his arms." My dramatic partner started fanning herself. "So then what happened?"

Looking at her, I shook my head. She honestly wanted me to give her a play-by-play. "Don't you have something better to do than worry about my personal life?"

Claudia pretended to consider my question for about three seconds, then shook her head. "No, I don't. Since I'm *suddenly* single, I guess I'll have to live vicariously through you." I didn't miss the note of bitterness in her tone.

"What happened to Joshua?" I asked, swinging around in my chair.

Claudia brought the Styrofoam cup to her lips and took another sip before she replied, "Josh decided he wasn't ready yet for a commitment."

"Wasn't ready? Goodness, you've been dating almost six months!"

She nodded her head, curls bobbing around her round face. "I know, and that's what I can't understand, because when we first started seeing each other he told me he was looking for a woman who was ready to settle down and start a family."

"Maybe he got cold feet," I said, trying to cheer her up.

"Or maybe he found someone else." Her voice rose enough in pitch to let me know she was in distress. Personally, I had always thought Joshua was too self-centered. He believed his women should be barefoot and pregnant. I guess he finally realized that Claudia was too independent for that.

"Hopefully, he'll realize how good he had it and come crawling back."

She shrugged a shoulder beneath a beige silk blouse. "Maybe, but I won't put much faith in that." She looked sad for a moment, then brought the cup to her lips again. "Anyway, enough about me. I want to hear about your date."

Oh, goodness. Enough already. "There isn't anything else to tell," I said, unable to look at her as I spoke.

She clearly wasn't convinced. "So you're trying to tell me he didn't kiss you again?"

I swallowed and met the curious look sparkling in her champagne eyes. "Yes … uhhh … we kissed," I replied, then shrugged like it was no big deal.

I noticed her brow drew in nice and tight as she studied me for several seconds. "And what else? *Oh my God*! You can't even look at me." She started bouncing on her seat. "You gave him some, didn't you?"

"No … of course not. Don't be ridiculous!" I denied. There was no way I was letting her know I gave away my goodies that easily. "He isn't even my type."

"Speak for yourself. A man that gorgeous is *every* woman's type."

My lips thinned before I smiled again. "We had a good time, but I don't plan on seeing him again."

"Not see him again. Why not?" she shook her head like I was clearly making a mistake.

"Because it was a mistake. We're worlds apart," I heard myself say, and realized I was lying. I would have possibly considered going out with him again, but that was before he had snuck out and then had the nerve to call with some lame-ass excuse. He'd scored a few points with the roses, but not near enough. "Dereon's a nice guy, but he really isn't my type."

Claudia snorted. "Yeah, right … tell that to someone who doesn't know you."

"I'm serious. What do we really have in common?"

"Who cares? The man can kiss," she squawked.

She was definitely right about that. *Among other things.* My body quivered just thinking about those other things. "I still can't believe he conned me into going out with him."

"And you liked it, admit it. You could have said no."

"Yes, I guess I could have, but that's it. No more. We had a good time, but I really need to draw that line between my personal and professional life. We've been hired to cater an event for him. Nothing more." I turned on my chair, hoping I came off like I really meant what I said, because inside I didn't. I didn't want to, but I yearned to see him again. More than anything I wanted an explanation.

"Who are you trying to convince, you or me?"

I fought to keep a straight face. "What do you mean?"

"What I mean is, I saw the way you looked at that man. Hell, I saw the way he was looking at you." She paused and started fanning herself again. "When I stepped into your office I heard a snap, crackle and a pop!"

I released a weary sigh. Claudia never did know how to let things go. "It was all in your head. And if it wasn't, well then that was lust you saw."

"Lust can be a good thing," she replied, eyes sparkling with mischief and possibility. "Sometimes that's better than the rest."

"Not in my book. I know what I want and Dereon isn't it."

"You are impossible. You know that? I don't know why you keep trying to deny it."

Because as long as I do, maybe I'll start believing it myself. "Claudia, you're not hearing me. It was dinner, nothing more."

We had always shared our personal lives with one another, but sleeping with Dereon was one thing I wasn't ready to share with anyone. I was still humiliated that I had given in to his wants. Okay, my wants as well. *I* was the one who was usually in control. The person who dictated when and where. But with Dereon, no matter how hard I had tried I couldn't think straight, and instead allowed myself to be led by my hormones. And you saw where that had gotten me.

"It looks like there's a lot more going on than you want to admit." Humor resonated in Claudia's throaty voice. She leaned back on the chair and stared across at me.

"Well, there isn't. He's a nice guy, really, but you and I both know the only reason I went out with him was because he had challenged me. What choice did I really have? We do have a reputation to uphold." I maintained a tone of displeasure. "If that isn't pressure, then what is?"

Claudia laughed. "Okay, I can see how going out with Dereon was a lot of pressure."

"I don't even know what the man does for a living, but I doubt it's anything that comes remotely close to making the type of money I'm looking for in a man," I said, hearing Jeanna's voice in my head.

Claudia pushed her hair behind her ear. "A man that fine, it wouldn't matter to me if he was a greeter at Walmart. Really, Christy. Relax and learn to have a little fun. Every man doesn't have to be husband material. There are so many other reasons to keep a man around who looks that good. Would you like for me to name a few?"

I lifted my head. "No, I think I can come off with a list of my own." In fact, it would probably take up more than one page. And mind-boggling would be right at the top of the list.

Claudia smiled. "See, I knew you liked him."

"I never said I didn't. I just said he wasn't my type and that I have no intentions of going out with him again." No matter what his explanation might be. The guy might be gorgeous, but he obviously had been after one thing—sex. Okay, so maybe he had called to apologize and had sent me a bouquet of gorgeous roses, but still there was no way I was letting him get over on me again. Sure, he was a wonderful lover. With every thrust into my body he had zapped any thoughts about his financial worth. Hell, for those few hours, I didn't care if Jeanna approved. All that had mattered was how good he had made me feel. Fortunately, I had eventually come to my senses.

"I don't believe you," Claudia said as she sipped her coffee.

"Believe what?"

Claudia pointed a perfectly manicured fingernail in my direction. "That you're not interested in Dereon. I bet if he asks you to go out with him again you will."

"He won't, and if he does I won't go," I pouted.

She sighed. "Come on, Christy. Aren't you the least bit curious?"

"Curious about what?"

"If he can fuck!"

"Claudia!" I screamed.

She waved her hand. "Oh puh-leeze. Don't act like you didn't notice the way he was licking his lips when he introduced himself. All I could do was imagine those lips and that tongue somewhere else. He looks like he knows what he's doing."

Oh, he knows. Too well. He was so good, just thinking about his tongue at my most intimate area had me fidgeting on the chair like a kid in church. Dereon was the definition of confidence and skill. Not once during our time together had anything seemed awkward. He'd known what he wanted and nothing stopped him from getting it. I blew out a breath. That's the reason I was so pissed off, because he had played me and gotten exactly what he had set out to get.

"I wonder what he's working with, or better yet, *how much* he's working with?"

I rose, ready to end the conversation. "Claudia, please find another man quick."

"Nah, I'm having much more fun sharing yours." She wagged her eyebrows and I had no choice but to laugh along with her.

"Good, then, take his folder and you can call and help him find a location." The less time he and I had to spend together, the better.

She rose in one fluid motion and purred playfully, "Mmmm, I look forward to it."

I finally got her out of my office, then spent the rest of the afternoon working on menus for two upcoming events. One was a wedding scheduled for next weekend and the other was a baby shower. Reaching for a notepad at the corner of my desk, I looked down and noticed the folder beside it labeled Dereon Sanders.

Dammit. I'd told Claudia to take that folder with her.

And I had been doing so good. Leaning back in my seat I found myself going over every second of our date, remembering, wishing I could forget, but at the same time I was grateful for the memories I couldn't seem to shake. It had been a night I probably would never forget. Dereon was a wonderful lover and an intriguing man. In so many ways he was everything I had ever looked for—funny, generous, outgoing personality, and extremely handsome. Yet he lacked the qualities that were most important in my life: Wealth.

Closing my eyes, I released a heavy breath. It pained me every time I thought about it. Was I really that shallow and self-centered? Was I really asking for too much? Jeanna didn't think so; therefore, neither could I. There was a man out there who would not only have money but make me feel as good as Dereon did.

Why are you kidding yourself?

I reached for a pen, and even though I had passed the task on to Claudia, I decided to work on the menu for his parent's anniversary dinner.

I took a few moments to glance over my notes. Dereon wanted something elegant and classy. How come he hadn't asked *Michele's* to cater? I had to chuckle at the thought of suggesting soul food at his parents' anniversary dinner. That was sure to get a rise out of him. But on the other hand, having a formal evening meant I would get to see Dereon in a suit. My stomach rolled at the thought of seeing him in something other than jeans. Hell, the man was gorgeous naked, and I was definitely one to know. My clit began to pulse and I groaned inwardly. Why couldn't I stop thinking about him? I'd had one-night stands before, had even felt instant physical attraction that was fulfilled in a matter of minutes, and then had gone on my merry way. Yet I had never reacted this strongly to a man before, especially knowing nothing could ever come of our relationship. He was so different from all the other guys I'd dated. They had been spoiled, rich and selfish. Like me. But Dereon was different.

Why was it I wanted something that was so wrong for me, like butter pecan ice cream or fresh fudge? I didn't need either, but couldn't seem to live without them. I pushed away the ridiculous thought. There was no way Dereon was going to become an addiction. I was confident I had made the right choice. I needed to stick to the plan and wait for my Mr. Right. Dereon was a client, nothing more.

Then quit thinking about him!

I decided it was time to leave for lunch. I grabbed my purse out of the bottom drawer of my desk and sashayed into the lobby. I smiled when I saw Mia sitting there with her smooth mocha face, a wild mass of short red curls, and warm brown eyes. The girl had a bubbly personality that brightened up the office, and I was so glad she had returned.

"Welcome back, Mia," I greeted. "How was your vacation?"

She gave me a warm, red lip-glossed smile. "Fabuloso! I'm ready for another one."

"That doesn't sound like a bad idea. I could use one myself." It had been more than a year since my last, and the joker who had taken me to Switzerland wasn't even worth talking about.

"You on your way to lunch?" She asked.

I nodded. "Yes, I am."

"Enjoy, and don't forget your two o'clock appointment."

"Thanks. I almost forgot." Another reason why Dereon was all wrong for me. Ever since he'd walked through my office I hadn't been able to think straight.

I stepped out the door and took a deep breath, glad to be outside. That was what I had needed all along, some fresh air to get my head on straight. A breeze stirred my hair around my face as I strolled down the sidewalk toward the parking lot on the side of the building and popped the door locks on my Jaguar. I was reaching for the handle when a pair of strong arms slid around from behind and pulled me close. I knew that tall, athletic body anywhere.

"Dereon," I gasped, then swung around. As soon as I saw that cocky smile I struggled to breathe normally. In the hours since I'd last seen him I had convinced myself that what I had felt was purely sexual attraction. Only, I found myself facing that same temptation again, but this time it was even more powerful.

"Friday night I went out with a beautiful woman with a slamming-ass body and the sexiest eyes. Since then I haven't been able to stop thinking about her."

I just stood there staring up into Dereon's face, in awe of his compliment. I should have known I would want him the second I saw him. Smiling, he held my gaze, looking as gorgeous as ever. My pounding heart refused to cooperate. "What are you doing here?"

"Claudia called me," he said, leaning closer to me until I was pinned between him and my car. "We gonna go check out a few banquet rooms so I can get an idea of what I'm looking for."

I felt a tinge of jealousy, which was ridiculous since I'd been the one who'd insisted Claudia take over most of the work. "You definitely need to book the location as soon as possible."

"So she says." Reaching up, he pushed a strand of hair from my face, then slid his finger along my collarbone. "I tried calling you yesterday."

"Yes, I know. I was … busy."

"Busy or tryna dodge me?" he said, mouth curving in a teasing smile that nearly had me breaking out into a sweat.

"Probably a little of both," I heard myself admit.

"At least you're honest." Dereon leaned in and kissed my lips so gently it was like a cool breeze, yet I felt a shot of adrenaline rush through my veins. "I wanna see you tonight."

Oh, how I wished that was possible, but there was really no point in starting something I had no intention of finishing. "Sorry, but I can't."

The smile on his lips was sensual and mocking. "Are we gonna go through this again?"

"No, like I said before, I had a good time with you, really I did, but I think it's best if we keep things professional between us."

"Uh-huh," he murmured and stared down at my lips for what felt like forever. Then he leaned forward again and claimed my mouth in a slow sensual kiss. As soon as our lips touched, I exhaled. Dereon's arms slid across my back and he pulled me closer so I had no chance of escaping. Not that I was planning on going anywhere. I leaned against my car for support as heat surged through my body. Dereon wasted no time slipping his tongue between my lips, then explored in long fluid strokes that clearly stated his intentions in ways that couldn't have been misinterpreted. His kisses were sweet, delicious and tasted like spearmint gum. I marveled at how he matched the swirl of my tongue, stroke for stroke, with enough skill that zipped through me like a shot of espresso.

Dereon deepened the kiss, moving in closer and rolling his hips, letting me feel his rock-hard length nudging right at my center. My breathing had become shallow. My body was aroused. With him touching me and smelling so good, I couldn't conjure up a rational thought in my head. And that was exactly what Dereon wanted. He wanted to put something on my mind so I wouldn't be able to think about anyone but him. I wish I could say his plan wasn't working, but if I had, I'd be lying.

As he continued to kiss me, his hand moved higher and palmed my breast through the fabric of my pink BCBG dress. I moaned and wiggled against him.

It was crazy. We were standing in the middle of a parking lot in broad daylight, a spectacle for anyone who had nothing better to do than to take notice, yet I didn't care about anything except the way he was making me feel. Dereon's lips traveled to my neck and shoulder, and at the same time I felt his other hand inching underneath the hem of my dress. Oh, my body was on fire! And when his fingers skated my delicate folds another moan slipped from between my lips.

"You like that?" he whispered.

"Yes," I whimpered. I parted my thighs, aching to be filled with something, anything, as long as it belonged to him. And when he brushed a thumb across my clit, I cried out with pleasure and heat surged through my body.

"Shhh," he whispered against my ear. "I'm gonna slide my finger inside of you but you gotta be quiet. You think you can handle that?" he asked as he pushed my panties aside and probed at my opening with his index finger. I nodded eagerly. I was willing to say or do whatever as long as he didn't stop. My body was aching for something only he could give me.

He slid two fingers between my moist folds, and I gulped air. Thank goodness I was resting my weight against the car. My legs were weak and I was trembling. I dropped my hands to his waist and used him as leverage.

"Look at me," Dereon ordered.

My eyelids fluttered open and met his intense and powerful gaze, filled with passion. I was wet and hot and every stroke brought me closer to orgasm.

"That's it, baby. Pretend that's me inside of you," he whispered and pumped deeper and longer, twisting his fingers and at the same time stroking my clit. I slid my thighs open as wide as I could. There was nothing going to stand in the way of me getting what I so badly needed.

Then Dereon started whispering in my ear, telling me how much he wanted me. How he couldn't wait to taste me … to be buried deep inside of me again.

He slid in a third finger and thrust deeper, and within seconds, my feminine walls clutched him tightly as an orgasms rocked through me. Dereon brought his mouth down over mine, capturing my screams of pure unquestionable pleasure. I collapsed and rested my head against his chest until my heart rate returned to normal.

Dereon brushed his lips against my forehead, and then way too soon he released me. I leaned back against the car and stared up at his face.

"We'll play it your way … for now," he murmured. His voice swirled around me as he grazed his thumb along my cheek and collarbone. A frustrated moan slipped from my throat and Dereon grinned. "I already know you'll be worth the wait." He made of show of licking each of his fingers one at a time, and my stomach did a slow roll. I wasn't ready for our relationship to end, no matter what I said. Unfortunately, Dereon knew it as well.

Without another word he turned and walked toward my office. I was left standing there long after he had gone inside, trying to catch my breath and wondering what the hell had just happened. It wasn't hard to figure out Dereon was trying to slowly break down my resistance by slowly seducing me.

Damn him!

TWELVE

I went to lunch and purposely stayed gone longer than an hour, because the last thing I wanted was to find Dereon still there. Face it. There was only so much I could take. Besides, I was embarrassed at how I had allowed him to tease me in the middle of a public parking lot. Unfortunately, Mia torpedoed me the second I stepped through the door.

"*Oh my goodness*, Christina. That man is freaking hot! You hear me? Hot!" Mia went on and on about how fine he was and I faked a smile and eventually made my way back into my office, where I pretended to work until my two o'clock appointment. Of course, the whole time I was watching the clock and wondering what the hell was taking Claudia so long. It was after three o'clock when she finally strolled back into the office.

"Christy, that's one helluva man," she commented while posing in my doorway.

I raised my head slowly and tried to pretend I had no idea who she was talking about. "What man?"

She gave me an incredulous look as she sauntered into my office. "Dereon, that's who."

"Dereon! Did I hear someone say Dereon?" Mia said as she scrambled into the room looking from me to Claudia. "Please, please say he asked about me during lunch."

Claudia frowned. "Chile, please. The only person he wanted to talk about was that chick sitting behind the desk."

Both heads turned in my direction, and it took everything I had to keep from smiling. He'd asked about me. Thank goodness I wasn't the only one with someone on their mind. I couldn't stop thinking about his hands sliding under my dress, brushing against my—

Before the two could figure out where my head was, I scowled and faked a frown. "I don't know why Dereon was talking about me because I made it clear I'm not interested," I said with a simple shrug.

"Then can I have him?" Mia asked, and the expression on her face said she was dead serious.

Claudia turned disapproving eyes on our twenty-something assistant. The petite mocha beauty couldn't keep a man to save her life. "Sorry, Charlie. That's Christina's man."

"He's *not* my man," I retorted. That's how rumors got started. Although I'll admit, it had a nice ring to it.

"Well, he *would* be your man if you'd act right." Claudia shook her head. "I don't know what to do with you." A phone rang in the front office and Mia trotted back out to her desk to answer it. As soon as she was gone Claudia frowned, then leaned in close and whispered. "You should have seen the way that girl was throwing herself at the poor man. I'm going to have a long talk with her."

I giggled. "She can't help it. We were both that way when we were her age."

"Speak for yourself," Claudia retorted. "I dated the same guy until my senior year of college before he decided he wanted to be a missionary and travel to Africa."

I was really laughing now.

Her champagne-colored eyes twinkled mischievously. "Seriously, I really like Dereon, and as God is my witness, if you don't go out with that man again, then I will."

A groan slipped from my throat. "Enough about Dereon. I've got work to do." To show her I was serious, I shooed her away with my hands and focused my attention on my computer.

"You're something else, you know that?" she huffed.

I looked up and smiled. "Yes, I'm afraid I do."

* * *

I worked late, then arrived home, had a frozen dinner, showered and decided to spend the rest of the evening curled up on the bed with a good book. I was a huge fan of James Patterson's Murder Club Series and had bought the tenth book last week. I figured it was going to take a good mystery to get Dereon off my mind. I had just begun chapter three when my cell phone rang. Reluctantly, I stuck the bookmark between the pages and reached for the phone. "Hello."

"Whassup, did I wake you?"

My pulse jumped. It was Dereon. "No, I'm reading," I told him. "Thought I'd take a little time this evening and do something I enjoyed."

"I know something else you enjoyed. Want me to come over and show you?"

My mouth turned dry and I sat up on the bed trying to shake off the arousing words. "No, I'd rather read."

"You're lying."

A shiver of delight ran through me. "Dereon, I thought I made myself clear this afternoon. Is there something you want?"

"Yeah, how about a phone date?"

"A phone date?" I repeated.

"Yep, since you won't go out with me, I'll take a phone date. You might find this hard to believe, but I miss you."

His confession startled me. That wasn't at all what I had expected to hear. "Dereon, a phone date is ridiculous, and this … this afternoon was so out of control. I don't know what came over me." I figure I might as well take some of the blame because I could have said no.

Apparently he hadn't heard a word I'd said. "I wish you were here right now so I could taste you," he said. "I like tasting you." The soft whisper sent warm shivers along my skin.

"You do?" My breath came out on a shaky sigh.

"Yes, I also love caressing your body."

I tossed the book aside and slid down onto the bed, resting my head on the pillow. His words had a way of getting to me. "Where would you touch me?" I heard myself ask. I couldn't help it. I just had to know.

"I'd start with your face," he replied in a voice deep and full of heat. "And work my way slowly down across your neck and shoulder. When I reached your breasts I would stop and play with your nipples until you moaned with pleasure."

"Really?" I dampened my lower lip.

"Really. I love your breasts. They're large and firm, with the prettiest chocolate nipples. I'd play with them until they were hard and you were moaning, then I'd put one in my mouth and suck until you were squirming on the bed."

My breasts were responding. Just thinking about him taking my nipples into his mouth made my panties wet. I gave a nervous laugh. "Then what?"

"Then I would traveled along your abdomen and play with your sexy belly button," he said, keeping his voice smooth and low.

"You really think my belly button is sexy?"

"Hell, yeah," Dereon replied. "I'd slip my tongue in and outta that tiny little hole."

With a sigh, I placed my hand over my belly button. I could almost feel his tongue there.

"Then I would travel down slowly and brush my hand over the patch of hair covering your pussy and stop there."

"Why do you like teasing me?" I asked with a shaky breath.

He chuckled softly into the phone. "It's more fun that way."

"Says who?"

"Woman, can I finish my fantasy?"

I laughed. "Sure, go ahead."

"I would then replace my hand with my mouth and travel slowly over to your sweet pussy and taste your lips, gently at first, until your hips begin to rock against my mouth." He moaned. "Damn, you're wet."

He didn't know the half of it. On my end of the phone there was nothing but heavy breathing. Goodness, I couldn't speak. Only feel.

"Baby, can you feel me touching you?"

"Yes," I whispered. "I can feel you." With the image he painted, I could also see him.

"Good. That's real good. Then I'd drop down onto my knees in front of you, spread your thighs and take your clit into my mouth. At the same time I'd slip two fingers inside. I love the way your juices coat my fingers."

"Do you?" Somehow my fingers had found their way underneath my gown and inside the waistband of my panties.

"Oh, yeah. I love the way you smell, taste. I'd suck and stroke you until you came in my mouth."

"Ooh," I moaned. I couldn't hold it in.

"That's it, baby. Imagine I'm playing with that pussy."

I pushed my fingers in and out slowly at first, but started picking up speed. I was lost in the image he had portrayed. It was him tasting, touching, fucking me.

"Baby, you're so wet you got me hard as hell," he cooed in my ear. "I'm holding it in my hand now."

My tongue swept across my lips and the speed of my fingers increased at the image he was creating.

"Those are your lips wrapped around my dick. First you're playing with the head, then you're sliding me deep inside your mouth before pulling out to the tip again."

"I'm teasing you the way you like to tease me."

"Yeah, and I'm gritting my teeth because it feels so good with your warm lips sliding up and down my dick."

"It tastes so good in my mouth. It's like sucking on a Tootsie Pop," I cooed.

"A Tootsie Pop, huh?"

"Absolutely. I'm trying to see how many licks it takes before I get to the sweet chewy center."

He grumbled into the receiver. "You better stop or I'm gonna come."

"Then that will make two of us." I stopped long enough to pull my panties down over my hips, then spread my thighs and slipped my fingers back inside while my thumb grazed across my clit. I hissed loudly into the phone.

"That's it, baby. I want to hear you come." He took a deep breath and I could almost feel its warmth through the phone.

"After you."

He hissed. "No, you first."

I swallowed to ease the dryness in my mouth. "What am I doing now?" I was so enjoying the fantasy.

"Now you're straddling me."

Oh my goodness.

"My hands are on your waist and I'm guiding you slowly down over the length of my penis."

I tried to laugh lightly, but it came out sounding more like a groan. "Wow." I could really feel him buried deep inside of me.

Dereon's voice had become dangerously low and shaky. "Now you're riding me. Slowly at first, coming almost completely out before pushing all of me deep inside of you again. My hands are at your waist, guiding you."

"Yesss," I moaned. My eyes rolled to the back of my head. I was soaring high over the bed. "You got me so wet."

"Baby, can you feel me sucking your nipples while you're riding my dick?"

My fingers dipped in and out of my body. "Yes, I can feel you."

"Say my name, baby."

"Dereon … I can feel you, Dereon."

There was heavy breathing coming through the phone and it didn't take a genius to know he was seconds away from coming himself. I could see myself staring down at him while I rode his beautiful length. Starting slowly, then building frantically.

"That's it, ride it. I love the way your muscles tighten around me when you come."

I no longer heard anything but the pounding of my heart. My entire body was on fire. I applied a little added pressure to my swollen nub and that was all it took. Waves of sensation swept over me, lifting me up and over, sending me soaring and crying out his name.

"That's it, Christina," he coaxed, then I heard a few grunts and pants of his own. "*Aughhh*!" he cried. We both sat there on the phone listening to each other breathe while our heart rates slowed.

"How's that for a phone date?" he replied with a chuckle.

I couldn't help it, I laughed along with him. "Good night, Dereon."

"Yo … Christina." I heard him called out.

"Yeah?"

"Sweet dreams, baby."

I ended the call, then lay there with a smile on my face, feeling quite satisfied yet more confused than ever.

THIRTEEN

I returned to the office after a quick lunch and a much-needed hair appointment. My amazingly flamboyant hairdresser Andre washed and dried my thin shoulder-length hair, then added weave for fullness before flat ironing my hair to perfection. My boy had skills.

Mia had already left for the day and a pink message slip was on the clipboard mounted to my door. I removed it and read the message to call Tamara, marked as urgent. As soon as I lowered into my chair I reached for my phone and dialed. "I got your message. Is something wrong with the baby?"

"No, nothing like that," Tamara snickered. "I spoke to Claudia while you were at lunch and she said you refused to go out with that Dereon guy again."

I dropped my head onto my desk and groaned. What was it with those two that they needed to be all up in my personal life? "She's right. I did say that." Although ever since our phone sexcapade I'd been rethinking my decision.

"Come on, Christina. You promised to go out with him *five* times. Think about the locket," she taunted, and I abruptly sat up on the chair. Goodness, how was it I kept forgetting about the locket?

That was the problem. When it came to Dereon I didn't know how to think. One minute he was all wrong for me and the next he was making me say his name. How was it one man had so much power over my mind and body? Well, whatever the reason, I needed to run for cover! Because being around Dereon was hazardous to my mental state. However, I'd been waiting all my life to get my hands on that locket, and it made me reconsider. It's a shame the things a woman has to go through to get the things she wants most.

Leaning back in my chair, I twirled the phone cord around my finger as I spoke. "Well, I guess if you put it that way, I could go out with him four more times." I mean, it wasn't like he wasn't gorgeous and couldn't have almost any woman he wanted. A smile tipped the corners of my lips at knowing I was going to see him again.

"Now that sounds more like it."

Actually, after our evening of phone sex I had spent the last week tossing and turning and rethinking my position. My body was craving that man, and even if he wasn't marriage material, Claudia was right. What's was wrong with having a little fun? The relationship would be strictly physical, of course, for the sole purpose of getting that man out of my system. Four more dates would be my chance to prove to everyone that I really did know how to relax and enjoy Mr. Right Now without there being any kind of ulterior motive . Well, other than the locket. Besides, sexual chemistry was the only thing Dereon and I had in common. I was so confident that's all there was, I was certain that by date number five my attraction to Dereon would have died a slow painful death. In the meantime I could have a little fun.

"Okay, I'll do it for the locket."

"Yeah, right. Who are you trying to fool? You know you want to see him again."

"Okay, maybe I do." Just thinking about him had my pulse racing and my forehead beading with sweat." Oh, shit!"

"What? What?"

I had been so embarrassed after the phone sexcapade I had called Dereon the following morning. "I left a message on Dereon's phone to never call me again."

"Is that all? Goodness, Christina! You scared me for nothing. Do you really want me to have this baby early?"

I chuckled. "Sorry about that."

"Your problem is easy to fix. Just call him and tell him you changed your mind."

Yes, I could do that, only I had never been the type of woman to run after a man after I had already told him no. Also, I'd been avoiding his calls ever since our kinky night of phone sex. Evidently he had finally gotten the hint, because for two days I hadn't had one missed call or a pink phone message from him.

"Have you forgotten? This is supposed to be about the new Christina, remember?"

Yes, she was right. I pulled my shoulders back. The new Christina. A woman who would have a no-strings-attached relationship with a man, even though she knew the relationship would never amount to anything. So what? I was young and deserved to have a little fun.

"Call him and ask him out. Pretend you're calling him to discuss details about the party, anything, just call that man." She was practically pleading with me.

"Okay, okay, I'll do it. But in the meantime, Missy, you need to put that locket in the jewelers and have it shining like a new brass penny for all the hoops you got me jumping through." She was cackling like a hyena as I hung up the phone.

I tapped a sculptured nail against my desk while I tried to think of every reason why calling Dereon was a big mistake. I decided to weigh my pros and cons. I reached for a pen and paper and made two columns: pros and cons. Whichever column was the longest would be the one I would accept.

I immediately wrote *cocky* at the top of my list, because Dereon definitely was that, although so far from everything I'd seen he had every reason to be, and to be honest, I truly liked that about him. So I erased the word and decided it was only fair to list it under the pros.

Next I scribbled *cheap*. After all, he had taken me to a hole-in-the-wall restaurant. I was sure our total bill for dinner had come up to less than one hundred dollars. Okay, maybe he was cheap, but I had to admit that the meal had been absolutely fabulous and the warm friendly atmosphere was like nothing I had experienced at any of the five-star restaurants my other dates had taken me to. So I blew out a frustrated breath as I started to erase cheap, then decided to keep it and put *wonderful dinner* under one column and leave *cheap* in the other. After all, just because he'd picked out a fabulous place to eat didn't change the fact that Dereon had gotten off cheap.

After sitting there a few minutes longer and not coming up with a single thing other than the word *hood*, I decided to work on the *pros* for awhile. I scribbled handsome, wonderful personality, great kisser, even better lover, and did I mention he was fine? I was scribbling as fast as the thoughts were coming and by the time I'd started describing every part of his delicious body I finally crumpled up the page and tossed it in the trash. "Fine! I'll call him," I muttered under my breath.

I removed his file from my drawer and flipped through my notes until I stumbled across Dereon's business card. I stared down at the fine script letters. Dereon Sanders, *Real Estate Investor*. How come I hadn't noticed that before? I wondered, and decided that maybe Claudia had placed it there. The title sounded as if he was someone important. *He is.* After one date—correction—one date, and one orgasm in the parking lot and phone sex, I couldn't stop thinking about him. I wasn't sure when it had started. It could have been the first kiss or possibly the second he'd walked through that door, or it could have been when he was kissing me up my inner thighs to my—

I pushed the images aside, took a deep breath, then reached for the phone. After several failed attempts, I heard ringing in my ear and my heart started pounding like crazy. *Please don't let him answer*, I kept chanting over and over and was preparing to leave a message when I heard someone pick up the line.

"Hello?"

Oh, no! Now that I'd called him I didn't know what to say.

"Hello?"

Goodness, I had to say something. Anything or make a totally fool of myself.

"Hello?"

I cleared my throat. "Hello? May I speak to Dereon?" As if I hadn't recognized the bass in his voice by now.

"You're speaking to him." Was that laughter I heard?

I cleared my throat a second time. "Hi, this is Christina."

"Hello, Christina."

His voice vibrated through me. He sounded so sexy my heart started racing and I wanted so desperately to pretend I had lost my signal and hung up. The only problem was I had called from the office instead of my cell phone.

"How have you been, Christy?"

I loved the way he used my nickname. His seductive tone turned me on more than one could begin to imagine. If he only knew I had been a basket case because I couldn't get him off my mind. "I've been busy. Really busy. Everybody wants an event catered."

"So are you trying to tell me the reason why I haven't heard from you in over a week is because you've been busy?"

I gasped. Had he really been hoping to hear from me? I tried to hide my excitement. "Yes, Claudia and I've been working some long hours. We catered a corporate luncheon yesterday."

"Then I guess I shouldn't feel insulted."

Insulted? I can't believe the nerve of this man. Did he really think that after having phone sex I was supposed to run after him? "I'm sorry, I don't remember your fingers being broke."

He chuckled openly. "Yo, I tried to holla at you but after you left a message on my phone telling me to *never* call you again, I figured unless I wanted to be arrested for stalking I needed to leave you alone."

Oh, yeah. I guess that made sense. "Well, that's why I'm calling now. I … uhhh … had some questions for you about the anniversary dinner."

There was a noticeable pause. "I was hoping you were calling to tell me you missed me."

Yes. Dear Lord, I missed you. His comment brought a smile to my face. "Actually, I would like to meet for lunch tomorrow to go over the menu."

"I'm meeting with my realtor tomorrow afternoon to look at a property. How about dinner tonight?"

Dinner? No way. I had really wanted to do lunch. It was a lot safer. Otherwise, we might really end up having sex in the front seat of his SUV. "Tonight isn't good for me, but I'm open for a late lunch."

"Make it dinner tomorrow and you have a deal."

I so wanted to say no … Okay, so I'm lying again. I wanted to see him, and then there was also the locket. Not that it took much to convince me. "Okay. As long as it's somewhere low fat."

He chuckled and I couldn't help but smile. "How about you pick the place for dinner? One rule, though."

"Oh, brother, I should have known there was going to be a catch to this."

"Absolutely. They've gotta serve hamburgers *and* I get to see that sexy ass in a pair of jeans."

"Jeans? For dinner?" I chuckled. "You're kidding, right?"

"No Christy, I'm serious. No suits, dresses or pantsuits. Jeans."

I tapped my index finger on the desk as I pondered the possibility. "Okay." Sure. People went to dinner in jeans all the time. I was certain to find a nice place. I would just have to ask around. How hard could that be to find some place other than fast food that had class but was casual enough for jeans and hamburgers?

Dereon had the nerve to laugh at me again. "This I gotta see. I'll pick you up at seven."

I hung up the phone and couldn't resist the smile that curled my lips. I was going to see Dereon again. Leaning back in the chair, I inhaled deeply and brought a hand to my aching breasts. I tried to convince myself I was seeing Dereon again for the locket, but deep down I knew there was more to it than that. I just wasn't ready yet to admit how much I was looking forward to tomorrow night.

FOURTEEN

"What do you think of these?"

We were shopping at Saks Fifth Avenue at the Plaza Frontenac. When I told Claudia I had a jeans date for dinner with Dereon, she got excited and insisted on going with me. I swung around and looked at the pair of Juicy Couture jeans Claudia was holding up in her hands and frowned. "Skinny jeans make my hips look wide."

"Wide!" she barked. "There is nothing wide about you but your head."

"Ha-ha! Funny." I don't know why she thinks I'm stuck on myself. Usually I'd brush the joke off, but this time I turned around and met her gaze. "Do you really think I'm big-headed?"

"Sweetheart, you know I love you, but I've told you before you need to come down a few pegs. Starting tonight, with this date."

"Okay, give me those jeans." I took them from her hands and moved into the dressing room. It took several tugs to pull the tight denim over my hips, but once I did they zipped with ease. Turning in front of the mirror, I couldn't help but grin at how good they fit. I scurried out of the dressing room. "How do I look?"

Claudia looked me up and down and nodded. "They look real good on you."

"You think so?" Her opinion meant a great deal to me.

"Definitely. Christina, Dereon's going to have a fit when he sees your ass in those jeans."

I chuckled. That was exactly the reaction I wanted him to have.

"Okay, now you need a cute top and some flats."

"Flats? Uh-uh." I shook my head. "That's where I draw the line."

Claudia's eyes sparkled with laughter. "I'm just playing. Come on. They're having a shoe sale next door."

I made it back to my condo with less than two hours to get ready. I showered, slipped into the jeans, put on a cute blouse and a pair of yellow espadrilles, courtesy of Jimmy Choo. After spraying a little Gucci parfum at my wrists, I moved to the mirror and grinned at what I saw. I looked absolutely fabulous. The dark skinny jeans rode low on my hips. The hem of the yellow and white camisole top ended at the dip of my waist, revealing my belly-button. After all, Dereon had mentioned how cute it was.

I allowed my jet-black hair to hang loose around my shoulders, then reached for my make-up. With a clear milk chocolate complexion, I didn't need much. Foundation. A little blusher. Nothing too heavy. I didn't want him to think I had gone to all this trouble for him, even though I had.

I applied a little mauve shadow to my brown eyelids and a touch of pink on my lips. As I applied mascara to my lashes I looked at my reflection and my heart skipped a beat. I was excited about the evening ahead. Every encounter we'd had so far had involved sex, so where else could the evening end?

Pulling my shoulders back I tried to convince myself it was a business dinner, even though the only thing we had to go over was the dinner menu. He and Claudia had already selected the pastries and the location. Nope, tonight was going to be about a lot more than food. No matter how hard I tried to deny it, I was hoping the evening would end with Dereon's having me for dessert.

Shortly after seven the doorbell rang and my heart started pounding so hard I had to stop to catch my breath. I had been waiting all evening for this, and now that the moment had arrived I was so nervous my knees were knocking together. I heard the bell a second time before I finally calmed my nerves enough to head to the door. I held onto the banister, then made my way down the stairs and to the door, where I took one final breath before opening it.

The second I saw him, Dereon swept my breath away. Was it possible for a man to be even sexier than the last time I'd seen him? The proof was standing right in front of me. Dereon was wearing a black fedora hat. I'd always thought the style was sexy on the R&B singer Ne-Yo, but he had nothing on the man standing in front of me. His was cocked to the side of his slick bald head and tilted just above his large golden eyes—powerfully piercing and hooded by thick black eyebrows and lush eyelashes. I had to swallow as my eyes traveled down his hard and powerful face to the delectable lips he was licking. I repressed a shiver. Goodness, a girl could only take so much, and Dereon looked downright sexy in stonewashed black jeans and a red polo shirt, with black and red Jordan's adding to the impression. I never found sneakers on a man's feet to be sexy until now. Clothes didn't make the man, but on Dereon the outfit looked like it wouldn't have looked on any one else—downright sexy. I had to force myself to finally speak. "Hey."

Dereon took one look at me and whistled long and low. "Damn, baby. You look good enough to eat."

And so do you. "Thanks." I stepped aside so he could enter.

"Speaking of food, where are we eating?"

As soon as he was inside, I shut the door and swung around. "One of my clients recommended a really nice restaurant in the Central West End. I hope you like hamburgers," I teased.

His lips curled with humor as he replied, "As long as I'm with you, I'll eat just about anything."

I laughed. "Glad you're willing to make an exception. Let me go and grab my purse." I turned and was heading to the kitchen when Dereon swung me around and pulled me close. My eyes flew open wide with surprise when I saw those beauties of his glittering darkly.

"Yo … Is that how you greet me?"

"I—"

Before I could find the words he'd captured my mouth with his. I would be lying if I said I hadn't been waiting for this, because I had. I clasped my hands around his neck and leaned deeper into the kiss, and when his tongue slipped inside I was ready. Once again he tasted delicious. I matched the rhythm of his strokes and the kiss could have gone on forever and it still wouldn't have been long enough. His mouth was so damned confident and demanding, and I decided if I didn't end the kiss now it would be to hell with hamburgers, and we'd be between the sheets gyrating to a different beat. I stepped back out of his reach.

"Mmmm, that will have to do for now," he said.

My breath caught in my throat as I stared into those mesmerizing eyes, and at the same time I was dangerously aware of the subtle smell of his cologne. "I-I'd better get my purse."

His eyes burned dangerously. "Yeah … you better," he taunted softly.

Relieved that I'd had a few moments to get myself together, I hurried into the kitchen, swung open the freezer and stuck my head inside. With only a brief kiss, my nipples had become agonizingly hard and my panties moist. I was on fire! Dereon had a way of knocking me off balance and making me painfully aware he was a sexy and virile man. He also made me feel beautiful and wanted, and that's what had my heart skipping an extra beat. If I wasn't careful he was going to be my downfall, and that I couldn't have.

Knowing I couldn't hide in the kitchen forever, I mentally squared my shoulders, grabbed my purse, then sashayed back into the living room and followed him out the door.

"Where's Nikki?" I asked when I noticed his Infiniti missing from my driveway.

"I decided to drive the old school today. I hope you don't mind?" I could see he was holding back laughter.

I followed the direction of his eyes to a 1978 Monte Carlo parked out in front of my condo with eighteen-inch rims and a metallic purple paint job. *Is he for real?* It looked like something a drug dealer would drive, yet I shook my head and mumbled, "No, it's no problem at all."

"Good."

I climbed inside and leaned back in my seat. I decided to wear my dark shades, at least until we left my neighborhood. After all, I had a reputation to protect.

"You hiding from someone?" Dereon asked with a chuckle.

Okay, maybe I was being a little ridiculous. "No, not at all." I sat up on the seat and cleared my throat. Once he'd pulled onto the highway I removed the sunglasses and started to relax. I gave him directions to the restaurant and we were on our way. After a while I forgot all about the car and focused on the gorgeous man sitting beside me.

* * *

"You said someone recommended this place?"

"Yes, a client of mine," I replied with a look of uncertainty, then glanced down at the menu again. I had asked around for a nice classy place to go that was casual dress with good hamburgers. Several people had raved about this place. But the second we stepped inside and were greeted by a hostess wearing all white and a waiter dressed in a shirt and tie, I knew this place was all wrong.

"Look at these prices! True Bleu Beef is a high-priced burger joint."

He was right. Forty-five dollars for an Angus steak burger and fries. "I guess this place isn't the type of burger joint you were looking for."

His brow rose with amusement. "No, I don't like spending fifty dollars for the same thing I can get as a number three at Burger King."

I giggled because it was actually funny. The way the hostess greeted us and walked us to a round table covered in fine linen and asked if we would like a glass of vintage white wine, I should have known. "Sorry, I was trying to impress you."

He leaned across the table. "Sweetheart, keep looking sexy like you are tonight and that's all the impressing you need to do."

I flushed at his low sensual voice. "I asked you out to dinner. So tonight is my treat. Go ahead and order a fifty-dollar hamburger if you'd like." I just hoped they tasted good.

"You don't really eat burgers, do you?"

I must have looked like a deer in front of headlights because he started chuckling uncontrollably. "Okay, so maybe I don't eat burgers on a regular basis, but I have had them. I just prefer a good steak instead."

"A caterer who doesn't eat burgers." Dereon shook his head. "Christy, baby, you are too much. Let's just go somewhere that you like. My treat."

"But I'm supposed to pay for dinner," I protested.

"Sorry, but I believe in taking a woman out. It's the way my parents raised me. Dad always said women are to be spoiled and made love to, and as long as I remembered those two things I could never go wrong," he added with a wink.

Goodness, how right he was. "Really, this, uh, restaurant is fine."

"Suit yourself." Dereon said, then studied his menu. "What do you think, Christina? Should I have the half pound burger with or without goat cheese?"

My eyes snapped up from the menu to meet his smirk. "Are you making fun of me?"

He shook his head and I could tell he was resisting the urge to grin. "Of course not."

"You better not be," I warned, then glanced at the menu, then back at him. "Actually, I think melted goat cheese and chives sound delicious." I noticed his lips turned down with surprise.

"Yo, you serious?" he asked.

I lowered the menu to the table and started laughing. "No, it sounds awful. If I have to eat a burger, then I expect it to be meat, cheese and a bun, nothing else."

"I'm with you," Dereon said with a sigh of relief, then rose from the chair. "C'mon, let's go," he said taking my hand.

"Where are we going?" I asked as he brought me to my feet.

"I'm going to show you what a good burger is."

Smiling, I reached for my purse and followed him out the door.

Thirty minutes later I was squirming on a rickety old bench. "Mmmm, where in the world did you find this place?"

Dereon shrugged. "My dad used to bring me here all the time."

We were sitting in Burger Creations, a restaurant on the north side of St. Louis. It was a small, no-frills establishment with wooden picnic tables, but what it lacked in class the restaurant made up for in taste. I took another bite of the delicious bacon cheeseburger and moaned out loud again. It was by far the best I'd had in years.

Dereon leaned across the bench and rested a hand on my upper thigh. "If you keep that up I'm gonna have to pull you into the supply room in back."

I swallowed hard and shifted on the seat. Just the image alone was enough to make me salivate. "You wouldn't dare," I challenged, even though the savage look in his eyes said he would.

"Try me."

I decided it was safer to finish my burger.

For the next half hour I enjoyed the one hundred percent steak burger that had been fired on a flaming grill. Trust me, Dereon insisted that the manager allow me in back just to prove it. We also had home-cooked fries and real chocolate milk shakes. By the time I had slurped the last of the chocolate delight through my straw I was ready to unsnap the button of my jeans. "Oh my goodness! I can't tell you the last time I've enjoyed a hamburger as much."

He looked pleased with my answer. "Good. I'm glad you liked it. And to think we both ate for under twenty dollars."

"Okay, I guess I deserved that one."

Chuckling huskily, Dereon draped an arm across my shoulders and led me back out to the parking lot and into the car that I decided was actually kind of cute. He had obviously spent quite a bit of money restoring its original look, although the only old cars I dared to own were expensive and vintage.

We were on 170 heading back to Ladue when I heard Dereon clearing his throat. "Remember the other night on the phone?"

Remember? Hell I couldn't get that sexcapade out of my head. "Yeah."

"I wanna see you play with yourself."

"What? Right now?" I gasped weakly.

"Yeah, right now."

I sputtered with laughter. "How old are you?"

"What does my age have to do with anything?" he asked.

"Nothing … everything … It just depends." I was sputtering like a fool.

"Depends on what?" he teased, and tipped his hat.

I swung on the seat, staring over at his beautiful teeth and panty-dripping smile.

"I want to know if you're of legal age." It sounded more ridiculous after I'd said it. Dereon obviously agreed, because he started laughing uncontrollably.

"Don't you think it's a little late for that? Especially since I already know every inch of that body?"

My stomach quivered remembering him licking me from head to toe me.

"Trust me … I'm old enough to handle my business."

Yes, he was. "Then why are you so mysterious? You won't even tell me what you do for a living … or your age."

"I told you I flip properties. Everything else you'll find out in time. Trust me. But right now I want you to close your eyes."

I released a shaky sigh. "Okay, my eyes are closed."

"Now, slide your jeans down and put your hand between your legs."

He was kidding, right? There was no way I could touch myself in front of him. It was one thing doing it over the phone, but here, in his Monte Carlo, with my jeans down and my fingers buried between my thighs, with him watching. I couldn't. I wouldn't. Or at least that's what my mind was saying, because my hand, which had a mind of its own, was unzipping my jeans and sliding them down over my thighs. It was Dereon, after all, and with him I was willing to try just about anything. I don't know what it was, but he made me feel wild and reckless. Besides, I wanted to turn him on. Make him want me so badly he'd drive with a heavy foot all the way back to my house.

"That's it, baby."

Goodness, I was stroking my inner thighs. When the hell did that happen? My head was back against the headrest with my eyes closed and my fingers were where he wanted them. "You know you're wrong for this, right?" I murmured as the tension began to climb.

"You're right," he growled. "I'm tryna watch you outta the corners of my eyes without having a wreck."

I chuckled. "Hmmm, I hadn't thought about that." For his viewing pleasure, I spread my thighs. That required pushing my jeans down to my ankles. *Next time I'll remember to wear a skirt.*

"Now that's what I'm talking about. Lean your seat all the way back … That's it. Now run your fingers along your thighs. Yeah … You like that?"

"Mmm-hmm."

"Now tell me who's touching you, Christy?"

"You are, Dereon."

"Do you like me touching you?" He took one hand from the steering wheel and reached across and stroked his fingers along the length of my thighs, starting at my knees and traveling upward at a snail's pace.

"Yes," I moaned, because this was what my body was aching for—Dereon's magic hands. But that was only the beginning. After that I needed something long, chocolate and preferably nine inches, as long as it was attached to the Mandingo sitting beside me.

"Tell me what you're thinking about," he said, as if he had read my mind.

"You … I need you inside me."

He returned his hand to the steering wheel. "So do I." Dereon's voice was low and strained, and his confession made my juices flow freely. Unconsciously, I started rocking my hips on the leather seat. "That's it," he coached. "Now slide your fingers along your pussy. Take your time. That's it, baby. Now tell me … are you wet?"

I couldn't answer. Hell, I could barely breathe as shudders raced up and down my spine. My hand, his voice and the vision dancing before my eyelids of him stroking and nibbling at my clit with his lips and tongue was enough to send me dangling over the edge.

"You remember how it felt when I was sucking your clit?"

"Yes … I remember." *Hell, how could I forget?* " Please, Dereon … touch me again. I need you to make me come."

I heard a soft rumble of laughter." I am touching you. Those are my fingers stroking you. Ooh, yeah, baby, you're coating my fingers with your juices," he hissed. "Dammit, I wanna be inside you so bad, Christy, I can't get to your place fast enough. In the meantime, I want you to come for me. Baby, can you do that for me?"

Damn right I could make myself come.

I thrust my fingers deep between my folds, pumping in and out, drawing closer and closer but never close enough, but then I opened my eyes and found Dereon had pulled to the side of the road and parked the car. He was sitting there watching me, as an orgasm ripped through me. My eyes rolled shut while my body bucked against my fingers. I pulled in several ragged breaths until the final wave passed.

I sat there slumped in the seat, breathing heavily and not ready for the moment to end. Because it wasn't enough. I needed more. I needed Dereon, not my own fingers buried deep inside of me.

"Damn!" Dereon hissed, then leaned over and captured my mouth with his in a kiss so explosive that when I felt his finger stroking my sensitive nub I bucked off the seat and came hard again with his lips crushed against mine. He kept on kissing me until my breathing returned to normal, then returned back to his seat.

I was thankful when the Monte Carlo was moving again and he was no longer staring at me with my jeans down at my ankles. With my eyes still closed, I sat there wondering what in the world he was doing to me. It was as if he had cast a spell over me. None of my other dates had ever asked anything so kinky, and trust me, they'd made some weird requests. Yet I hadn't been willing to do anything out of the ordinary unless it benefited me in some way. Vacations, jewelry, shoes, but nothing had come close to what Dereon had just asked. But with him it was different. I was willing to do just about anything, and that's what frightened me.

Dereon pulled to a red light and brought the car to a stop. I opened my eyes and pulled up my jeans.

"You okay?" he asked. I looked over and found him staring at me with his eyes soft with concern.

"Yes, I'm fine." *I had just come not once but twice in a span of fifteen minutes.* I started chuckling. "I'm better than fine."

"Yes … you … are. You're sexy as hell. How much farther to your place?" he replied with strangle laughter.

I glanced out the window and realized he had gotten off on Page Road, which wasn't anywhere near my condo. "How in the world did you end up over here?"

"I was so caught up in what you were doing, I think I missed our turn a couple of times," Dereon said, and I laughed.

We turned around and a few minutes later he pulled into my driveway and turned the engine off. He climbed out and walked around and helped me out of the car. I smiled. Dereon was such a gentleman, nothing at all like that asshole Logan, who had yet to apologize for trying to play me. We moved to the door holding hands. I put the key in the lock, opened the door and turned and faced him.

Dereon stepped forward so our bodies were touching. "I hope you're inviting me in."

I swallowed. "Yes, I am."

"Good, because vampires can't enter unless they've been invited," he murmured, nibbling playfully along my neck and causing me to wiggle with laughter as I hurried into the house.

FIFTEEN

Giggling, I shut the door, swung around and froze. Humor had suddenly been replaced by heated desire as I stared up into his glorious eyes.

"Tell me what you're thinking about," Dereon said, reaching up and pushing his fingers through my hair.

My lips moved but words refused to come out. I had been waiting all evening for this moment and was so excited I couldn't think straight.

Dereon smiled and was standing so close I could smell the breath mints on his breath. "What? Cat got your tongue?" he murmured. "Okay. Then how about I tell you what I'm thinking?"

Oh, yes, please tell me.

Dereon ground his hips against me, making certain I was aware he was aroused. Trust me … he wasn't the only one. My hands were trembling, and when he told me exactly what he planned to do to me, I almost dropped to my knees.

"I want you to go upstairs, take off your clothes and lie down on the bed with your legs spread. As soon as I undress I plan to crawl into bed and taste you, starting at your neck, until I reach your sweet wet pussy."

I heard a whimper and it took me a moment to realize that sound had come from little old me. I couldn't help it. Dereon's words were erotic and had my kitty purring with anticipation.

"You like when I talk dirty to you, don't you Christy?" he whispered near my ear.

Like it? Oh no, I love it. My heart hammered loudly against my chest in agreement.

He didn't even wait for a response, which was a good thing considering my lips and my head—hell my entire body—refused to move. I was sure I looked like a freaking mannequin. But what did he expect? Hearing he had every intention of taking his time had my body immobilized and burning with heat.

Reaching up, Dereon cupped my breasts in his hands. I was braless, so the shirt was no barrier against the heat I instantly felt on contact. My nipples were hard and erect and straining toward the palm of his hand. I closed my eyes and enjoyed the feel of his strong hand squeezing my aching breast. When his thumb grazed my nipple, a single moan escaped my lips. "Dereon."

"That's your spot, isn't it?" he asked, whispering close to my ear again. "I figured it out the other night when you were lying on your back. Your nipples were hard and begging to be sucked," he murmured appreciatively. "And the second I wrapped my lips around them your body began to tremble." He pinched my nipple gently, causing my breathing to come out in short bursts. "I'm hard as hell just thinking about how good you look." His lips traveled down along my neck, teasing in its path. "You want me to suck them, don't you?"

I leaned forward as he pinched and squeezed some more. "Yes," I moaned. My breasts were aching for him to take one between his teeth and suckle it. "Yes please," I whispered.

"Yes?" he whimpered against my lips. "Please, what? Tell me what you want Christy?"

"You," I moaned. "I want you."

"You want me?" he whispered. "Tell me what you want me to do."

Before I could find the words to speak, Dereon had tossed his hat onto the chair, dropped his mouth to mine, and slipped his tongue inside. Thank goodness he was holding me because my body went limp in his arms. I returned the kiss eagerly, desperate for everything he had to offer, but no matter how urgently he kissed, it still wasn't enough. My clit was throbbing with anticipation. I wanted more than petting and kissing. I wanted to feel him inside of me. Buried deep.

When he finally ended the kiss, my breathing was coming hard and fast.

Slowly, I opened my eyes and gasped at what I saw. Hunger. Raw and powerful. A quiver traveled through my body, because the look on his face was a mirror image of everything I was feeling.

Dereon brought a hand to my breast and leaned into me. He captured my lips once again. I arched my breasts high, causing friction both from his hand and the material.

I couldn't think or breathe. All I could do was feel. His hand was so arousing that I was ready to beg him to carry me upstairs and make love to me. It had been too long since I'd had him inside me and I needed him now. Once was not enough and I wasn't sure if it would ever be again.

Before I could find my voice, Dereon lowered his hand down to my belly button. My stomach muscles tightened involuntarily on contact.

"What's wrong, Christy?" he teased as his hands traveled up my stomach, pulling the blouse up over my head and onto the floor, exposing my breasts. Standing there, half naked, I watched the hunger heating his eyes as he reached up and traced the shape and size with his fingertips.

"Oh … "Aching for his touch, I moaned and arched my back to push my breast into his palm. He massaged my nipple with his fingers and finally lowered his head and captured it between his lips. First he flicked his tongue over the peak, then suckled gently.

I squirmed, feeling both aroused and so damn frustrated I couldn't think straight. "Dereon, please," I cried.

"Please, what?" he said, while his tongue circle my areola, then captured my nipple again as he suckled hungrily. With his other hand he reached up and teased my left nipple between his fingers.

"Yes!" I cried, my hips gyrating against his erection. My jeans grazed my clit with every motion, causing the heat to build. "Yes, oh yes!"

I was seconds away from a release when he lifted his mouth from my breast and licked a trail to the other nipple, giving it equal tender loving care. I gasped and squirmed, desperate for what had been building all evening.

By the time he looked up at me I was fighting for an orgasm that was within reach. "Damn you, Dereon!" I hissed. He was going to make me beg.

"What do you want, Christy?" he demanded. "Tell me."

"I …" It was impossible to think with his hot sweet breath fanning across my moist nipples.

"Tell me, Christina. Tell me what you want and I'll give it to you," he coaxed as his lips traveled back up to my mouth, giving me a brief, hot kiss. As the expression goes, *I ain't too proud to beg.*

"I need you inside of me. Please, I want you to fuck me!"

When I looked up at him, his gazed heat was an exquisite combination of hunger and desire. Oh God, I wanted him inside of me.

Reaching down, he found the zipper of my jeans and lowered it. "You wet?"

Ya think? After all the teasing, I was soaked. Dereon lowered my jeans over my hips to allow for better access, then slipped a long finger inside the crotch of my panties, between my slippery folds, and pushed inside in one swift move. "Oh," I cried out, my hips rocking and my kitty clamped down around his intruding finger.

"Damn, baby, you're wet," he hissed, leading me slowly over to the couch without our bodies losing contact, pushing my butt back against the edge of the couch. Dereon slipped in a second finger while using his thumb to stroke my throbbing clit. "So very wet." He thrust his fingers into me, slowly in and out, stroking my g-spot along the way.

I was going mad with desire and started bucking my hips wildly, meeting the steady rhythm of his fingers while once again wishing I hadn't worn jeans because they were definitely in the way. My body was burning up and desperate for release. It was right there within reach, yet no matter how hard I pumped or how often his index finger tickled my g-spot, Dereon refused to give it to me. Damn that man for holding out on me!

"What … what is it?" When I refused to answer, Dereon chuckled and slid me over so my back was lying flat on the couch. "Let me look at you," he growled, his voice sounding low and aroused.

I watched his eyes travel down between my legs where his fingers continued to stroke and tease, moving in and out, slow then fast, traveling even deeper into me. I moaned, rocked against his hand, and begged him to make love to me and end the torture, but dammit, he refused to take me out of my misery. My moans turned into whimpers, and I was certain I was getting ready to cry when he finally pressed his thumb firmly against my clit, causing me to moan with pleasure. The stimulation was too much and felt so much better than the toy I kept in the nightstand beside my bed. Sparks of pleasure shot through my body, sending darts of heat down to my sex. Rubbing circles against my clit while slipping his fingers back inside was my undoing. The convulsions started deep, shooting through my body. I squeezed his fingers as I cried out into an orgasm. "Yessss … yessss!"

It was a short time later before I found the strength to speak. "Thanks." I opened my eyes and stared up into his gorgeous eyes, shimmering with heat. For the longest time we simply gazed at each other. Then Dereon broke the trance.

"We're just getting started," he said. He rose and in one swoop lifted me over his shoulder and carried me upstairs to my bedroom. Once there he lowered me gently onto the bed.

He stepped back and shed his shirt, followed by his jeans, and as I watched my breathing became sporadic. Dereon was beautiful. Sexy. Breathtaking. Everything a woman dreamed a man to be.

As he slid his boxers down his hips I admired how his waist melted seamlessly into narrow hips and a round ass. His penis was thick and hard, surrounded by a nest of dark brown hair. I took in his massive size and length and remembered how good he had felt inside me.

"You see something you want?" he asked with a cocky grin on his handsome face. He knew damn well what I wanted. I lay their licking my lips, aching to touch him as he took his time. There was no doubt in my mind Dereon knew what he was doing. Ever since I'd met him my equilibrium had seemed off, and when he was around I was left feeling off balance, like I had vertigo.

As he removed his shirt I stared at his dark brown nipples, itching to reach out and run my hands along his hard muscles and travel downward until his erection was firmly in my hands. By the time he had rolled the condom on, I lay there trembling with anticipation for what was soon coming my way.

Dereon moved closer to the bed. "I think these are in the way," he commented. I raised my hips and allowed him to slide my jeans down over my hips and onto the floor. My panties followed. I then slid up further onto the bed and lay back with my legs spread invitingly.

He climbed onto the bed. My legs started trembling as he settled between my thighs and lowered on top of me. Finally, after an entire evening of yearning, my desires were about to be fulfilled. The head of his penis nudged my slick opening.

"You ready for me?" he whispered.

My mind was spinning while my body tingled. "Yes, Dereon … I'm ready."

With a small thrust he pushed the head in and stopped. Dereon was inside me, not all the way, but there, joined with mine in the way I had been yearning for. But I wanted more. Why was he still teasing me?

He kissed me softly. I sighed and surrendered to the power of his tender lips moving back and forth over me. His tongue slipped inside just as he pushed his hips forward, just a bit more, filling me a little deeper.

I caught my breath and whimpered softly into his mouth. "Baby, please."

"Please what? Tell me Christy," he commanded.

"I need to feel all of you."

With one quick thrust he pushed deep and I gasped. Dereon was inside me again. The thought swirled through my mind as he stretched me open and filled me completely with his manliness. Pleasure radiated throughout my body. I wrapped my legs around him, pulling him deeper, while I rained kisses along his neck and jaw.

Dereon whispered heated words in my ear, letting me know how good it felt being inside of me, and my breathing became heavy. As I drew closer, Dereon raised up on his arms and pumped deeper and harder into my body. The feeling brewing inside was intoxicating. I opened my eyes and admired the way the muscles in his arms flexed and tensed with each thrust.

Dereon groaned and moved faster.

I was on the verge of another orgasm but I wanted to wait so we could come together. I bucked my hips against him and squeezed my walls, tightening around his length. He groaned each time and moved in a more fevered rhythm.

"I'm getting ready to come!" he hissed. Then he tensed and dropped his lips to mine. He let out a raspy breath and I felt his penis pulse inside me. The tension ran out of his body and he collapsed, covering my body with his and breathing heavily against my shoulder.

I buried my face in his neck and inhaled his masculine scent. With my arms wrapped around him, I wished we could stay here like this forever. As long as we were here in my room, in my bed, nothing outside this door mattered.

But that wasn't real life. I had a career, an image and a mother. There was no way I could be seen in my circle with a man whose jeans sat low on his hips and who preferred to wear sneakers instead of Ferragamo loafers. And I could just imagine pulling up in front of Jeanna's mini-mansion in Dereon's Monte Carlo. Although that idea was almost tempting, just to see the startled look on Jeanna's face.

After a few moments, Dereon rolled over onto his back and my eyes swept his magnificent body. I don't know. As long as he looked that good, I might consider quitting my job, packing my stuff and running off together to a deserted island.

"Yo ... what are you over there thinking about?" He finally said with a lazy smile on his lips.

"How good you look lying there." If only I could put him in an Armani suit, maybe no one would even know the difference.

He grinned and tucked a hand beneath his head so he could see me better. In the moonlight, our eyes locked. "You don't look so bad yourself," he replied with a wink.

"Are you ready to discuss your parents' dinner menu?" I teased.

"No ... what I'm ready for is for you to come over here and ride me."

Before I could object, Dereon lifted me up so I was straddling him. As soon as I felt his length pulsing against my opening I gasped. "You couldn't possibly be hard again that soon."

"I'm in physically good shape. You eat and live right ... a man can get it up as often as he likes."

I'll have to make sure I only date athletic men from now on.

He reached up and started fondling my breasts. My eyelids lowered and I was arching my back toward him again. The instant he touched my spot a quiver of awareness caused them to swell and my nipples to engorge to a pleasurable ache against the palm of his hands, and I moaned.

Dereon chuckled. "I told you I knew your spot."

My eyes rolled open and I pushed his hands away. He was too cocky for his own good.

"You know you like it, so I don't know why you keep playing hard to get," he said, still laughing at me.

"Yeah, whatever," I mumbled and stared down at him, trying to appear mad, but he was too cute for that to last long.

"I also know what else you like." He brought his hands to my waist and lifted me up over his length and entered me in one push. I exhaled at the exquisite feeling of him being inside of me again.

"That's it, baby … now ride it."

He didn't have to tell me twice. I started gyrating my hips, loving the way his erection felt sliding in and out of my heat. I was so wet that if I rode him too deep, he kept slipping out. Using my hand, I clasped my fingers around the base to hold him firmly in place, then rode him long and hard, coming out to the tip and thrusting down onto him.

"Shit, that feels good," he moaned. Dereon started rocking upward, meeting me halfway. Desire starting spiraling through me and my lips parted and I moaned with pleasure.

"Yeah … that's it … ride that dick," he chanted over and over and his voice, low and seductive, had me pumping wildly over his length. I move up and down, loving the way the head tickled my g-spot with every downward thrust. Dereon reached down between us and rubbed my clit in quick little circles, matching the fast heated rhythm of my thrusts.

I lowered my eyes to the handsome face below me. As soon as I saw the confidence burning in their depth, I gasped with pleasure. He was so fine. Dereon held onto my waist, slamming my body down onto his penis, and within seconds we both came. I lowered my limp body over his.

"You're something else, you know that?"

"Yes, that's what I've been told," I joked, then closed my eyes. I was drifting off to sleep when I heard the soft chirp of Dereon's cell phone.

He sighed and I rolled off him, allowing him to lean over the side of the bed and retrieve it. Under narrowed lids I watched him glance down at the screen and mumble something under his breath.

"What's wrong?"

His head snapped around and he looked at me as if he'd suddenly remembered I was there. You can image what that did for my ego.

"That was one of my tenants. The central air is out in her unit."

Why did I get the feeling he was lying? Maybe it had something to do with him staring up at the ceiling instead of looking over at me.

"Oh, so you're a landlord?"

He gave me a fleeting look, then rose from the bed. "Uhhh, yeah. I thought I told you that?"

"Well yeah, I guess you did." I used my arm to prop myself on the bed and sat there admiring his gorgeous body. Muscles on top of muscles. I couldn't find an ounce of fat on his body. He was truly a distraction. "How many properties do you own?" I figured if he said a few dozen and they were located in some prestigious areas of St. Louis I just might be able to get him past Jeanna.

"One."

"One? One what? Apartment complex?"

He slipped on his boxers. "No, one fourplex."

Okay maybe it wasn't as bad as I thought. "Really? Where at?"

"In Jennings, off of Goodfellow."

Okay, it was worse than I thought. Jennings was one of the worst areas on the north side. Goodness. "Oh, I guess when I saw *Real Estate Investor* on your business card, I guess I expected … more."

His eyes sparkled with amusement. "I flip houses. I've got one my crew is working on right now, and another I just made an offer on. The idea is to buy and sell homes, not keep them."

That was something, wasn't it? Although it would have been better if he'd owned real estate all across the city. Preferably several high-end homes, but I guess everyone has to start somewhere. Right? I watched him finish getting dressed and sighed. He was so sexy. I just wished he was rich.

"Listen, I know you gotta get up in the morning, so I'll holla at you tomorrow," he finally said and jingled his keys.

Part of me was hoping he was planning to come back, but that's what I get for wishing.

"Sure."

He leaned across the bed and pressed his lips to mine in a kiss that was starting to get heated when he finally raised his head. "Walk me to the door." He pulled me to my feet and down the hall.

"Can I put some clothes on first?" I laughed.

"Nah … I prefer you like this."

Holding his hand, I followed his lead down the stairs and to the door. Once there he swung around and pulled me flush against this body. My nipples beaded instantly.

"You gonna call me tomorrow?"

I gazed hypnotically into his beautiful eyes. "Yes."

"That's what I was hoping you'd say." He lowered his head and tasted my mouth in a kiss that had me ready to knock him onto the floor and straddle him again.

"Good night, Christy," he said when he finally released me.

"Good night."

He settled his fedora hat back on his head and I moved behind the door while he opened it. Mr. Peters across the street was an eighty-year-old peeping Tom. If he caught sight of me in my naked glory I would never get rid of him.

I shut the door and moved over to the window, peering out between the blinds. As I watched him walk all I could do was shake my head. That brotha had swagger out of this world. If I could find a way to package it, we'd both be rich.

SIXTEEN

I strutted into the Cheesecake Factory looking and feeling fabulous in a purple BCBG Max Azria wrap dress paired with black peep-toed shoes. I scanned the area over the tops of my Versace sunglasses and spotted Tamara sitting at a booth in the corner, waving, trying to get my attention. I brushed past the hostess and sashayed over to where she was sitting, my arms weighed down with bags. I couldn't help myself. There was a sale at Nordstrom and credit cards are a girl's best friend.

"Hey, chick!" I greeted and leaned over and kissed my pregnant cousin on her round cheek.

"It took you long enough," she scolded. "I've already had two glasses of lemonade."

I lowered onto the seat across from her, admiring her soft yellow sleeveless dress. Tamara made pregnant look good. "Sorry, I saw this cream blouse I had to have, and then once I tried it on I had to buy accessories to go with it."

"You're too much," she said shaking her head with a knowing smile.

The waitress arrived and I ordered a sour apple martini and Tai lettuce wraps for the two of us to share.

"So what did you want to talk about?" I asked after the waitress left to check on the customers at the next table.

"We'll talk about that in a minute," Tamara began with a dismissive wave. "Right now I want to hear about your man. How was your fourth date?"

Sometimes I think she and Claudia are secretly conspiring. "It was nice. I don't think barbecue ribs ever tasted so good." I watched the way her brows rose quizzically.

"Burgers … now ribs? You sure you're feeling well?"

I laughed. "I'm fine. I actually enjoyed it." I paused and shrugged a slender shoulder. "I don't know what it is about Dereon, but he makes me want to explore things I never thought about doing before."

Since my disastrous gourmet burger date, Dereon and I had been seeing quite a bit of each other. A movie, barbecue at Harold's Rib Shack. He had even taken me through his old neighborhood in Pine Lawn and showed me where he was born. But what I enjoyed most was at the end of the night, when he brought me back home and carried me off to bed and made sweet love to me. After four dates, I still couldn't come up with a way to express what I was feeling. One minute I thought Dereon was all wrong for me and I was ready to end the relationship, but the moment he pulled me into his arms I didn't care about anything in the world, or what others would say. All I cared about was how he made me feel.

"I'm still trying to get over you eating meat with your precious hands. Ribs? You?" And then she was laughing so uncontrollably the couple at the other table glanced over in our direction.

I frowned at her. "Very funny. I cook with my hands. It's really no different."

"Oh, *I've* been eating ribs for years. It's *you* who couldn't stomach picking meat off a bone. Remember? You said it was too much work."

Okay, she did have a point, but I can't help it if that's the way I was raised. Jeanna always said ribs were a messy waste of time. After eating the smoked meat, I was hooked. "Did you really invite me to lunch to tease me about my picky eating habits?"

Tamara shook her head. "No, I want to hear about that sexy man of yours. Please, please tell me you have a picture of him on your phone or something."

"Yes, I do, but it's not anything I can share," I said with a suggestive wag of my brows, and the two of us started laughing. Dereon had sent me a photograph so I could see how much he was truly missing me. Goodness, I stared at that photograph practically the entire night.

Tamara reached for her lemonade and took another sip. "Sounds like things are getting serious."

The waitress returned with my martini and I thanked her and took a sip, grateful for a few moments to think about my answer.

"No … I wouldn't call what's happening between us serious. I think we're enjoying the moment."

"The moment?" she sniffed delicately. "Come on, Christy, don't tell me you're still stuck on finding a rich man."

"Yes, but that doesn't have anything to do with Dereon. He makes me laugh and the sex is explosive, but there is still something not right about our relationship."

"Meaning … ?" she trailed off pointedly.

"Meaning, I don't even know where he lives and he's never stayed the night at my place."

Her lips thinned thoughtfully. I figured she would be just as puzzled about the situation as I was. "What reason does he give for not spending the night?" I could tell she was still trying to give him the benefit of the doubt.

"It's always some kind of emergency. Sure he stays until after the clock strikes midnight, so I know a fairy godfather isn't somehow involved in all this."

Her smile deepened. "I'm glad you can see the humor in all of this."

"Barely. But with me never going over to his place and he never spending the night … correct me if I'm wrong … but I'm starting to think that maybe he might be married."

"Wow!" There was a long pause . "I can clearly see how you came to that conclusion," she replied, with her hand resting comfortably on her belly.

"I really like Dereon. I don't think I've ever had this much fun with a man before, but you and I both know there are two kinds of men I won't do."

She nodded. "Broke and married."

"Okay, so maybe I'm making an exception with the broke part. However, married is one thing that goes against everything I believe in."

"I wish Aunt Jeanna could hear you right now choosing handsome and broke or loaded and married."

I laughed and took another sip. "Can we be serious for a moment?"

"Sorry," Tamara said with a sheepish grin. "Why don't you just come out and ask him?"

"Because then it will seem like it really matters to me."

She raised a brow. "Probably because it does. Come on. You have a right to know if the man is married, or even living with someone."

"You're right." I guess part of me was afraid to make the relationship more than it was. We're having fun. That's it. No building a future or anything, just two people enjoying each other's company, and as long as I think he's hiding something, there's no chance of me losing my heart to him.

"You have a right to know what you're getting yourself into. The last thing you need is some crazed baby mama coming after you."

I still hadn't gotten over Logan's wife knocking on my front door. There were so many different ways that situation could have ended. Thank goodness it was with everyone's teeth still intact.

"Okay, next time I see him I'll ask him if he's living with someone."

"Good girl. I hope he isn't, because it would spoil all the fun. I can't remember the last time I've seen you this happy." She stared at me with her full coral lips pressed firmly together. "Girl, you're practically glowing, and I'm the one who's supposed to be pregnant."

"You're silly."

A server arrived with our wraps and Tamara and I chitchatted about the sales at Nordstrom's while we fed our faces. As bad as I had been eating lately, I was pleased to be having something that I could *almost* consider healthy.

"Okay, you still haven't told me what you needed to talk to me about," I said as I took another sip of my apple martini.

While Tamara chewed, her expression became serious, yet she made me wait until she swallowed and flushed it down with some lemonade before finally saying, "I ran into your father yesterday."

That was not at all what I was expecting to hear. "My father? Carlos?"

She nodded. "I was coming out of the office when I spotted him in the hallway. One of the senior partners is representing him in a possible merger with Anheuser Busch."

My father was in town. "How did he look?"

"Handsome as ever in a Billy Dee Williams kinda way. He's probably the only good-looking man I've ever seen Aunt Jeanna with." She laughed, trying to soften the mood, but I was still stuck on him being in St. Louis. Especially since his corporate headquarters were located in Miami.

"Anyway, he said he'd really like to see you but wasn't sure how to approach you since you never seem to return any of his calls."

I sniffed. "Calls? He only calls on my birthday and Christmas, and that's only because he feels guilty for ignoring me all these years," I said mockingly.

"I don't know, Christina," she began with uneasiness. "He really seemed sincere. I think you should give him a call and see what he has to say."

"I'll think about it." I pouted. I knew I sounded like a spoiled brat, but all my life my father used money to substitute for what I had yearned for—a man in my life. Where had he been when I'd won the national spelling bee, made captain of the swim team, or when I'd had the starring role in my high school play? Instead of being there he had sent a card with a signature stamp and a check for a ridiculous amount that Jeanna so graciously deposited. I never wanted the money. All I wanted was a father. My father.

I brought my martini to my lips and finished half the glass in one swallow, then signaled for my waitress. "Can I have another one of these?" I asked.

"You know I'm hating you right about now."

I glanced across the table and caught Tamara eyeing my drink like a recovering alcoholic, and started giggling.

"How can you have a martini when you know it's my favorite and I can't have one?" she protested.

"Sorry," I replied apologetically. "I guess I forgot the reason why you were sitting over there drinking lemonade."

We talked some more, and after we settled the bill I kissed Tamara goodbye and headed back across the mall and through Nordstrom's. I was thinking about Dereon and how I was going to approach him about his living arrangements when I ran smack into someone coming the other way.

"Excuse me." As soon as I swung around I spotted a tall man in front of me.

"Sorry about that. I must not have been looking."

I gasped with recognition. "Harold Harmon … is that you?"

He paused and stared at me for a few seconds before a smile curled his succulent lips. "Well, I'll be damned! Christina Holloway." I watched the way his eyes perused my curves with approval. I'll admit he wasn't the only one who was impressed. *Dayum!* Ten years had definitely been good to him.

Harold was wearing Khaki slacks and a blue button-down Ralph Lauren shirt, and on his feet were leather Gucci sandals. His hair was close cropped and looked perfect against his round face. He had a thin mustache and a perfectly trimmed beard. There was no doubt about it. Harold Harmon was sexy as all getout.

"Jeanna told me you were in town."

He chuckled a little louder than needed and said, "I see you're still calling your mother by her first name."

"Old habits," I said with a shrug and a smile.

He clasped my hands, his eyes roaming my face. "Grams told me you were gorgeous, but she didn't tell me you looked like this. Man, you look tasty!"

Tasty? Goodness, that sounded so gay. "Thank you. You don't look bad yourself."

He shrugged. "I spend a lot of time in the gym when I'm not practicing law."

"Oh, so you're a lawyer?" I asked like I didn't already know.

"Yes, I'm partners at a prestigious law firm in Massachusetts," he boasted and I guessed that at his age he had every right to be proud.

"That's wonderful." And I meant it. The more I looked at him the better he looked. Don't get me wrong. Although he had smoky grey eyes and a smooth sun-kissed complexion, he was a little light for my taste. That is, since my recent addiction to dark chocolate.

"I hear you started your own catering business and that you're quite successful."

Wow. I guess my mother does talk about me. I nodded. "Thank you."

He smiled, revealing white even teeth. "I'll be in town for the next few weeks taking care of my grandfather's estate. I'd love to spend some time together, catching up."

"I'd like that, too."And I meant it. He was handsome, rich and successful. Everything I wanted in a man. And Jeanna would be so proud.

We exchanged cell phone numbers and promised to get together in the next few days. I walked back out to my car with a smile on my face. Maybe he was the distraction I needed. But instead of thinking about Harold and what the future could hold, I couldn't shake the need to be held in Dereon's arms again.

SEVENTEEN

"Okay, what do you think?"

I stood back with a hand to my hips while Claudia reached for a spoon, stuck it in the dip I had just concocted, and brought it to her mouth. "Mmmm, that is delicious," she moaned. "What is it?"

I smiled, quite pleased with her reaction. "A seafood dip I've been working on." To the left of *Cater to You* was a full-service state-of-the-art industrial-sized kitchen. After our catering orders had begun to blossom there were too many orders for our small kitchens at home. When the suite next door became available we purchased it and had the kitchen installed.

Claudia spooned some more dip on a cracker and brought it to her mouth. Closing her eyes, she crooned, "Oh, this is going to be a hit."

"I hope so. I'm nervous about the appetizer selections."

"They'll be a hit. I'm just looking forward to being on the yacht." Claudia paused and worried her bottom lip. "Mindy is due to deliver any day now so we still need to find another person to man the carving station. You know I don't trust just anyone with the prime rib. I have an ad over at the culinary arts school. Hopefully there's someone taking summer classes looking for a job."

"That's a good idea. We'll need all the help we can get to make the evening a success. I'll also contact the temporary service." Over the years we had built relationships with career counselors at the culinary art school where students were eager for intermittent work and gain hands-on experience for credits, but finding help was always difficult during the summer, which was our busiest time of the year.

Claudia pointed at the boxes on the table. "As soon as I deliver this food to the Ladies Auxiliary Council I'm going to meet the mayor's personal assistant so we can go over the meal. The sooner we can have the menu approved the better." We spent the rest of the morning going over the menu selections and thinking about table décor and flowers.

"Look what someone sent you," Mia announced as she stepped into the kitchen carrying a huge edible arrangement of chocolate and fresh fruits. "It seems you've got a secret admirer you haven't told us about."

Claudia's eyes were glimmering with intrigue as she walked around the large island and reached for the envelope. "Who could that be from? Or do we even need to bother to ask?"

"None of your business. That's who," I replied and snatched the card from her hand , slipping it into my apron pocket.

Smiling, I took the bouquet from my assistant with excitement dancing around my chest. I didn't need to read the card to know who it was from.

It almost felt like there was more going on between Dereon and me than just sex. But there was no way I was allowing my mind to go there.

Claudia moved over to the arrangement and plucked off a strawberry. "Fine. Keep your little secrets," she pouted playfully. "If that's from you-know-who, then you'd better be enjoying every second of it."

Mia stamped her feet. "I knew I should have read the card before I carried it in."

"Mia!" Claudia gasped.

Pouting, she shrugged. "I'm serious. They're from Dereon, aren't they?"

I didn't answer.

"Of course they are," Claudia replied. "He's feeling my girl here."

With a look of envy, Mia sighed. "Some of us get all the luck." She was almost out the door when she looked over her shoulder and said, "Don't forget Macy Maxwell will be here at three. I think she's bringing a couple of her sorority sisters with her to sample the sweets."

I nodded. I loved doing sorority fund-raising events.

Claudia removed a pan of assorted quiches from the oven. "When are you going to see him again?" she asked after Mia had returned to her desk.

I bit into a piece of pineapple and shrugged. "Don't know. We haven't made any plans."

"You're kidding, right?"

"No, I'm not. In the meantime, I have a date tonight with an old friend."

"Let me guess. This friend is rich."

Nodding, I moved over to the sink and reached for the hand soap. "He's the son of one of my mother's friends."

"And your mother wants you to go out with him," she said with a disapproving look.

"Actually, I decided to see him." I told her about running into Harold at the mall two nights ago and agreeing to get together. Then the second I had gotten home my mother was calling, with Kathy on the other line. In truth, I would have been arm wrestled into going out with Harold if I'd refused.

I would much rather go out with Dereon, whom I hadn't heard from him since Sunday. When Harold had called yesterday and asked me to dinner, I'd agreed, since his breath no longer seemed to be a problem. "Where's he taking you?"

"Prime Meats."

Her brow arched, showing she was clearly impressed. The restaurant was á la carte. There was nothing cheap on that menu, including the bottled water. "I love that place."

I reached for a knife and walked over to the table. "So do I, which is why I agreed to go out with him."

"I guess." Claudia looked as if she was pondering something. "What about Dereon?" she finally asked.

"What about him? I haven't talked to him in two days." As I sliced the chocolate cake, I tried to act like it was no big deal. But I was starting to think that maybe there was another woman involved.

"Have you called him?"

"Now why in the world would I do that?" One thing I didn't do was run after a man. I was old school and believed a man should chase a woman, not the other way around.

While she argued my point, we boxed up the quiches and loaded up Claudia's car with all the food. After she left to deliver, I went back into the kitchen and removed a sausage lasagna from the oven. I smiled, pleased to see it was bubbling hot and the top was perfect. Nothing worse than burnt cheese. I removed fresh Parmesan cheese from the refrigerator, put it inside a grater and sprinkled it generously all over the top.

I spent the rest of the afternoon getting the desserts ready for my three o'clock and had just finished icing a red velvet cake when I heard someone clear his throat behind me.

"I see you got your delicious arrangement."

I looked over my shoulder and grinned as I watched Dereon step into the kitchen. "Yes, I did. Thank you." He looked wonderful in a navy blue t-shirt and denim shorts. My eyes traveled down to his mahogany legs and I felt my pulse do a back flip. Nothing attracted me more than a man with beautiful legs.

Dereon walked around the spacious room, admiring the industrial-sized stainless steel appliances and butcher block countertops. "Impressive. I guess this is why I haven't been able to reach you all morning."

I giggled, pleased he had finally called. "This is my home away from home."

"I can see that." He gazed down at the presentation of baked goods I had displayed on the table. I rocked back on my heels, beaming with pride. I was proud of the work I did and was glad to see him admiring it.

"Would you like a taste?"

Incredulously, he stared at me. "Seriously? These aren't for someone?"

"No, they're for sampling." I walked to the end of the table covered in fine white linen as I spoke. "I have an appointment in an hour. What I usually do is slice up the desserts and arrange them on the table for tasting."

"Sounds delicious."

"It is. Now taste this." I reached for a slice of my popular coconut cake and handed him a fork.

Smiling, he took it from my outstretched hand. "Did I tell you this is my favorite cake?"

I shook my head and smiled. "No, but if it's your favorite then you're in for a treat."

He didn't look convinced, but then he brought a forkful of cake to his mouth and chewed. Within seconds his eyelids closed and a moan slipped from his juicy lips. I chuckled inwardly. *Works every time.*

"Damn, that's good! What's in it?"

"Uh-uh," I replied, wagging a finger in front of his face. "That's for me to know. It's a family secret."

"Secret, huh?" He took the plate from my hand and took another bite. "This is the bomb! You can keep your secret as long as you make me a cake like this."

"You want one for your parents' anniversary dinner?" I asked.

He shook his head. "No, my mother loves Italian cream. I want one for me."

I giggled. It was Grandma Celeste's recipe that she'd passed on to me. I used to spend hours in her kitchen helping her cook. "I think that can be arranged."

Dereon finished the cake and reached for a napkin. He moved over to the island where I was sifting flour into a large bowl, and I was clearly aware of his watching me. "Is there something I can do for you, Mr. Sanders?"

"Yeah, there is. You can come over here and give me a kiss."

I startled, then my lips turned downward. "Why should I? I haven't spoken to you in days," I said with a playful pout.

He scowled. "Sorry about that. My realtor and I've been out looking at buildings. And when I wasn't doing that I was busy working on a house I needed to flip as soon as possible."

"Really? Where's it located?" I asked, looking over at him.

"Kirkwood."

Kirkwood. I lowered the sifter, giving him my attention. The small west county town was known for its down home charm and community pride. "That sounds interesting."

"If you're good to me I'll take you by to see it. Now c'mere."

Smiling, I removed my apron and walked over to where he was standing and waiting patiently.

Dereon looked down at me with an intensity that was scorching. Our eyes were locked as I stepped closer, pressing my body to his and tilting my head upward. He met me halfway and pressed his lips firmly against mine, then slipped his tongue inside. My arms moved around his waist while I met each stroke with my own. His mouth was delicious and flavorful and better than any slice of cake I had on the table. He slid his hand down my body and under my shirt, caressing my breasts. When his thumb grazed my nipple, a shudder rushed through my body.

"We better stop before someone comes in here," I insisted.

Reluctantly, he removed his hand and released me, and my eyes traveled down to the sizable bulge that was evident in his shorts. I licked my lips. My body was already craving his.

Dereon took my hand and led me to the door in the corner. "What's in that room?"

"That's the supply closet," I whispered.

"Perfect."

He opened the door and I followed him inside with laughter bubbling up inside of me. Once the door was shut I was in his arms again, loving the feel of his body against me and the taste of his sweet lips tasting mine.

"Get rid of your bra," he breathed against my lips.

Reaching behind me, I released the clasps and my eager breasts sprang free. What the hell had gotten into me? I didn't have a clue, and at that moment I honestly didn't care. All I knew was I couldn't survive another minute without Dereon touching me. The kiss deepened, with his tongue dancing a familiar dance with mine. Then without missing a beat, Dereon reached up and released the buttons of my blouse. There were several agonizing seconds before he finally pushed the material aside. He squeezed my breasts, kneading them with his hands. My nipples pebbled as he rolled them with his eager fingertips. His lips traveled down across my cheek and throat and across my collarbone before he finally captured a nipple between his teeth and sucked.

I arched my back, granting him better access to my breasts, and when he began to lavish one a whimper slipped from my parted lips.

"I missed these," he confessed between hungry sucks while his fingers tweaked and caressed the other.

"That's what you get for staying away so long," I managed between breaths.

"I guess we'll have to do something about that."

Yes. Oh yes. I leaned back against the wall, eyes closed, lips parted, so caught up in the way he was making me feel. The door wasn't locked and Mia could walk in at any moment, but I didn't care. All I cared about was him being buried deep inside my body. My legs were trembling and I brought my hands to his shoulders and held on.

I was acting like a horny teenager, although in high school I'd never felt anything as intense as what I was feeling with Dereon. I wanted him and there was nothing juvenile about that. As he continued to play with my breasts, my hands moved all across his body, skimming his head, down across his wide shoulders and muscular back and finally down to cup his tight ass, holding him firmly in place while his tongue swept across my nipple. The only sound in the pantry was breathless panting.

When I felt him bite down with his teeth, I jerked, hitting him in the shoulder and sending him back against the shelf, and a can came tumbling down onto the floor.

"Shhh," I whispered, laughing.

"Sorry about that," he muttered under his breath.

I giggled again and wrapped my arms around his middle and kicked the can out of our way.

"Why don't you turn on the light so we can see what we're doing?"

I reached along the wall until I found the switch and turned it on. I blinked a few seconds and gazed up into his handsome face.

"There, now I can see your face when I slide inside of you."

Without breaking eye contact, his hand dropped to my slacks and he lowered the zipper. I held my breath and waited while he slid them down over my hips. He reached out and stroked my crotch with his hand, while a wave of pleasure swept through me and I rocked my hips, stroking my clit against his thumb. I was wet. My panties soaked.

Reaching up, I lowered his mouth to mine and devoured him as he slid my panties down and onto the floor. Eagerly, I reached for his jeans, and after several fumbled attempts I got them unfastened. I freed him and held his magnificent length as it pulsed in my hand.

"You got a condom?" My body was on fire.

"Yeah," he groaned. "In my wallet."

I reached around to his back pocket and within seconds I had his jeans and boxers down to his knees and had rolled the condom slowly over his size while he gritted his teeth.

"Bend over," he whispered.

I leaned against the wall and Dereon moved behind me and spread my thighs. He then slid in with one hard thrust, as if he had never left. I sighed, and a smile of satisfaction curled my lips because he was back where he belonged. His thrusts pushed me against the door and I braced myself as he pumped into my body repeatedly. A soft sound came from my throat as I rocked back, meeting his strokes. As he moved faster so did I, racing together toward the finish line. I clenched my jaws, trying to muffle my cries of pleasure, but the closer I got to climaxing, the harder it got to keep quiet. Dereon swept a hand across my back and over to my breasts where he ran a hand across my hardened nipple before it traveled downward to the patch of curls between my legs. Without slowing his strokes, his thumb found my clit. And as soon as he applied pressure I came hard, tightening my walls around his penis and squeezing him tightly. I heard his breathing quicken and together we came.

I collapsed against the wall laughing. "Goodness," I said in a breath. "I needed that."

Chuckling, Dereon pulled me into his arms. I can't remember the last time I had laughed so much with a man. We had fun together. He made me feel so alive.

He kissed me once, twice, three times, then we straightened our clothes and opened the door. I went out first and made sure the kitchen was still empty, then held the door open for Dereon. He came up behind me and wrapped his arms around my middle and leaned in close.

"Yo, you might wanna fix your hair."

"What?" My hand shot up to my head. While he chuckled, I made sure there wasn't a hair out of place. "How's it look now?"

"Beautiful," he said with another kiss, then he pulled back and gazed down at me. His lips were moist and wet and I craved to lick every drop away. "I want to see you tonight."

Oh, and I wanted to see him. My body was already crying out to him to take me again. "I already have plans."

"Cancel them."

Oh, how I wish I could. I shook my head. "I can't."

He gazed at me and I noticed a muscle at his jaw pulse before he finally nodded.

"Can I ask you a question?" I figured it was as good a time as any.

"You can ask me anything as long as I can have another piece of that cake."

"When are you going to invite me to your place?"

He rubbed a hand across his head. "How about I invite you to my place tonight?"

"Nice try."

Chuckling, he pulled me close to him again. "You can't blame a brotha for trying."

I couldn't help but smile. I don't know if it was because I was pleased he was inviting me over, or knowing he lived alone.

"Give me a couple of days to clean up my place, then you can come over. In the meantime, how about lunch tomorrow?"

"Lunch sounds wonderful."

"Matter of fact, take the afternoon off. I wanna spend some quality time with you."

I nodded.

"I better go," he finally said.

I blinked twice and forced myself to put my head on straight and nodded. Dereon leaned in and kissed me firmly on the mouth. "I wasn't lying about that cake. Make one for me." He then winked, grabbed another piece, and headed to the door.

I watched him leave and stood there thinking no man had ever made me feel that way. Never. So why now with a man who was so wrong for me?

The rest of the day I was in a daze as I tried to stop thinking about Dereon and focus my thoughts on Harold and our date, but it was useless.

Claudia called me while she was down at the mayor's office and told me to meet her at Port Charles Harbor so we could get a feel of the yacht's layout.

Lady Marmalade was over 170 feet long, with a sundeck, a gym, indoor and outdoor bars, a dining room and full galley, four guestrooms and an owner's suite. I climbed back out onto the upper deck, completely impressed. This was the life my mother wanted me to have. Riches, wealth and the opportunity to never work another day in my life. Even though I was crazy about Dereon, he could never give me this. When we were together it didn't matter. However, as I looked around at the beautiful craftsmanship, I had to wonder if maybe I was making a mistake spending so much time with him.

I brushed the ridiculous thought aside and remembered the conversation I'd had with Claudia. Every man I dated didn't have to be husband material. I could just have fun. Well, that's what Dereon was to me, fun. Harold, on the other hand, was husband potential, and not to mention Jeanna would be so happy. The last thing in the world I ever wanted to do was disappoint my mother. But I was starting to think that it was maybe time I started living my own life and doing what made me happy.

Nevertheless, on the drive home I picked up my cell phone several times, preparing to cancel my afternoon with Dereon tomorrow. I had a business to run and didn't have time to be playing hooky, but I couldn't do it because sometimes the body wants what the mind doesn't. I knew it was better to end the relationship while I still could, but as I got ready to dial his number I remembered that I still had one more date before the locket would be mine. Sighing with relief, I tried to convince myself that that was the only reason I was meeting him for lunch tomorrow and nothing more. But I knew better than that. Wrong or right, I couldn't wait to see Dereon and have him hold me in his arms again.

EIGHTEEN

It was barely ten o'clock when I stepped into my condo and waved goodbye to Harold, who was waiting for me to get inside safely. A smile curled my lips as I shut the door. Harold was a wonderful guy and would make someone a fabulous husband, but unfortunately that person wasn't me. He was polite, funny, and smart, and was planning to run for city council, but no matter how hard I tried to imagine a life as Mrs. Harmon, the only man I could see being with was Dereon. I really think I needed to get my head examined because I had a future on a gold platter right in front of me, yet I wasn't interested.

What in hell was happening to me?

I was moving upstairs when I heard my house phone ring. Swiftly, I walked down the hall to the last room on the left and grabbed the phone from the side of my bed on the third ring.

"Hello?"

"I was hoping you were home by now."

Jeanna.

I fell back onto the bed with a groan. "Hello, *Mother*."

"I couldn't possibly go to bed until I found out how your date went with Harold," she said in an animated voice, the way girl friends did when discussing their first kiss.

I closed my eyes and thought about the kiss we'd had as he'd said good-bye, the kiss that had done absolutely nothing for me. "It was fine, Mother."

"Well, where did he take you? What were you wearing?" she pushed impatiently. When Jeanna got like this the best thing to do was give her what she wanted. Otherwise she'd never get off the phone.

I rose from the bed and unzipped my dress . "We went to Prime Meats for dinner, and I was wearing Christian Louboutin heels and that cute black Prada dress you love so much."

"Perfect." She sounded happy, and I was pleased. "Darling, I have a good feeling about you and Harold," she began and went into her usual spiel while I half listened. I was too busy comparing him to Dereon. Harold wasn't dark enough, his eyes weren't light enough, his lips weren't near as soft and his hands lacked calluses and strength. I knew it wasn't fair comparing the two men, but I couldn't help it. I actually liked having a man who knew the meaning of hard work.

I was standing in the middle of my room in blue panties and a matching strapless bra when Jeanna finally came up for air.

"Wait until I call Kathy! She's going to be so excited."

"Mother," I warned as I padded on bare feet over to the closet. "We've only gone out once."

"But that's only the beginning. Harold is handsome, successful and rich. And it's time for you to settle down and start a family. I want to know that my girls' futures are secure."

I slipped into a pink robe and released a heavy sigh. A couple of weeks ago Harold would have been perfect, but then something changed all that.

Dereon.

That man made me feel like no one else. If only I could take Dereon's qualities and Harold's money, I would have the perfect man.

"Are we still on for luncheon next week?" I heard her ask.

"Yes, I'll be there."

"Very well," she said sighing dramatically before continuing, "well, you go ahead and rest up and I'll talk to you tomorrow."

I hung up the phone and took a seat on the bed. Knowing Jeanna, tomorrow she'd be out shopping for a wedding gown with Kathy. She was truly a trip.

Sighing, I reached for my purse to retrieve my cell phone and got ready to plug it into the charger when I glanced down and noticed I had a text message. I tapped the screen.

You look sexy as hell in that blue bra.

My lips curled upward at Dereon's message and I was plugging in the charger when the realization sank in. I gasped. There was only one way he'd know what I was wearing. I scrambled over to the window and looked down. There was his Infiniti parked right across the street. Excitedly, I tightened the belt on my robe, slipped my feet in a pair of slippers and hurried down the stairs. I flung the door open and stood there, heart pounding, as I watched Dereon step out of the SUV and start toward me.

* * *

All I can say is I don't know what I'm doing anymore. One minute he's all wrong for me and the next I can't seem to survive another second without seeing him. There is something about Dereon I'm drawn to. Every time he walks into a room the hairs on my neck stand up, and when he turns that beautiful smile on me all I want to do is smile back at him, and every problem laying heavy on my mind seems to fade away.

As he walked toward me with all that swagger, I licked my dry lips and my body started to heat up because I knew that in a few seconds he was going to pull me into his arms and hold me close. When he's around my body seems to have a mind of its own.

"Whassup, sexy," he said in greeting as he climbed the stairs onto the porch and stood directly in front of me. I tilted my head and gazed up at his gorgeous face.

"Hello." I wanted to touch him and hold him close to me. "What are you doing here? I thought we were meeting for lunch tomorrow."

"I came to claim what's mine." Dereon lifted me into his arms and carried me inside and upstairs to bed. As soon as we stripped our clothes and lay between the sheets, my teeth chattered with anticipation of what was to come.

The second Dereon lay on top of me and pushed inside I knew my body had been made for his. He moved, stroking me in all the places that other men knew nothing about. But not Dereon. He was experienced enough to make sure he paid extra attention. As he plunged deeper and deeper I could feel the heat of my body rising like a covered pot on the stove, boiling until it spilled over. I couldn't get enough of the way he made me feel. No matter how often we made love I wanted more.

Each day I looked forward to his delicious kisses and him filling my body with his own. Yes, it was a wild mixed-up feeling and I truly didn't think I'd ever felt this crazy and confused over a man before, but now I could truly say I knew what it was to find your soul mate, because that's how I felt each and every time we came together. Dereon touched my soul.

I wrapped my legs around him and met his powerful strokes, and within minutes we came together and collapsed in each other's arms. I lay there with a smile on my lips and realized I didn't want to share my life with anyone but him.

I know this might sound insane, but I finally understood how people became obsessed and how others became stalkers and how so many women were willing to sacrifice everything for the sake of their men. I can say for once I knew what it was to feel that level of attraction for someone. Was it lust? Absolutely not. Lust was something that came fast and died out even faster. What I felt for Dereon was a steady feeling that made my stomach ache and my heart pound.

So this is what love is.

I released a shaky breath as the revelation hit me.

NINETEEN

"So, Portia, tell me how does it feel to be married?"

She smiled across the patio table at me. "Wonderful. I can't even begin to describe it in words."

I looked over at my sister's lovely almond face and she radiated happiness. "You know I hate you, right?"

Tamara had invited us over for brunch out on her patio. She had a beautiful thirty-six-hundred-foot, two-story stucco home in Chesterfield with wide hallways, high ceilings, gleaming oak floors and whitewashed walls. We spent the last hour sitting beside the pool, enjoying the wonderful June weather and looking at honeymoon pictures from my sister's trip to Morocco. It looked like they'd had a wonderful time. Portia's cheeks were round and it appeared that Moroccan food had been too good to pass up.

"Sis, I was hoping you were happy for me," she replied with concern in her eyes. *Goodness, would she ever learn how to take a joke?*

The petite woman was sitting beside me in a cute leopard print bikini showing off her firm abs and generous breasts. With a round face and large eyes everything about her was so damn delicate. "I'm very happy for you, just a little jealous," I added with a wink. She smiled and appeared pleased by my response. My sister has always needed the praise and approval of not only Jeanna, but her big sister as well.

Tamara slid open the patio doors and came out carrying a fresh pitcher of lemonade. She looked fabulous in a designer maternity two-piece swim suit beneath a red cover-up. "It took you long enough," I huffed playfully.

"Sorry, but Pierre came into the kitchen and one thing led to another and, well … " she wagged her brow suggestively.

I glanced down at the tray she sat at the center of the patio table and frowned. "Eeww! Please tell me you weren't anywhere near the lemonade."

Portia was giggling, probably because she and her new husband had been doing the exact same thing for the last six weeks.

"Relax, Christy." She flopped down in the chair across from me and reached for a pitcher, filling three glasses with ice-cold lemonade. It was warm for June, so I was thankful for something cold to drink.

Tamara was seated at the head of the patio table, with Portia at her left. I was on her right. A wide overhead umbrella blocked the sun. "Did you see your obstetrician Tuesday?" I asked. When she nodded I added, "What did she say?"

A grin tilted her lips. "We're having a boy."

"Oh, I'm so happy for you!" I sprang from my seat and came around the table and hugged Tamara. Portia did the same.

Her smile was radiant. "Thanks, you two. Pierre is so happy. He went out yesterday and bought a football."

I was grinning so hard you would have thought I was having the baby. "I am so jealous."

"Oh, please," Tamara began with a dismissive wave. "You could have the same thing if you wanted."

Portia choked on her drink, then started laughing. "My sister? Pregnant? Right. The only way she's having a baby is if someone else carries it. Lord forbid something should happen to her figure."

"I can't believe you're saying that."

Portia rolled her eyes playfully. "It's true. You had a fit when you got a scar on your leg. Heaven forbid you get stretch marks."

Tamara laughed and nodded her head in agreement. "Sorry, cousin, but we know you too well."

I was a little stung by their remarks, no matter how true they might be.

Tamara smoothed a hand over her rounded stomach. "Portia, I'll have to admit your sister has been pretty busy since you left."

Portia sat upright in the chair, then looked from me to Tamara and back to me. I gave Tamara a hard look. If I'd wanted my sister to know I would have told her myself.

"Chris, what's going on?"

Tamara leaned back in the chair. "I was getting ready to ask her the same thing. Come on, cousin, I'm dying to know how date number four went."

"Date number four? Okay, back up. What millionaire is she dating this time?" Portia demanded to know.

Tamara took a deep swallow from her drink. "Who says he's rich?"

Portia gasped and put her drink down on the table. "Chris, what is Tamara talking about?"

I reached for my lemonade, took a sip and pretended it was no big deal, although my heart was beating heavily just thinking about Wednesday night, when Dereon showed up at my townhouse unannounced. "I've been dating one of my clients."

Portia's eyebrow quirked. "Ooh, a client. What's he look like?"

I leaned back in my chair and was unable to contain the smile on my face. "He's gorgeous. Everything a woman would want in a man and then some."

Tamara must have seen something on my face because her eyes grew round. "Oh, my goodness. He's good in bed, isn't he?" She and Portia leaned across the table hanging on a breath, waiting for me to speak. I opened my mouth ready to deny it, then decided, what the hell. If I didn't tell someone soon I was going to burst.

"Yes, he is."

Tamara started screaming at the top of her lungs so loudly that Pierre came rushing out the French doors. I shook my head and waved at him that everything was okay. He'd been married to my cousin long enough to know she could be a little too over the top at times. He nodded and went back into the house.

Portia stared at me, as if silently debating what stand she should take, and finally shook her head. "I don't know if I like hearing that my sister is sleeping with a man after only four dates."

Oh, brother, leave it to my sister. She'd been a virgin until she met Evan, and even then she made him wait six months. Unlike her, I didn't have that kind of patience. There was no way I would waste six months with a man unless I had some guarantees he was going to be worth my time. Besides, I slept with him on the first date, not the fourth, but I decided to keep that bit of information to myself. "Believe me, we've been seeing a lot more of each other than four dates." I paused and licked my lips. "Besides, if you saw how gorgeous he was you would have slept with him, too."

"That cute, huh?" Portia looked intrigued.

As I thought about the dimples on either side of Dereon's face, I smiled slowly. "He gives Iris Elba a run for his money."

Crossing her legs, she leaned closer. "Now *that* is fine. I guess I would have slept with him, too." The three of us shared a chuckle and it was good to see my sister loosening up and enjoying a casual conversation that just happened to be about sex. Marriage had definitely been good for her. I hadn't seen her this relaxed since middle school.

Holding up her hand, Portia said softly. "Whoa … wait a minute! I just remembered Mother saying something about you seeing Harold,". Her eyebrows bunched with confusion.

"Oh, pooh," I said with a scowl. "That's Jeanna living in her own fantasy world. Harold and I went out one time and he's nice, but he doesn't do it for me."

"Hmmm," she said, appearing puzzled. I guess passing up a man who would eventually inherit millions was hard for her to digest. With my track record I couldn't blame her.

"So come on, spill it. You know I'm not letting you leave here until you give me some details," Tamara said impatiently.

"You're so nosy," I said, although I had every intention of sharing my news.

"I wanna hear about some of your dates," Tamara said, leaning in.

"Well …" I began, smiling. "One evening he insisted I wear jeans to dinner."

"Jeans?" Portia obviously couldn't believe her ears. "He took you to a restaurant and you wore jeans?" Tamara looked at Portia with an incredulous look on her face.

I tilted my head and cocked an eyebrow. "Actually, I picked out the restaurant. It was in the Central West End."

Portia raised a hand. "Hold on. Give me a moment. I still can't get past you wearing jeans to dinner. Not you."

I frowned. They were trying to make me sound like I was truly stuck-up. Okay, so maybe I am. "You want me to finish my story or not?"

"By all means, finish the story," Tamara chimed in.

"After dinner we went roller skating. And—"

"What?" Tamara screeched in surprise.

Portia held up her hands. "Okay, time out. Now I know you're lying. You don't even know how to roller skate."

"True, I don't, but I had fun letting him teach me." Actually, I *was* lying, but it sounded too good to pass up.

Tamara just sat there with this far-off look in her eyes while she shook her head. "Unbelievable."

"Seriously, I went roller skating. Here, look. I've got a scar on my elbow to prove it." I turned my wrists so they could see the bruise on the back of my arm that I really had gotten banging the end of my desk. The two of them looked at each other and started shaking their heads in disbelief.

"Keep going. I'm waiting for the good part," Tamara said and rested her elbow on the table as she waited. You would have thought she was watching her morning soap operas.

Smiling, I continued. "Afterwards, he took me home. I invited him in and one thing led to another, and before I knew it I was breathing heavily and lying in his arms."

Tamara started fanning herself. "Oooh, this is just like one of those romance novels! My cousin got her some."

"And not a moment too soon." I had to stop and take a breath. "Tamara, that man did things to me I'd never had done before."

Portia's eyes grew wide knowingly. "I know exactly how you feel."

"I'm serious. I'm ready for an encore."

"So does that mean there will be date number five?" Tamara asked.

"Of course. After all, that's the only way I can get my hands on Grandma Celeste's locket, right?"

Portia's jaw dropped as she stared at me and Tamara. "Hold up. The two of you were betting on a locket?"

Tamara nodded. "Only partially. I just wanted your sister to step out of her comfort zone and date an average man. That's all."

My sister's brow rose. "Average? What do you mean, average? Christy, what does your mystery man *do* for a living?"

I looked at her then shrugged. "I don't know. Flipping homes. Maybe."

Portia scrunched her face as if sucking a lemon. "You're kidding, right? You're involved with a man you know nothing about?"

"Actually, I know quite a bit about him," I replied with a smirk.

Tamara leaned over near Portia and whispered, "Chris … got herself a thug."

"A thug!" Portia gasped and practically spilled her glass.

"Relax, he's not a thug," I replied defensively. "Just someone who's keeping it real."

"Oh, brother. She's already starting to talk like him." Portia shook her head, and her reddish brown curls moved with a life of their own. "Christina, what would Mother say if she knew?"

"Who said she has to find out?" I shrugged a narrow shoulder. "I mean, it's not like it's anything serious. Just two consenting adults enjoying each other's company. What's wrong with that?"

Portia eyes widened indignantly but she chose not to comment. I never realized how much like my mother she really was.

"Personally, I don't see anything wrong with having a little fun," Tamara replied in my defense.

Neither did I, but the look on Portia's face said she thought otherwise. *So would Jeanna.* I suddenly felt uncomfortable and regretted discussing Dereon with her. I was doing what made me happy, so why did I feel so guilty?

There was an uncomfortable silence as we each sat back enjoying our drinks and getting lost in our own thoughts, and then Tamara decided to splash around in the pool and Portia and I followed.

I stayed until dinner, after which Portia said goodbye to rush home to Evan. I left shortly after. I could just see her running over to see Jeanna tomorrow so she could tell on me, the way she used to do when we were kids. If she did, I would never hear the end of it.

Speaking of Dereon, my cell phone beeped, and I smiled when the LCD flashed his name on the screen.

"Hey, where you at?" he asked in a cheerful voice that made my smile widen.

"Just leaving my cousin's house."

"I just ordered a pizza. Why don't you come by and help me eat it?" he drawled.

Yes! Yes! He was finally inviting me to his place. I quickly cleared my throat and tried to play it cool. "Sure, just give me directions." He rattled off his address and I typed it into my GPS while trying not to run into the car in front of me. "I'll be there shortly." I hung up, tingling with excitement. I hadn't seen him since Wednesday night, and I hoped he had more than food on his mind.

As I drove, I realized that Dereon and I had yet to discuss our relationship. I was starting to wonder what was really happening between us. I loved him and wanted to know how he felt about me. Not that I'd shared my feelings, either, but at least if I knew where his head was maybe I could screw my own on right. Sure, we spent a lot of time together, but neither of us had defined our relationship. I cared about him and even loved him and that was what scared me the most. I was in love with a man my family would never approve of, and because of that I felt guilty. I wasn't sure if the guilt was because I was dating Dereon and I wasn't ready yet to share him with the world or because I was ashamed of who he was. That was something I needed to figure out, and fast.

I pulled off the highway. As soon as I saw the decaying homes and heard the loud gangster rap coming from an Impala idling at the stoplight beside me, I started to have a feeling of uneasiness at the pit of my stomach again. You better believe this was not at all the life I wanted to live. The light turned green and I made a left onto Hamilton and frowned when I spotted a bunch of thugs standing in front of a corner store. I drove slow, looking left to right, until I spotted Dereon's SUV in front of a two-story red-brick building with white shutters.

"Goodness, Christy, come on. What did you expect?" I whispered, feeling slightly lightheaded as I pulled over to the curb and parked behind a car that appeared to be more rust than paint.

My eyes traveled nervously up and down his street. There were mostly small old homes that seemed to have been well maintained for the most part. No thugs or crack heads hanging around. I climbed out, made sure my Jaguar was secure, then sashayed up the sidewalk in a green wrap dress and white sandals. The yard was neat and trimmed and there was no litter in the front yard, so that was a good sign. Nothing worse than a man who kept a messy home. I was coming up the stairs when the screen door swung open and Dereon appeared. My mouth began to water at the sight of him in loose-fitting Nike shorts and a wifebeater. His feet were bare and his chiseled pecs and biceps were on display. He set me on fire with one hot glance.

"Hey baby," he greeted with an adorable grin.

"Hi, yourself," I said and couldn't resist a smile of my own.

As soon as I hit the top step, Dereon leaned forward and kissed my lips. "Welcome to my world," he chuckled.

Goodness, was he nervous? I'm sure I heard it in his laughter and there was even a hint of uncertainty in his eyes. Silly me. I'd been so worried about what I was going to think I never even thought that he might be uncomfortable with me seeing how he lived. Goodness, I can be so self-centered at times.

"Good evening, Mrs. Larkins!" he yelled across the street.

I followed his gaze to an elderly stout woman who was out sweeping her front porch.

"Hello, dear. Make sure you come by tomorrow and pick up some tomatoes!"

He nodded, and said, "I will." Then focused his attention on me.

I stared up at him, grinning. I had a soft spot for a man who went out of his way to be nice to the elderly. Dereon took my hand and led me inside the building.

"Remember when I told you I owned a fourplex? Well, I live in one of the bottom units and rent out the other three," he said by way of explanation. He walked to the first apartment on the right and pushed open the door to his apartment. I held my breath, preparing for the worst, then stepped inside. Quickly, my eyes darted around the room, and by the time Dereon had shut the door I took one look at him and started laughing.

"What's wrong?" he asked with a silly smirk.

I shook my head. "You have no idea!"

He chuckled quietly. "Oh, I can imagine."

No, he couldn't. His place was sleek and modern. The entire inside had been totally remodeled. Fresh paint, new oak flooring. I strolled through the rest of the apartment and was clearly impressed. Updated travertine tile bathroom, upgraded kitchen, two good-sized bedrooms and a fabulous living room with built-in bookshelves and crown molding. The place was small, yet so cute.

Dereon was leaning against the wall with his arms crossed. "You thought I lived in a dump, didn't you?"

I nodded. "Yes, I did. As soon as I pulled into Jennings, I figured this place was going to be so bad I was going to spend the entire time kicking cockroaches off my shoes."

"Oh, now *that*'s cold!" he chuckled. "I can't believe you even went there."

I was cracking up. "I did. I took it there."

He smiled and slowly shook his head. "What did I tell you about judging a book by its cover?" he smugly reminded me. Well, at least he looked amused.

"I know, I know. I was wrong and I'm sorry," I replied, holding my palm up in surrender.

"I forgive you. Although I'll admit this place looked exactly like what you envisioned when I first bought it. A crew and I totally gutted it and remodeled all four units."

"I'm really impressed." And I was. I was also starting to feel better about us, because now I knew he hadn't been lying. "To be honest, I also thought you had a woman living with you."

"A woman?" he mocked.

"Well, yeah. You've never stayed over at my place, so I figured you had a wife to run home to."

Dereon tossed his head back with laughter. "Nothing like that. Believe me, my mother decorated my place. And as for staying, I was trying not to crowd your space. All you had to do was ask."

I walked over and wrapped my arms tightly around his neck. He lifted me off my feet and into his arms.

"The only woman in my life is you."

My heart started pounding heavily. His words were music to my ears. Dereon captured my mouth, then slipped his tongue inside. I leaned in and deepened the kiss. It wasn't long before he groaned and pulled back. "Food first. Then I plan to eat you."

I loved the way he just said whatever was on his mind, because it was exactly what I'd been thinking.

He lowered me to my feet, then took my hand and I followed him back into the kitchen with stainless steel appliances and granite countertops. I took a seat at a small table near the window. Dereon carried a pizza box over and we dug in while he talked about investing in the building and all the work it had required.

"What made you get into the business?" I asked between chews.

He leaned forward in his seat. "I worked construction in high school and have always been good with my hands. I knew a guy who was in the business. He taught me the ropes and I was hooked. I bought and flipped my first home five years ago and have been doing it ever since."

"I'm impressed."

We finished the entire pepperoni pizza while he talked about the business of flipping homes. I must say I was truly intrigued. He bought foreclosures at jaw-dropping prices, then he and a team spent no more than ninety days renovating the property. He had a fabulous realtor who immediately put it back on the market. The plan was to buy and sell the property within a span of six months. But with the economy the way it was, he had to be prepared to wait longer if needed. It sounded like a wonderful investment. Something I could consider investing in.

He led me back into the living room and over to a large overstuffed burgundy chair, where he lowered me onto his lap. "Why's your hair damp?" he said while running his fingers through it. I dipped my head back before he had a chance to feel my tracks.

"I spent the afternoon hanging out at the pool with my sister and my cousin and we decided to play in the pool. Trust me, I wasn't trying to get my weave wet but my sister kept splashing me," I replied as my fingers traced the defined lines of his flat belly.

He shook his head. "I don't know why women wear weave. Especially when they already have a head full of hair."

I batted my eyes. "Because it makes my hair look fuller, that's why." Men, they just didn't understand women.

"If you say so," he replied with a ridiculous look on his face. "Now let's get back to that bathing suit."

"I had on a string bikini," I purred seductively.

"*Wroof! Wroof!*" he barked, and I started laughing. "You sure know how to hurt a brotha."

"Yeah, right," I giggled.

"Well, while you were having a good time I spent the afternoon helping my father in the yard. He thinks he can still get out and take care of the yard like he used to, but since he had a stroke three years ago we've been trying to get him to take it easy. He's pig-headed, so I try to rush over and do the yard before he gets a chance."

I leaned against him, resting my head on his chest and smiling as I listened to him talk about his father and how he wanted him to be around for as long as possible, and if that meant taking away all his power tools, then so be it. What I would have given to have that type of relationship. My mind drifted to Carlos and for a few seconds I found myself once again yearning to have his love the way I used to as a child. And for the first time since my luncheon with Tamara, I couldn't help wondering why Carlos wanted to see me.

"What's on your mind?"

Pulling back slightly, I looked at his eyes filled with compassion. "I was thinking about my own father. He's in town."

A slow crooked smile appeared. "You gonna see him?"

"I'm not sure," I replied honestly. "I haven't seen him in a while."

"How long is a while?"

"My college graduation. He showed up with some hooker," I said bitterly.

"A hooker?"

Heat stole into my cheeks. "Okay, maybe not a hooker, but some chick around my age wearing a short dress."

"Mmmm, how short?"

I punched Dereon playfully in the arm and he bellowed with laughter, then he squeezed me tight. "I'm just playing."

"Anyway, he's in St. Louis negotiating a contract and told my cousin he would like to see me."

His brow rose. "Sounds like he's trying to reach out to you."

I leaned my head against him again and sighed. "Maybe," I said although not totally convinced. He hadn't reached out to me in years, so why now?

There was a prolonged silence before I heard Dereon ask, "What's the problem? Are you afraid to see him?"

I shivered slightly. "Yes … I guess I am." I raised my head from his chest and met the concern in his eyes. "If I decide to see him, will you go with me?"

Dereon appeared surprised by my request, but not as surprised as I was. I couldn't believe the words came out of my mouth and I was ready to take them back when an irresistible grin curled his lips.

"I would feel honored."

I sighed, feeling a sense of relief, and knowing he was willing to go with me gave me something to think about. Maybe I'd see my father. Maybe I wouldn't, but at least Dereon would be right by my side if I did. "Thank you." I lowered my mouth to his and kissed him, expressing every emotion I was feeling. "I mean it. Thank you."

"No problem. Do you wanna watch a movie or go in my room and make our own?" he suggested, and then gave me one of those coochie-clenching grins of his.

My eyes crinkled with laughter. "How about we skip making the movie and just go to your room?"

"Bet." Dereon rose with me in his arms and carried me down the hall to his bedroom, then lowered me gently onto his bed and lay beside me. I stared up at him, lips parted, heart pounding heavily beneath my breasts. Desire was burning in the depths of his eyes and had my entire body pulsing.

"I'm glad you came to see me," he replied as he loosened the belt on my dress and opened it, exposing me all the way down to my thigh. "I missed these." He slid the dress down over my shoulders, my bra as well, then captured one of my breasts in his hand and gently caressed my nipple. On contact, I rose up off the bed, bringing my body closer to him.

"You like that?" he asked capturing my gaze.

"Uh-huh," I moaned and turned into his touch. His hand glided over to the other breast . I closed my eyes and savored the feel of his strong fingers against my skin.

"I know what else you like," he growled against my lips. He kissed me gently at first, then increased the pressure and pushed between my lips and mated his tongue with mine. I met his strokes eagerly while my body was conscious of his hand that had traveled down past my belly button and began to fondle me. He was right. I liked when he stroked me between my thighs. I parted my legs, allowing him complete access as his fingers played along my folds before he finally slipped a finger inside.

"Yesss," I whispered against his lips as he continued to kiss me. It was hard to focus on his mouth when his fingers were doing things to me that felt heavenly.

"How's that feel, Christy?" he asked between kisses.

"Good," I whimpered. "Sooo good." I rocked my hips with the rhythm of his fingers. Dereon drove deeper, then used his thumb to stroke my clit and I almost came off the bed. He increased the pressure, and within seconds I was rocking hard against his finger and crying out in ecstasy. Before I could even catch my breath, he slid down on the bed, lowered his mouth between my thighs and suckled my overly sensitive clit.

Goodness, what was it about this man that made me go against everything I had been raised to believe was important? Because all that seemed to matter was him and me. Within minutes he had me squirming and crying out his name. While I lay there breathing hard, he grinned and slowly slid up onto the bed beside me. He was so adorable.

"You like that?" he asked with a cocky chuckle.

"You know I do. That's why you're laying there wearing a shit-eating grin." He tried to give me an innocent look, then started laughing. In one swift motion I rolled over and straddled him. "You're laughing now, but we'll see how you feel in about twenty seconds." I slid down past his knees and reached for the waistband of his shorts, signaling for him to lift up.

"What are you doing?" he asked with a nervous laugh, although he was completely cooperative.

"You'll see," I replied and tugged his shorts and boxers down over his waist. The second I wrapped my hand around his erection, Dereon squeezed his eyes shut and groaned.

"Baby, what's wrong?" I asked innocently.

His answer was a combination of a grunt and a moan. I chuckled quietly, then leaned forward and blew across the tip.

"Shit." He tightened his hands into fists, and when I started licking, sucking, teasing, his jaws clenched.

"You like that?" I asked.

"Hell, yeah."

"I'm sorry. Did you say you wanted me to stop?" I taunted.

"Don't you even think about it," he said, then opened his eyes and stared down at me.

I pushed my hair away so I wouldn't miss his expression. Our eyes were locked as I lowered my mouth over his erection as far down as I could manage, then wrapped my fingers around the rest.

"You look sexy as hell sucking my dick," he hissed.

Together my lips and hand worked his entire length while he continued to watch me, eyes glazed and soft low groans coming from the back of his throat. He started squeezing my ass in rhythm with my long deep strokes. I moved up and down, again and again, and Dereon flinched and gasped. I flicked my tongue across the head and applied pressure to the large vein right near the tip and realized it was his spot.

"Shit, you about to make me come," he moaned, and it felt good knowing I had that level of control. I moved faster this time, trying to deep throat him, and within minutes I heard a ragged cry and he came, his penis pulsing inside my mouth. I sucked him vigorously and swallowed. Dereon collapsed and lay there, breathing heavily.

"Damn!" he finally shouted, then pulled me up beside him and started kissing me across my neck and along my shoulder. I giggled. "What are you giggling about?"

"I'm not giggling. I'm ticklish!"

"Oh, yeah? Well how about here and there?" he said playfully.

"Yes! Yes!" I screamed and squirmed on the bed as he tickled me. "Please, stop, please!" Laughing, he complied and pulled me over into his arms and covered my mouth with his.

TWENTY

"Come on, Dereon. You have to admit it was a good movie."

Dereon stopped walking and made an animated show of sticking his finger down his throat. "Yeah, if you like sappy movies with happy endings."

Reaching down, I clasped my fingers with his as we exited the theater. "What's wrong with happy endings?"

"Nothing, but c'mon. This dude was left half dead … learned martial arts in one month … traveled to Europe, then single-handedly rescued his high school sweetheart from a drug smuggler."

I chuckled. "I guess when you put it that way, the movie *was* a little cheesy."

"A little?" he smirked.

I met the incredulous look in his eyes and couldn't help the laughter that pierced my lips. He pulled me closer to him and draped an arm across my shoulders as we followed the crowd toward the main exit doors.

The Fourth of July weekend had been amazing. We had gone downtown to the annual fireworks. There were vendors and the Temptations performed live on a makeshift stage near the Arch. What I'd enjoyed most was that Dereon had spent the entire weekend at my place. The more time we spent together, the more I discovered how lucky I was to have him in my life.

"You wanna go and get some ice cream?" he suggested as he pushed open one of the double doors and held it open for me.

"That sounds nice, as long as they have butter pecan."

He slapped a fist to his chest. "Yuck! I'm a green mint man myself."

We were heading to the SUV, debating ice cream flavors, when Dereon suddenly stopped walking. I followed the direction of his eyes to a beautiful Latina female with long silky black hair and a body like J-Lo. Who wouldn't have noticed her? She was a rich shade of honey, with high cheekbones, a perfect round face, small nose, and large brown eyes. As soon as she spotted him, the smile on her lips hardened.

"What do we have here?" she asked, looking from me to him as she closed the distance between us.

Dereon's grip suddenly tightened. "Milagros … so nice to see you."

"The same here." She looked down at our fingers locked and faked a smile. "How cozy. Who is this?" she inquired as her eyes perused my beige Coach sandals and a chocolate Donna Karan sundress. Trust me, I was keeping it cute, and obviously she noticed.

"This is a good friend of mine, Christina," he said by way of introduction, like I was no big deal. "Milagros, how was your holiday?"

"Obviously not as good as yours," she replied, and didn't even bother to hide the bitterness in her voice. Okay, what the hell was really going on?

"Well … good seeing you. I'll holla at you." Dereon led me away from her and toward his SUV before I had a chance to see if she was even there with a date. He remained quiet and I waited until he pulled away from the parking lot before I finally broke the silence.

"Who was that woman?" I asked curiously.

I watched the muscle at his jaw twitch before he finally replied. "No one important."

So, in other words … none of my business. "Fine. Keep your little secrets." I knew I was pouting and acting like a spoiled brat, but I didn't care.

Dereon ran a frustrated hand across his face. "She's a … business associate."

I wanted to ask if she was also a girl friend, because it seemed pretty obvious there was more than business brewing between them. I mean, it wasn't like I was about to become a stalker, but a woman likes to know who her competition is. I don't know why I felt threatened by the beautiful woman, because lately Dereon had been spending the majority of his time with was me, but I was.

He took his eyes off the road long enough to toss me one of his beautiful smiles. "You still want that ice cream?"

I forced a smile of my own. "Of course I do."

We ended up sharing a banana split and joking around, but I could tell he was distracted.

"Is something wrong?"

He shook his head. "No, I'm fine." I then heard his cell phone vibrating in his pocket again. It had been going off since we'd left the theater.

"Aren't you going to get that?"

Dereon released an impatient sigh, reached inside his pocket and removed his phone. As soon as he stared down at the screen I heard him curse under his breath. "I need to drop you off at home."

I remained quiet and waited for whatever excuse was coming my way, but it never came.

"Will you be coming by later?" I heard myself ask.

It felt like forever before I finally heard him say. "No, but I'll call you later."

We finished our ice cream, but the mood had been ruined. Maybe I'm crazy, but I had a feeling that woman we'd seen earlier, Milagros, was somehow responsible for the sudden change in Dereon's behavior. Or maybe I was just being silly.

Dereon clasped his fingers with mine while he drove with his other hand. He talked about his mother calling this morning and his father being under the weather and having an appointment to see his physician in the morning. He and his sister both planned to be there. I couldn't help but wonder that if anything ever happened to my father before we'd had a chance to talk, would I have any regrets? The answer was yes.

Dereon pulled in front of my condo, and when he left the engine running I knew he had no intention of coming in. It was just the same. The mood was ruined.

"Thanks for the movie."

His golden eyes twinkled. "Any time, sweetheart. I'll call you later."

I wasn't going to get my hopes up. He leaned over the seat and kissed me hard on the mouth. "I'll call you," he repeated. He kissed me once more, and then I opened the door and climbed out.

I stepped into my condo, slipped out of my sandals and left them at the door, then tossed my purse on the couch and headed into the kitchen for a bottle of water.

My mind was racing with all kinds of thoughts. Was Dereon going to see that woman? I couldn't help but think about how beautiful she was and the way her eyes narrowed dangerously when she saw us together. There was something going on between them. If not now, then definitely in the past. I just wished I knew what it was.

I opened the refrigerator and started mumbling all kinds of crazy off-the-wall stuff under my breath. What was wrong with me? I had never been a jealous woman. In fact, I was clearly confident that I had what it took to keep a man. However, being in love was an altogether different ball game. It left your heart opened, exposed, and easy to be broken, something I swore I'd never allow any man to do. I knew what happened to women with broken hearts. They ended up using men the way my mother did. And one thing I knew for sure. I didn't want to end up bitter like Jeanna had become after my father left her.

Taking a deep breath, I stepped back into the living and took a seat on the couch. I sat there staring out the large picture window for several minutes, thinking, before I reached inside my purse for my cell phone, scrolled through the phone numbers and dialed. As soon as it started ringing I noticed my hands were shaking.

Finally a man answered the phone. "Hello?"

"Is … is this Carlos Holloway?"

There was a slight pause. "Christina, sweetheart, is that you?"

A sob caught in my throat. "Yes, daddy … it's me."

TWENTY-ONE

The following morning I was still watching a phone that never rang, which was probably for the best. I was meeting my father for lunch this afternoon and I had decided it was better if I went on my own. I had things I wanted to say to my father in private.

I spent most of the morning on the phone with Culinary Resources, a staffing service for temporary personnel in the food and hospitality industry. We'd used them several times in the past because they provided us the flexibility to hire additional staff only when needed. I scheduled a few interviews for the rest of the week. We required at least six servers for the dinner cruise.

At eleven-thirty, I reached for my purse and sashayed out of my office. "Mia, I'll be out at least until two. Call my cell phone if you need me."

She twirled around on her seat. "Ooh, you're all dressed up. You must be meeting a man!"

I tried to keep a straight face. She can be so nosy. "No I'm meeting a potential client."

She glanced down briefly at the calendar on her desk. "Really? Then why isn't it on the calendar?"

"Because I made the appointment myself," I said without making eye contact. "I'll see you later." I turned and hurried out of the building before she started asking more questions. Meeting my father was something I wasn't ready yet to share with anyone.

I made it to Cardwell's in plenty of time, and surprisingly there was parking nearby, which doesn't happen too often in Clayton. Thankful for the extra time, I fixed my make-up, then stared at my reflection in the mirror. "You can do this," I said aloud, because I needed to hear it. I wasn't sure what I was going to say, or even why

I had finally decided to call Carlos, except that I felt I was at a point in my life when I needed answers.

My cell phone rang and I glanced down and noticed it was Jeanna calling. Goodness, talk about timing! I knew why she was calling. I was supposed to be at Kathy's luncheon. But there was no way I could tell Jeanna I had decided to have lunch with my father instead. She would never understand how important seeing him meant to me. I turned down the volume and put my phone back in my purse. I couldn't allow myself to get sidetracked by what Jeanna would think. I'd done that all my life.

At noon, I took a deep breath, climbed out of the car and fed four quarters into the meter. I sashayed up the sidewalk and caught my reflection in the window of several shops. I had made a good choice wearing an off-white sleeveless pants suit and chocolate pumps. Those were the colors that made me feel most confident.

I stepped into the restaurant and was met by a rush of cool air. The hostess immediately greeted me, and I informed her I had made reservations for a private room. This afternoon was too important for interruptions.

She led the way and I took a deep breath and gasped when I spotted Carlos already seated at our table. The second he saw me he rose from his chair.

Looking at him, my hands began to shake. He'd aged so well I had forgotten how handsome he was. Tall, six-one, medium build with salt-and-pepper curls, caramel brown skin and walnut-colored eyes. He was sporting a mustache and a neatly trimmed beard.

"Christina," he said in a voice I missed hearing. His smile was wide and looked so sincere. As soon as I reached him, he wrapped his arms around me and hugged me close, and I found myself closing my eyes and holding him tight. "I missed you, young lady," he whispered, then kissed my cheek before releasing me. "Please, have a seat." The smile remained but there was something else in his eyes that I couldn't quite place. Sadness, maybe? I wondered if he was as nervous as I was.

I took the seat across from him. "You're early." I commented because I didn't know what else to say.

"I wanted to make sure I wasn't late."

My lips parted, surprised by his response. Being on time had never been important before.

"Would you like to order?" he asked.

I nodded, and that gave me a few minutes to focus on the menu and get my nerves under control. When our waiter arrived and took our orders, I asked for a Cobb salad and Carlos ordered the Pecan Wood Smoked Shrimp.

"Tamara mentioned something about you being in negotiations with Anheuser Busch," I said, hoping to get the conversation underway.

"Yes, I'm thinking of selling my company to them."

"What?" I couldn't believe it. "But you love that company."

He nodded. "Yes, but at the rate I've been going, I'll be dead in five years."

I gasped at his words and searched his eyes for meaning.

"I had a mild heart attack in April."

"Oh, no!" I cried. "Why didn't you tell me?"

He gave me a sympathetic smile. "I did, but you didn't return my calls."

He was probably right. If he'd called I would have ignored him the way he had done me all those years. An eye for an eye. It seemed so stupid now. "I'm so sorry."

Carlos held my gaze. "Thank you, but I didn't come here to have you feel sorry for me. I'm here because having the heart attack made me realize what's most important in life …" he blinked and cleared his throat. "And that, sweetheart, is you."

"W-Wow," I sputtered. "I don't know what to say." Because I didn't. Who was this man, and what had he done with my father? Maybe I needed to check the tabloids and see if there had been any alien sightings lately.

"You don't have to say anything except that you'll give me a chance to make it up to you." His voice was raw with emotion as he reached across the table and covered my hands with his. "I know I haven't been there for you. I've put my job and personal life before my own daughter, and I'm ashamed and sorry. But no more. I'm selling the business and freeing up my schedule. I dumped my girlfriend and I'm thinking about planting a garden. But what matters most is being in my daughter's life. I have missed you so much. Can you forgive me?"

I looked across the table and saw the remorse and sadness gleaming in his eyes, and my heart squeezed as I thought of all the time we had lost. But I was thankful there was still a chance for us to develop a relationship. Despite everything I had said about not wanting anything to do with Carlos, I knew it had all been a lie.

I gazed into his eyes through a sheen of tears and whispered, "You have no idea how long I've been waiting to hear you say those words. Of course I forgive you."

"Thank you." His face creased into a smile and his brown eyes grew warm and crinkly. Carlos reached across the table and took my hand and told me about the heart attack while I lectured him on cutting the stress from his life and about healthy eating. We both began to relax and even shared laughter. We were getting along so well, one would have thought we had always been a part of each others' lives. Carlos didn't release my hand until our food arrived.

"How's your mother?" he asked between bites.

I wiped my mouth with a linen napkin before speaking. "Remarried, still trying to run everyone's life."

"I guess some things just never change," he said with a throaty chuckle.

You can say that again.

* * *

I slowed down the speed on the treadmill to a slow walk, then reached for a towel and mopped the sweat from my forehead. I had been working out for the last hour and hoped to have burned off some of the extra calories from the afternoon.

After lunch my father and I had gone to Sweet Creations for fudge, and then ended up next door for gourmet coffee. Afterwards, I'd taken him back to the office and introduced him to Claudia and Mia. He seemed interested in hearing everything about our business and even gave us a few pointers about expanding regionally. The entire time he was talking I sat there watching him, full of admiration for the brilliant man I could finally call my father. Not once did he pick up his cell phone, even though I had heard it vibrating in his pocket. Instead, he focused all his time and attention on me. By the time he'd left, I was sorry to see him go. But we made plans to get together for dinner before he departed St. Louis.

Finally, I had my father in my life. I wanted so badly to tell Dereon about my day, but I had yet to hear from him.

I slowed to a brisk walk for another ten minutes, then moved down the hall to my bedroom, stripped my clothes off and headed straight for the shower. I sighed as soon as I moved under the spray of hot water. It had been a long day, but quite rewarding.

I was lying across the bed, watching *House Hunters* on HGTV when Dereon called. I considered not answering the phone but my heart wouldn't let me.

"Yes?" I said by way of a greeting.

"Yes? Is that how you greet your man?" he chuckled into the phone.

I rolled over onto my back and stared up at the ceiling. "Who said you're my man?" I replied with attitude.

Dereon paused and blew out a long heavy breath. "Yo, don't be mad at me. I've been at the hospital with my father."

I abruptly sat up on the bed. "Oh, no! What's wrong?"

"While he was in the office seeing his doctor, he started having numbness and tingling in his left side and they decided to admit him."

I felt so bad for thinking the worst. I suddenly thought about my father and his heart attack. "Is he okay?"

"Yeah, thank God," he began, voice raw with emotion. "For a moment there we thought he was having another stroke, but they can't find any evidence of that."

"That's a relief."

He blew out a deep breath. "Tell me about it. Anyway, baby, I just needed to hear your voice. I'm gonna stick around here until visiting hours are over, then I'm going home to shower and crash."

"I understand. You make sure you get some rest."

"What you got up this weekend?"

It only took a second to remember I already had plans. "I have a wedding to cater on Saturday."

"Then how about Friday afternoon I take you on a picnic?"

"Picnic!" I gasped, because I hadn't done anything like that in years. "Where at?"

"That's a surprise," he whispered.

I giggled. "Okay, mystery man. How about *I* bring the picnic basket?"

"As long as you make me a cake."

I was really laughing now, and it felt so good. "Sounds good. I'll call you tomorrow." I ended the call and lay there staring at nothing in particular before I finally shook my head. I was ashamed of myself for all the negative things I had been thinking. Dereon wasn't with another woman, he had been with his father. "Christina, you've gotta stop jumping to conclusions," I murmured, then curled on the bed with a wide grin. I had my father and a wonderful man both in my life, so what more could a girl want?

TWENTY-TWO

There were a lot of places I would have considered for a picnic, but I almost wet my panties when I discovered where we were headed.

"You're kidding, right?"

Chuckling, Dereon shook his head. "Why's it gotta be all that?"

I gaped at him in horror. "Because you said we were going to a park to have a picnic. You didn't say anything at all about going to the zoo."

I guess he found my behavior amusing, because he gave a hearty laugh as he pulled into the parking lot and killed the engine. Personally, I didn't find anything amusing at all. "Christy, don't tell me you've never been to the zoo."

"Of course. Who hasn't when they were a child? But that was many moons ago." I think I'd been only once, and that was on a fifth grade field trip. I remembered being scared to death because Jeanna raised me to believe animal were filthy creatures, breeding disease and rabies.

"Well, if it's been years then you'll have a good time," Dereon said with certainty.

I hesitated. "But you don't expect me to eat around them, do you?"

"No, baby, we're going to picnic over there in Forest Park after we're done."

Okay, I could do that. I breathed a sigh of relief. The last thing I wanted was for him to think I wasn't any fun and didn't appreciate him trying to be romantic, because I did. A man had never done anything remotely close to this, although that was probably a good thing, because before Dereon walked into my life I would have flat-out refused and told the fool to lose my number.

I unfastened my seat belt and swung my purse strap over my shoulder and reached for the door handle.

"Hey."

I looked to my left and Dereon looked so serious.

"C'mere." He gestured with a tilt of the head. I leaned forward and allowed him to capture my mouth in a swooping kiss that caused a stir at the pit of my stomach. "Hmmm, that should tide me over until later."

Later. I loved that word. I was hoping Dereon was planning to spend the evening with me. I was starting to hate sleeping alone.

He climbed out of the SUV and came around and opened the door for me. I smiled. He was such a gentleman. I took his hand and stepped out and was pleased when he laced his fingers with mine and headed toward the zoo entrance. I made a quick sweep of the other visitors dressed in shorts and t-shirts and frowned as I looked down at my pink sundress and slinky white sandals. Overdressed as usual.

I guess Dereon had read my mind again. "Don't you think you'll be more comfortable in a pair of flat shoes? We can stop by one of the shops and see if we can find you a pair of flip-flops."

Flip-flops? Was he crazy? Men don't understand. I can't wear a designer sundress with flip-flops. There are rules in fashion, and that was definitely one of those. "No, I'll be just fine."

Dereon gave me a long look then shook his head. "Okay, suit yourself."

We spent the next hour walking around, holding hands and seeing the animals. I have to admit I was really enjoying myself, mainly because we were spending time together. I saw the admiring glances Dereon was receiving from a few women and I felt territorial and squeezed his hand. As usual, he looked sexy in khaki shorts, an orange tank top and leather sandals. Meanwhile, my feet were screaming, but there was no way in the world I was letting Dereon know my three-hundred-dollar shoes were killing me, not after he'd advised me to buy something more comfortable.

"You wanna go see the sea lion show?"

"Sure." *If it means I get to sit down.*

"Okay, then we better hurry. The show's about to start."

Yes. Hurrying sounded like a wonderful idea. He took my hand and practically dragged me to what I felt was all the way over to the other side of the zoo. I cringed and gritted my teeth. You better believe I was planning on taking these shoes back to the store tomorrow and demanding the manager give me store credit. I was all about looking fabulous and dealing with slight discomfort, but *this* was beyond ridiculous.

We followed the path through a brush of trees and I almost cried out loud *yes, yes,* when I saw the sea lion arena straight ahead. I practically pushed my way through the crowd, and to hell with wiping off the seat first. I flopped down on the bleachers with a sigh. Mild chuckling to my left caught my attention.

"What's so funny?" I hissed.

"You're feet are hurting in them shoes aren't they?" he challenged, raising a thick brow.

I pulled in a long breath and gave him an innocent look. "No. Whatever gave you that idea?" Dereon stared into my eyes while I struggled to keep a straight face. Thank goodness the show started and his attention was diverted to the sea lions and not me. I watched and was so intrigued I felt like a child again. Those little critters were so cute and well trained. I found myself clapping right along with them. In fact, despite obvious reasons, I was disappointed to see the show end. Leaving meant I had to walk in those shoes again. They were definitely beautiful to look at, but walking was another story altogether.

Dereon stood and reached for my hand. I reluctantly gave it to him and rose to my feet wearing a pained smile. "Where to next?" I asked, because I was hoping it wasn't too far away. "I'm starting to get hungry."

His eyes twinkled as he suggested, "How about we go back to the car and retrieve your basket? I'm dying to find out what you have inside."

I smiled. Going back to the car sounded like a wonderful idea to me. Too bad that meant I had to walk.

We made it to the car, and not a moment too soon. I was practically limping, and I swear I now have corns on both of my pinky toes. Damn shoes!

"How about we drive around to the other side of the park and find a cozy spot?" Dereon suggested as soon as we both had our seat belts on.

"Sure," I sighed with relief, and leaned back in the chair. The farther he drove the better. I closed my eyes. *You can bear it*, I chanted over and over as he drove. As soon as we were done eating we would pack up and be on our way.

I groaned when I spotted him pulling into a part of the park lined with benches sooner than I had hoped. Dereon climbed out and I waited until he came around and opened the door for me before I made any attempt to move off the seat. He was reaching in the rear for the basket and his back was turned before I mumbled, "Ouch." under my breath.

"Did you say something?" Dereon asked as he swung around holding the basket in one hand and a blanket in the other.

"No, nothing," I replied then quickly changed the subject. "Hey, what's the blanket for?"

He shook his head and grinned. "Babe, it's not a picnic without a blanket."

I was in too much pain to argue that a picnic bench would do nicely. Instead, I accepted his outstretched hand and followed him down the path. I couldn't help it, but after a few steps I started limping. The pain had become unbearable.

He paused. "Baby, you okay?"

I took one look at the concern in his eyes and I couldn't hold back a second longer. "Noooo! My feet hurt!" I replied like a whiny baby.

"I was wondering how much longer before you told me the truth." I could tell he wanted to laugh but was glad he didn't. Instead he led me over to a large tree and spread out the blanket and set the basket beside it. "Now sit."

I wasn't one for taking orders from a man, but this was one time I wasn't about to argue. I flopped down in my expensive sundress and sighed with relief as Dereon slipped the sandals from my feet. "*Oh God*, that feels wonderful."

Dereon tossed his head back and chuckled heartily. "Maybe next time you'll listen to me."

I shrugged. "Maybe and maybe not."

"You are one stubborn female."

"And obviously you like it," I retorted.

"Yes, Lawd!" he shouted, drawing laughter from me as he lowered on the blanket beside the basket. "Poor thing. Give me your feet."

I draped my legs over his and immediately he began to massage my feet. "How's that feel?"

"Wonderful."

"I aim to please." Oh, he was definitely doing that. "I don't get how females wear shoes that put corns on their feet."

"Corns? I have a corn?" I snatched my foot back and stared down at my toes. I couldn't believe how red the blisters were on my pinky toes. There was no way I could be caught again in sandals until it faded.

"Yo, quit tripping. Give me your feet and relax."

Sighing, I placed my feet back in his lap, then said, "I guess wearing those shoes to the zoo wasn't such a good idea."

"Ya think?" he said mockingly.

"But they were cute and I've been dying for the perfect day to wear them," I said, trying to justify my reason.

"I ain't gonna lie. You were wearing the hell out of them shoes."

I grinned at the compliment and it almost made it worth the blisters.

Dereon leaned his head back and stared up into the trees. "When I was young I used to love watching my Mama wear heels. I used to love the way her legs felt in pantyhose."

"You used to rub on your mother's legs?"

He nodded and switched to my other foot. "Yep, but back then I thought they were really her legs. My Dad used to say, boy, don't nobody feel on my woman's legs but me. Anyway, Mama used to strut around in those heels and daddy would just watch the way she moved and mumble under his breath stuff a child wasn't supposed to understand."

I sent him a sly smile. "See, even your mother wore high heels."

"Yeah, but you better believe the second Mama got home from school she exchanged them for slippers."

"Well, my mother *lives* in heels. I don't think she ever wore flats. She's a tall woman who loves towering over people and feeling empowered. As soon as I was old enough she taught me how to wear heels and I've been wearing them ever since. I can't imagine wearing anything else. What can I say?"

"I can say I like what I see … everything." He winked. "How's that feel?"

"Much better, thank you." I sighed, then curled my feet underneath me. "Ready to eat?"

He rubbed his palms together. "Oh, yeah! I've been waiting all afternoon to see what's in that basket."

I reached for a bottle of hand sanitizer from my purse, put some on my hands and handed it to him. He chuckled.

"I guess we can't have toe jam on my food."

"Toe jam!" I playfully swung my hand and swatted him on the shoulder. Dereon laughed, then wrestled me down onto to the blanket and met my gaze. "Your toes are pretty enough to suck. But right now I want to suck on something else." He lowered his mouth and captured mine, then sucked gently on my bottom lip before slipping his tongue inside. I wrapped my arms around his neck and pulled him closer and deepened the kiss.

"I think we should eat," I murmured after several seconds.

With a growl he finally released me. "Probably a good idea."

I sat up straight while Dereon rubbed his hands together eagerly. "Let's see what's inside." He reached into the basket and pulled out the first container. "What do we have here?"

"There's roast beef sandwiches, potato salad, fresh fruit,, and homemade coconut cake."

"A woman after my own heart." His words made my heart pound. *Was he ready to give me his heart?* "Baby, everything looks good." He swooped in and planted a loud kiss to my cheek.

We ate and laughed and talked about nothing in particular, but it didn't matter. I was having more fun than I did shopping at the mall.

Dereon moaned with approval with every bite. "You're really something, you know that?"

"Really?" I said between chews. "Something like what?"

"You can cook, you're educated, sexy and gorgeous. You got me walking with my chest stuck out."

"Whatever," I mumbled, and tried to act like it was no big deal when it really was.

"Seriously, Christy. I'm really feeling you."

I was grinning so hard I was afraid my face was going to split. "You know how to make a girl feel good."

"I try to put my education to work," he joked.

"You went to college?" I asked between bites.

"Why do you seem so surprised?"

I shrugged. "Probably because you haven't said much about yourself personally."

Nodding, he reached for a soda can and popped the tab. "You're right. Actually I graduated from UMSL."

"What did you study?"

"Accounting," he announced with a grin.

My eyes widened. "You're kidding!"

"No, I'm afraid not. It was my mother's dream. It wasn't until after I graduated and I got a job with a CPA firm that I realized accounting was boring as hell. I couldn't see being confined to a desk staring at spreadsheets for the rest of my life."

We talked and ate and when we were finished he packed up the basket while I was supposed to be folding the blanket. I rose, and as soon as I applied pressure to my feet, I groaned. "I hate to put these shoes back on."

"Then don't."

My eyes narrowed. "Don't?"

Dereon chuckled. "You heard me. Don't. Just wiggle your toes and walk back to my SUV barefoot. Trust me, women do it all the time."

Yes, but I'm not like other women. Although I must say taking a chance of getting dirt on the bottom of my feet was less painful than slipping my blistered toes back in those shoes. I could *always* get a pedicure tomorrow. "Okay, I guess I could walk in the grass."

Dereon turned up his nose. "People walk their dogs around here."

Eeww! I hopped from one foot to the other while searching the grass for evidence of dog crap. "On second thought, wearing those shoes isn't such a bad idea. What's a little pain for a few minutes?"

"Hold up … I've got a better idea." He draped the blanket over my arm, then reached down for my shoes and placed them in the basket.

"Hey, put me down!" I demanded with a laugh when he scooped me into his arms.

"Hush, and let your man carry you."

I draped my arms around his neck and smiled, then suddenly I stilled. Wait a minute did he say *your man?* "My man? This is the second time you've said that. Are you trying to tell me something?" I asked with a nervous smile.

"Yeah, I am. You gotta problem with that?" he answered with his breath warming my lips.

I stared into his eyes, heart pounding wildly. "No … I guess I don't."

"Now, that's what's up." Dereon leaned in and pressed his mouth to mine. I allowed my eyes to flutter shut and gave in to the kiss. The entire time my mind was racing for a meaning behind the words. *My man. Dereon's woman.* Just thinking about being in a relationship, a real relationship, with this gorgeous man made my body heat up profusely.

He finally ended the kiss and gazed at me. "Glad we could come to an understanding." Dereon adjusted me in his arms, reached down for the basket and headed toward the SUV. I started laughing and he joined in.

"Christina Darcy Holloway, what in the world are you doing?"

My head snapped around and I froze when I noticed the woman standing before me with a hand planted firmly at her narrow waist.

Jeanna.

TWENTY-THREE

I blinked several times while I search for my voice and spoke. "Mother, what are you doing here?"

"I should be asking you the same thing," she retorted with a disapproving look. I noticed her eyes traveling from Dereon's t-shirt down to the sandals on his feet. "I 'm on my way to a Board of Director's meeting. The Society Ladies are hosting their annual fundraiser and we're meeting in one of the banquet rooms. The zoo has so graciously donated the space."

Mother and her charity events. Dereon lowered me slowly back onto my feet.

"Now, tell me why my daughter is in a park wearing a wrinkled dress and no shoes?"

Self-consciously my eyes traveled down to the material. Sure enough, I was a wrinkled mess.

Dereon decided to come to my rescue. "She's on a date with me."

"A date? At the zoo?" Jeanna gasped. "And who might you be?"

"Dereon Sanders, ma'am." He stepped forward and held out his hand. Well, at least he didn't greet her with *whassup*.

Jeanna glanced down at his hand like she might contract something if she touched him before finally shaking his hand, but afterward she quickly released it.

"So *you're* the mystery man. Christina you've been keeping secrets." She gave a fake smile and glanced over at me. I could see the wheels in her head were already turning.

"No secrets, Jeanna. We're just friends."

She wasn't buying that at all. "Since when do friends carry friends across the park barefoot?"

"I just mentioned to Christy I would love to meet her family." My eyes snapped to Dereon and silently begged him to quit lying.

"Christy, huh?" Mother returned her attention to Dereon, and as her eyes perused his body a slow grin curled her lips. "I wish I could continue this conversation, but I hate to be late for my meeting."

Heaven forbid that ever happened.

"How about dinner Friday night at my house? Say, around seven?"

"Mother, I already have plans," I blurted out in panic.

She gave me a dismissive wave. "Then change them. I expect to see you there, and Dereon, you'll be coming as well, correct?"

He nodded and flashed his signature grin. "Yes, ma'am. It would be my pleasure."

"Very well. I'll see the two of you on Friday. Christina, I'll be calling you later. Young lady, you have a lot of explaining to do." With that she sashayed up the sidewalk toward a large white building. As soon as she was far enough away I groaned loud enough for Dereon to hear. He chuckled.

"Now I see where you get it."

My head whipped around. "Get what? Me and my mother are nothing alike." Like I was really going to admit that even being possible.

He was laughing his butt off. "Oh, yes you are! Trust me, the fruit doesn't fall far from the tree."

I rolled my eyes and stormed off to his vehicle.

He called after me. "Yo, you want me to carry you?"

"No, I can walk on my own." *How dare he say I acted like my mother?* I'd rather get glass in my foot than for someone to think I acted as snobbish as she did.

We were quiet all the way back to his SUV. Dereon waited until we were both inside before he spoke. "Christy, talk to me."

"There's nothing to talk about." How could I begin to explain to him how embarrassed I was by my mother's behavior?

"Hey." He cupped my chin then turned my head so I was forced to look at him. "What's going through that head of yours?"

"Nothing. Sorry. My mother's a piece of work."

"Yeah, I kinda figured that." Laughing, he kissed my cheek then put the key in the ignition.

I leaned back in the seat and tried not to think of Jeanna. The second her meeting was over she was going to call me to ask questions I wasn't prepared to answer.

"What time do you want me to pick you up on Friday?"

I glanced out the window and announced, "I'm not going."

"Why not?"

I released a heavy sigh. "Because I don't want to give my mother the wrong idea."

"Wrong like I'm not the type of man she would approve of?"

How did he know that? I didn't want to hurt his feelings, so I tried to find a way to soften the blow. "My mother will want to know everything there is to know about your parents, and then she'll want to know how much money you have and what you do for a living."

"So what you're saying is she wouldn't approve."

"Pretty much."

There was a pregnant pause before Dereon spoke again. "The way I see it, the only thing that should matter is what you think."

I love you. However I couldn't say that because so far I had no idea where I stood with him. He said he was my man, but what exactly did that mean? Dereon had opened up about so much, yet told me so little. There was still something he was hiding from me. I could feel it in my gut. I wasn't ready to go up against my mother when I wasn't sure who the man was I was with. The only thing I was certain of was that I was in love with him.

I turned on the seat and studied his profile. "All my mother wants is for me to be happy."

"And are you happy?" I watched him lick his lips.

Nodding, I replied, "Yes."

"Then that's all that should matter."

He was right. That's all that should matter, but it wasn't. "You're right." I forced a smile and tried to act like everything was going to be okay.

I made up some excuse about having to finalize a few details for the wedding tomorrow and asked Dereon to drop me by the office. It was only partially true. I needed to be alone long enough to think. Mia had gotten off at two and Claudia had gone to Chicago with one of her sisters. She'd be back in the morning.

"How are you getting home?" he asked.

I gave a dismissive wave. "No big deal. I'll just take a cab." Before he could ask any further question, I leaned over, kissed his lips and climbed out of the car. Then I suddenly remember how bad my feet hurt. Thank goodness I had a pair of comfortable mules in my office closet. I waved at Dereon and padded over to the building and unlocked the suite. I turned on the main light and walked across the reception area to my office and went inside. The carpeting under my feet felt heavenly.

I flopped down in my seat with a sigh. My life was a mess. Now that Jeanna knew I was seeing someone I was never going to hear the end of it. When she asked what he did for a living, what in the world was I going to say?

I picked up the phone and dialed the one person who would understand.

"What's wrong, chica?" Tamara said after we said our hellos.

I leaned back in my chair and groaned after I told her about my date in the park. "For once I'm in love with a man who is so wrong for me."

"Who says he's all wrong?"

"No one's said, but … " I purposely allowed my voice to trail off.

"But what? Didn't you just tell me you loved this man?"

"Yes. I love him." I didn't think I'd ever hear myself say those words out loud before. Yet it felt as natural as breathing.

"Then that's all that matters. I felt the same way when I started dating Pierre. I knew my Dad wouldn't understand, but after a while I didn't care anymore what he thought of me. The only thing that mattered was that I loved Pierre and he loved me."

I closed my eyes thinking about what Tamara had just said. She was right. Nothing should matter except how Dereon and I felt about each other. That was another problem. I had yet to find out how he really felt about me. Sure, we were in a relationship, but no rules had been set. No parameters. I had no idea where I stood with him.

"Quit thinking so hard, Christina. If you don't learn how to let go and enjoy life, you are going to end up losing the best thing to ever happen to you."

I expelled a long breath. I couldn't imagine Dereon not being part of my life.

"Take him to Aunt Jeanna's and hold your head high. If anything, she'll have to respect you more for doing what feels right for you." With that last comment I thought the baby was starting to suck up a little too much of Tamara's oxygen. Nevertheless, she was right.

"Okay … you're right. I love him and that's all that should matter." I couldn't keep allowing my mother to dictate my life. I had to do what was right for me. We talked a few more minutes, then I hung up and leaned back in my chair, deep in thought. I don't know what it was, but I always felt stronger when Tamara was coaching me, but the second I hung up, sitting all alone in my office, I felt overwhelmed with uncertainty again. I was so pathetic.

"Whatever it is, it must be serious."

I gasped and my eyes snapped up toward the door where Dereon was standing. "What are you doing back here?"

"I felt like I needed to come back." He pushed away from the frame and stepped into the room. "C'mere." I rose from my chair and closed the distance that separated us and moved into his arms.

Dereon brought his lips to my forehead. "Baby, you can lean on me. Whatever it is, we can get through it together."

Together. I loved the way that sounded.

He pressed his lips to mine in a passionate kiss, lifted me off the floor and carried me over to the edge of my desk. Dereon reached underneath my dress and pulled my panties down over my hips and down past my ankles. "I can't wait a second longer to be inside you," he growled impatiently.

Quickly, I reached down and unzipped his shorts and they fell down to his feet with a *swoosh.* Then I slipped inside his boxers for what my body was craving. It was hard enough to hammer nails into a board.

"Christy," he groaned as he fumbled in his back pocket for protection.

He slid on the condom and I guided him to my slick wetness. He was inside with one push. "Yes, Dereon."

"Wrap your legs around my waist," he commanded. I locked my ankles against his butt and leaned back, using my arms to brace my weight against the top of my desk.

"Don't close your eyes. I want you to watch."

I loved the way he always wanted me in the most primitive way. Staring down between us, I watched as Dereon thrust slowly, filling me completely. His erection was buried so deep I had to raise my legs to his lower back in order to allow for deeper penetration. The impact caused my body to shudder.

"Oh, that's feels good," I gasped. "So good." I held onto the end of the desk, circling my hips to grind against him.

I stared up into his beautiful face. His lips were parted, panting, and his eyes were narrow and low. Dereon leaned forward and I met his lips as he kissed me, tongues tangling, while he continued his powerful thrusts.

"You like that?" he asked, his breath fanning my nose.

"Yes, baby, I like that." I managed between breaths. "I love … having you … inside me."

He kissed me once more, then concentrated on thrusting deeper. With our eyes locked and Dereon watching my facial expressions, it made it even more arousing.

"Oh, Dereon," I whimpered as my clit started to throb like a heartbeat, then heated. The sensitive nub rubbed against his body, the friction clearly exquisite, while he continued to stroke me long and deep. Dereon groaned softly, then reached between us and grazed my clit with his thumb.

"Yesss," I moaned unable to tear my eyes away from his. "Oh yes, Dereon, *yesss*." Then I came, hard, flinching off the desk, and I knew he felt it because his eyes were round as I pulsated all around his length, suffocating him.

"Christy," he groaned. "I love you."

I was panting, trying to make sure I'd heard him right, while Dereon adjusted his hold and started thrusting hard and fast. I was speechless as I tried to find my voice, but the combination of what he'd said and how good he was making me feel was too overwhelming to put to words.

"Tell me," he growled. "I already know how you feel. I heard you on the phone."

I stared into his eyes and I saw everything he was feeling sparkling in their depths. "I love you, Dereon."

He then growled and his strokes became quick and powerful, and within seconds I had a second orgasm while I felt him come with a force that brought us both laughing and falling onto the carpeted floor.

"You are something else, Christina Holloway," he chuckled, then pulled me into his arms.

"So are you," I whispered. "So are you."

TWENTY-FOUR

Dereon's brow rose. "Nice place." A whistle escaped his lips, but the unenthusiastic expression on his face said he wasn't really all that impressed.

"I know you're lying," I replied after we greeted the butler and stepped into the foyer.

It had taken years before I realized that my mother's house was nothing more than a museum. A showcase. A place for Jeanna to show off her worldly possessions. Nothing out of place. She had a live-in housekeeper, so there was not a speck of dust. No shoes near the door. No coasters. Everything was black, grey and white, bland and depressing. White furnishing, black accents and gleaming floors. Boring artwork on the walls and priceless sculptures surrounded the room. Nothing about the impersonal house showed that it was even lived in.

The butler shut the door and I took Dereon by the hand and led him through the large foyer that was elegantly decorated with marble columns and a massive crystal chandelier overhead. As we passed a double staircase toward the formal dining room, I heard footsteps coming across the marble floor at the other end of the hallway.

"You made it!"

I breathed a sigh of relief when I saw Portia coming around the corner looking amazing in a cream pants suit and peach Christian Louboutin pumps. Her hair was pulled up in a sophisticated ponytail with tapered bangs showing off the diamond drop earrings dangling in her ears. Smiling, I moved over and gave her a hug. "Thank God you're here," I whispered for her ears only. "I don't think I could deal with *her* by myself."

Portia gave me a worried look as she released me. "Well, I'll warn you. Mother's been sipping wine since long before I got here."

Damn, that meant she would be loose at the tongue. I rolled my eyes, took a deep breath and smiled. "Portia, *this* is Dereon."

"I see," she replied. I noticed the appreciation in her gaze as she checked him out from head to toe, taking in the outfit I had insisted on buying him—navy pleated slacks, white shirt, blue tie and leather loafers—before returning to his face with a generous smile. "Nice to finally meet you. I've heard so much about you."

"Same here." Dereon shook her hand, and the second he flashed her with one of his irresistible grins, I noticed the way her eyelashes fluttered flirtatiously. Yeah, he had that effect on all the women. "I hear you're a newlywed."

At the mention of her husband, Portia blinked as if suddenly coming out of a daze. "Oh … yes, and I left him in the kitchen with Mother. I'd better get back in there before he divorces me." She gave a two-finger wave and hurried back toward the rear of the house.

I laughed, knowing good and well Evan adored Portia. It would take a lot more than Jeanna to get rid of him. I sighed and silently prayed for the strength to get through the evening. Dereon must have sensed my hesitation because he moved up beside me and brought a hand to my waist.

"Did I mention how beautiful you look in that blue dress?"

"Yes, but it doesn't hurt to hear it again." I smoothed down the front of the sleeveless, button-down Gucci dress, making sure there wasn't a wrinkle in place. He kissed my cheek and guided me through the double doors into the formal dining room, which was dominated by a long white linen covered table that was beautifully set with Grandma Celeste's china and a glowing candle centerpiece. A silk rug covered the floor. A mahogany china cabinet was against one wall and a matching buffet on the other. There were French doors to the right that led out onto a beautiful deck surrounded by a lush garden. Walter and Evan were engrossed in conversation.

As soon as he noticed our arrival, the tall balding man rose and immediately came over to greet us. He kissed my cheek, then turned and shook Dereon's hand.

"Welcome to my home," Walter said with a huge goofy smile.

I placed a hand on his arm. "Dereon, this is my stepfather, Walter, and my brother-in-law, Evan."

"Congratulations, man, on your nuptials." They exchanged head nods and greetings the way men do, just as Portia stepped into the room, followed by Jeanna, carrying a beautiful prime rib.

"Well, look who *finally* made it," Jeanna said with a saccharine smile. "Dereon, welcome." As Jeanna carried the platter over and set it at the center of the table, I noticed she was wearing an apron. She mopped her forehead. "I feel like I've been slaving in the kitchen *all* morning."

Portia and I exchanged looks. The closest thing we'd ever seen Jeanna do that resembled cooking was TV dinners in the microwave. As usual, her housekeeper Jillian had done all the cooking, and then mother gave her the rest of the day off so she could take all the credit.

I heard voices and looked up to see Kathy and Harold strolling through the door. *What the hell?* My eyes snapped to my mother, who was trying her best to hide a mischievous grin. There was no way their being here was a coincidence. She was still trying to fix me up.

"Kathy … Harold … so glad you could join us," she said by way of greeting. Jeanna sauntered over and she and Kathy exchanged air kisses.

Dereon's brow rose curiously and I gave an awkward shrug. "They're friends of the family," I explained.

Harold and I made eye contact and he winked. I couldn't help but smile because it was obvious by the exaggerated eye rolls he didn't want to be here either.

"Come on." I took Dereon's hand and led him over to the group. "I would like you all to meet my boyfriend, Dereon."

Kathy's brow rose and she sputtered with disbelief. That was before Dereon reached down for her hand and brought it to his lips.

"Pleasure meeting you, ma'am. Who is this? Your brother?"

She patted her horrible wig and started blushing and laughing flirtatiously. "Oh, you're too kind! Christina, where in the world did you find this nice young man?"

Dereon winked, and it took everything I had to keep a straight face, as he had to practically pry his hand away from Kathy.

"Dereon, this is a good friend of mine … Harold."

The two nodded and had a friendly exchange while my eyes traveled over to my mother, who was whispering in Portia's ear. The way her hands were moving indicated she wasn't too happy. *What else was new?*

"We missed you at lunch last week," Harold said softly.

"I'm sure I didn't miss much," I mumbled under my breath.

"Not at all. I ended up sneaking out the back door."

I cupped my mouth and chuckled.

During dinner Jeanna was loud and laughed way too much. Walter tried taking her glass, but she kept pushing his hand away. I wasn't sure if she was trying to impress Harold or Dereon, although I was certain Harold was used to her behavior by now.

"Christina, did you hear that Evan is going into private practice?"

Oh, brother, here we go. I finished chewing my prime rib and wiped my mouth with a linen napkin before saying, "That's wonderful."

Portia gazed over at her husband with adoration. "It's a big decision, but we feel confident things will work out."

"Of course they will." A handsome pediatrician. He'd have every single woman in the city falling all over herself to have her children as his new patients. I speared an asparagus and felt the heat of Jeanna's gaze.

"Did you know that Harold just made partner?" Kathy gushed. I knew it was only a matter of time before Kathy added her two cents. "His father and I are *so* proud of him."

Harold stuck a finger down his throat when his mother wasn't looking. He was just as bored by the entire evening as I was. Mother went on bragging about Walter's new peach-flavored vitamin water hitting the market in the fall. Then the men got into a long discussion about power drinks. I hurried to clear the table for dessert. But the second the crème brulée was brought out my mother cleared her throat and focused her attention directly across the table. At me. "I'm sorry, Christina. What did you say Dereon did again?"

I choked and reached for my water glass.

Dereon tapped me lightly on the back and whispered, "Baby, you okay?"I nodded, not trusting myself to speak.

He reached for my hand under the table, then flashed that kilowatt smile on Jeanna. "To answer your question, I flip houses."

It was mother's turn to choke. "D-Did you say you flipped houses?"

He nodded. "Yes, I've been doing it for years."

Kathy snickered behind her napkin.

"Mother, he also owns rental property," I quickly added.

That caused her eyes to spark with interest. "Really? How many buildings?"

Dereon sliced into the dessert and brought it to his mouth as he replied, "Just the one I'm living in."

Jeanna gave a rude snort.

"Mother!" I snapped. How dare she be rude to my guest!

Kathy smirked. "I'm sure your parents are quite proud of you."

"Yeah … they are." He either had no idea they were making fun of him or he just didn't care.

"And what do *they* do for a living?" Jeanna asked.

Okay, it was time to put a stop to this line of questioning. "Enough! Dereon, you don't have to answer."

"Why not? I don't have anything to be ashamed of," he said, as he lowered his fork to the table. "My mother's a retired school teacher and my father has owned a corner store for years."

The second he announced what they did for a living, Jeanna's lips were compressed and unsmiling. Portia dropped her head and refused to look over at me. Evan leaned back in his chair, stroking his wife's arm. Kathy looked like the wheels were already turning in her head. I bet the second she left she was going to be on the phone gossiping to all their friends. Harold was the only one who looked sympathetic. Dereon squeezed my leg underneath the table, but I couldn't bring myself to look at him. I just focused on my dessert.

Mother spent the rest of the meal praising Evan and complimenting Portia on making such a wise choice. She made several wisecracks about the working class and Dereon didn't seem to mind at all. I, on the other hand, had had enough, and by the time coffee was served I had a splitting headache. Coming over was a big mistake.

After the table was cleared I rose and went into the kitchen. Jeanna's housekeeper would be in bright and early, but I was never one for leaving work I could do myself for someone else. I was loading the dishwasher when I felt Jeanna's presence darken the room.

"How dare you bring that man to my house?" Jeanna hissed.

"What?" I spun around and pressed a finger to my lips. "Please lower you voice."

She gave an exaggerated eye roll. "Oh, please."

"What's wrong with him?" I asked with a hand planted to my hip.

"Do I have to spell it out to you? Everything," she chuckled. "You couldn't possibly be that naïve."

"Jeanna, he's a nice person. If you'd just give him a chance you'd see that."

She shook her head and moved in closer. "Why would you waste your life with him when someone like Harold is interested in you?"

"Because I enjoy being around him. He makes me laugh. He puts a smile on my face. What's wrong with that?"

"Everything!" she cried impatiently.

I glanced nervously at the door, then back at her. "Why can't you just be happy for me?" I whispered.

Jeaned crossed her arms over her ample breasts and leaned a slender hip against the granite countertop. "Because you're wasting your life. You're beautiful enough to marry a doctor or the next Barack Obama."

"You mean someone with money so I can be miserable like you?"

She dropped her gaze momentarily. "I'm quite fond of Walter."

"Fond? What about love, Mother?"

She raised mocking brows. "Love won't keep you warm at night or put a roof over your head. Didn't I teach you anything?"

"Yes, in fact you did. You taught me how to put money and power before everything ,and until now I never saw that." I noted dryly.

"Sweetheart, what do you even know about that man?" Jeanna said in exasperation.

My mouth tightened further at the criticism. "I know Dereon has more compassion in his pinky than you have in your entire body."

"Did I hear my name?"

I looked over at the door to find him standing there with a dimpled smile and panicked.

"Is something wrong?" he asked, brow narrowing with concern as his gaze traveled to Jeanna, then back to me.

Jeanna tried to shoo him away like a pesky fly. "Could you excuse us? I'm trying to have a *private* conversation with my daughter."

I stubbornly stood my grounds. "No, he can stay."

Her eyebrow arched. "What did you say?" It wasn't often that I stood up to my mother.

"I said he can stay." I emphasized each word. "If you're going to talk about Dereon, then at least say it to his face."

Jeanna pulled her shoulders back and narrowed her gaze in his direction. "Very well. Dereon, you might be a nice man, but I think my daughter can do much better."

I was so embarrassed by the comment I couldn't even find the words to speak. Dereon, on the other hand, had no problem defending himself. He looked from me to her, and when their eyes met his lips curved in a slow, lazy smile.

"I agree. Christy is a beautiful and talented woman and she could have done a helluva lot better, and because of that, I feel honored she chose me."

My eyes met his and I saw the passion. I never had anyone stand up for me before. "Thanks, babe."

He winked. "You're welcome."

Turning to Jeanna, I frowned. "Thank you for dinner, but we're leaving." I swung around, took Dereon's hand and led him back through the dining room. All heads turned when we entered. Of course, Jeanna's tipsy ass stumbled into the room behind us.

"Christina, don't you dare turn your back on me!"

"Why not? You have." I walked around to my chair and retrieved my purse.

She shook her head and sighed dramatically. "I'm so disappointed in you."

"So am I." For allowing her to dictate my life all these years. "You know what? I met my father for lunch last week. And after spending half the day getting to know him, I can see why he wouldn't marry you. You're too much maintenance!" I screamed at the top of my lungs.

There was a collective gasp before Jeanna stuck her chest out and sashayed around to her chair to retrieve her glass. "Portia … please … talk some sense into your sister," she insisted.

My sister glanced over at me, her eyes pleading with me to listen. She was such a coward. Kathy's eyes were wide and animated. Apparently, she had picked the perfect night to come over for dinner. Walter looked sad. He was another one of Jeanna's puppets.

"Harold, it was a pleasure seeing you again, but I'm leaving," I said.

"Wait, Christina," Harold said, then tapped his fork lightly against his wine glass. "Since this evening is a night full of revelations, I have one of my own."

Kathy patted his hand, her tanned face beaming. "Go ahead, baby. Share your wonderful news."

"Well at least someone has *something* important to say," Jeanna drawled as she poured herself another glass of wine.

I rolled my eyes and was ready to walk out the door, but I wanted to hear Harold's announcement. I figured he was ready to share with his mother his decision to run for city council.

"Go ahead, dear. The floor is yours," she urged.

Harold rose and smiled. His mother stared up at him with adoration. "Christina, I want to thank you so much for hanging out with me a few weeks ago. It isn't often I get to be in the company of a smart and beautiful woman. Listening to you talk about stepping out on faith and starting your own business made me realize I have to start living for myself and not for others. Mother … everybody … I'm gay."

My jaw dropped. Portia and Jeanna gasped while Kathy shrieked and fainted. While Evan hurried around the table to assist her, I glanced over at Dereon and tried to keep a straight face. The night had gotten quite interesting.

* * *

"I guess I should have warned you that my mother's dinners are usually … dysfunctional."

Chuckling, Dereon opened the door to his apartment and stepped aside so I could enter. "Yeah, but it's good to see that rich folks have problems too."

It was nice to be able to laugh about that whole situation, although I wouldn't admit how embarrassed I was at the way Dereon had been treated. I followed him to his room, slipped off my shoes and sighed with relief.

"Them dogs howling?" he joked.

"You know they were." I laughed, then hopped onto his bed and flicked on the television.

Dereon lowered onto the bed and motioned for me to slide over beside him. "Hey."

I looked up and met his penetrating gaze. "What?"

"Thanks for having my back over there."

"Any time," I purred and leaned in to kiss him. "When I said I loved you, I meant it."

He pulled me into his arms, and within minutes we were undressed and touching and feeling. By the time he'd reached down and slid his fingers along my slippery folds, I was primed and ready.

"Oh," I moaned as Dereon plunged a finger deep inside. He thrust in and out, then added a second finger. I whimpered and rocked against him. I wanted him. I was hot, needy and hungry. He played some more, dragging his fingers up and down, in and out. I was panting, my breath coming in quick puffs. When he finally stroked my clit, I nearly jumped off the bed as I came. Dereon deepened the kiss, stifling my screams. I continued to buck as he applied pressure, until I couldn't take it any longer.

"Please, baby, make love to me," I begged.

"Grab a condom out of the drawer for me."

I rolled away from him and opened the top drawer of his nightstand and gasped when I saw the gun inside. I abruptly sat up on the bed. "Dereon, why do you have a gun in your drawer?"

He stilled and mumbled something under his breath, then rolled over next to me. "For protection, baby, why else?"

It wasn't like I hadn't seen a gun before, but why did he have it beside the bed? *Did he need protection from something?*

"Does it bother you?" he asked.

I nodded. "Yes, guns give me the creeps."

He rose, removed it from the drawer and carried it over to the closet. I watched him walking, admiring his tight ass. A girl could get used to looking at that every day. "Hmm-hmm-hmmm, look at that body!"

He glanced over his shoulder, grinning, and put the gun on the top shelf and closed the door. "Now where were we?"

Smiling, I waved a foil packet in the air.

Dereon chuckled and then dived onto the bed, causing me to erupt with laughter. He took the condom from my hand, ripped open the packet and quickly rolled it on. I was still laughing when he climbed on top of me, braced his weight with his arms and plunged inside. He rode me for what seemed like forever. And when he came he crushed his mouth to mine, burying his tongue deep into my mouth, claiming me every way he could.

I spent the rest of the evening and the entire night wrapped in his arms. I was in heaven. Let me tell you. Dereon made me feel like a real woman. His woman.

I woke up the next morning and almost cried when he told me to lie there while he made breakfast for us. The man made biscuits from scratch. Can you believe it? Scrambled eggs with cheese, and the bacon was a little on the burnt side, but all that mattered was that he had been considerate and cared enough to try.

I was in love and I wasn't letting my family or anyone else ruin it for me.

TWENTY-FIVE

A week later I pulled into the large circle driveway and gasped as the magnificent five-thousand-square-foot home came into view. Built in the tradition of the Governor's Palace, the stately Georgian was prominently positioned on nearly three acres of lush green land. I had barely parked the car in front of the double mahogany doors when Portia came hurrying out the door to greet me. I climbed out of my Jaguar and rounded the vehicle as she reached the bottom step.

"I was wondering if you were going to make it," she said with a playful pout.

"I had an appointment that ran late. Oh my goodness! Look at this place!"

She beamed, pleased that I loved her new home. "Thank you. Come on, let me show you the rest of the house." She grabbed my hand and practically yanked me up the stairs and into the spacious foyer.

The house didn't disappoint. There was a grand double staircase and there were five spacious bedrooms on the second floor, each with its own private bath. Then there was a formal living and dining room and half a dozen other rooms that made my head spin. The entire first floor opened up to a large terrace that spanned the entire length of the house.

But what impressed me most was the chef's kitchen, with every amenity I could desire. It was something Portia knew I had always wanted of my own.

"Look at these countertops!" Beautiful black marble engulfed the entire room. I ran my hands across the cool surface as I glanced around at the pots and pans hanging over a massive island with six stools.

"Isn't it the grandest thing? I'm so happy you like it," Portia cried, then threw her arms around me and we hugged. I was so happy for my sister.

"Wow! That's all I can say. Where did you find this place?" The house was tucked away in a charming community in Ladue close to shopping and entertainment. I only lived a few minutes away and never knew this area existed.

"Mother found it, but the second Evan and I saw it we knew we had to have it."

I should have known Jeanna was somehow involved. Although I couldn't blame her for falling in love with this one. "Mother always did have good taste," I muttered sarcastically.

"Would you like something to drink? My housekeeper doesn't start until next week, so we've been eating takeout, but I do have some leftover French food if you're hungry."

I shook my head. "No, water will be fine." It's a shame my sister didn't know how to cook, but at least she had hired someone who would fully appreciate the kitchen. I moved over to the island and took a seat on one of the stools. "You did well, little sister."

"Thank you." She closed the refrigerator and came over carrying a bottle of Fiji water and handed it to me. Portia then leaned across the counter and tapped her perfectly manicured nails against the countertop. "Christina, you're not really serious about that guy, are you?"

I popped the cap off the bottle before answering. "If you're referring to Dereon, then yes, I am."

She took a moment to brush a few curls from her face as if they were in her eyes, but with Portia nothing was ever out of place. "You couldn't possibly be serious?" she said, and had the nerve to laugh as if I would joke about something like that.

My eyes narrowed to slits. "Why wouldn't I be? He makes me feel like no other man I've ever been with. Isn't that how you felt when you met Evan?"

"Yes, but Evan's a pediatrician."

"And what does that have to do with anything?" I retorted.

"It has everything to do with it, don't you see? With Dereon you'll never have a house like this," she added with a dramatic sweep of her hands.

I glared across the counter at her and thought about grabbing one of those pots overhead and popping her upside the head, but decided that was probably not a smart move. "I'd rather be in a one-bedroom apartment with him than married and miserable with someone like Walter."

Portia's mouth twisted. "Now you're being ridiculous."

"No, *you're* the one who's ridiculous," I exclaimed indignantly. "I'll admit I used to think snagging a rich husband was what was most important, but I've learned a lot since I've met Dereon, and that that you can't put a price tag on love. It doesn't work that way. Love is something that just happens. I'm starting to think there's really a cupid in the heavens shooting down his arrows, because I never expected to feel like this about him, but I do."

Portia stared at me as if I had a pimple growing on the end of my nose. "Mother's so disappointed."

Had she not heard a word I'd said? "I can't live my life for my mother. If she wants to go to bed every night with that shriveled-up old prune, then that's on her, because I know what I have, and trust me, I have no complaints."

Portia gave me an envious look, then just as quickly her lips turned up with disapproval. "I really think you need to reconsider, Christina." Then as an afterthought she added, "In fact, Evan and I are hosting a dinner party next weekend and have invited several of his single colleagues. Why don't you come? Never know … you might be able to snag a doctor yourself."

Her words were like a massive blow, like the one I yearned to give her with that copper pot. I sat there as realization began to sink in. Is this how I'd been behaving all my life? I stared at my sister, with her perfect hair caressing her slender shoulders and cosmetics that looked as if applied by a L'Oreal professional. She was dressed in black slacks and a cream button-down blouse and two-tone pumps that alone cost more than six hundred dollars, but other than being Mrs. Evan Smith she had absolutely nothing going for her beside looks. She'd sacrificed an education and a career to be a rich housewife. All those were things I'd been raised to believe I, too, had wanted, but as I stared over at my sister with her nose up in the air, I felt nothing for her but pity.

"You know what, Portia? You act just like Jeanna. Tell me this, when Evan decides to leave you for an independent woman with a career and her own money, what are you going to do?"

Stunned, she stood there, eyelashes blinking for several seconds before she finally replied with a smug smile, "Then I guess I'll just have to find myself another husband."

Shaking my head, I took one final swallow and lowered the bottle hard enough that it splashed over onto the counter. "I feel so sorry for you." I rose and swung my purse over my shoulder. "With Dereon I'm following my heart, not a checkbook. So you can either be happy for me, little sister, or you won't have to worry about me ever setting foot in your house again." I turned on my heels and headed toward the door.

I was so mad I tripped on the bottom step and had to catch myself. Damn her and Jeanna! I was reaching for the driver's door when Portia came rushing down the stairs.

"Christina ! Hold up before I fall!" she cried.

I huffed impatiently and planted a hand to my slender hip as I waited for Portia to walk to my car.

"Goodness, Christina, you could have at least met me halfway," she pouted.

"Are you serious? Portia, I don't have time for games." I swung away ready to get home because I was too through with my family, when Portia grabbed my arm.

"Christina, please … listen to me for a minute," she pleaded.

I looked over my shoulders and saw tears streaming down her face. Slowly I turned around and Portia took my hands and clasped them with hers, the way we did when we were little girls.

"I'm sorry, Christina. Maybe I have been acting like a spoiled brat, but you are my big sister and I need you in my life."

I scowled. "Dereon is in my life, too."

Portia nodded and sniffled. "I know, and if you love him then I need to learn to love him as well."

I stared into her watery eyes. "Do you really mean that?"

She nodded. "Yes, absolutely. I love you too much to lose you. Besides, that man of yours is easy on the eyes. I don't think it's going to take much for me to fall in love with him," she added with a playful wag of her brow.

I chuckled, then hugged her close. Maybe there was some hope for her after all.

* * *

Much later that evening I opened the door and my heart did serious thumps as I gazed at the handsome man standing on my porch. "Why are you all dressed up? Not that I'm complaining." Dereon was wearing charcoal slacks and a white shirt and tie.

He kissed my lips and strutted inside. "I put in an offer on a strip of commercial property in Dellwood."

I shut the door and swung around, grinning. "Look at my baby moving up in the world!"

He winked. "I'm tryna be like you when I grow up."

Laughing, I reached for his tie and pulled him close, then pressed my lips to his. Dereon's tongue swept into my mouth, twirling with mine. I steeled my grip on his tie, wrapping the slippery material around my fists and holding his mouth captive.

"I missed you," I whispered.

"Tell me again."

"I missed you."

When Dereon kissed me all that mattered was tasting him, devouring those succulent lips, pressing the heat of my body against his while I rubbed my fingers across his smooth bald head. Within seconds my body was on fire. My clit was throbbing from the rough brushing of his slacks against my skin and his groans encouraged me to sway forward. Dereon reached up, cupping my breasts and teasing my nipples through my cotton bra. The sensation shot straight down to my sex. I loosened my hold on his tie but didn't let go. He deepened the kiss and slipped a hand underneath my blouse. I squirmed against him, releasing his mouth and whispering. "I'm in charge this evening."

"My bad," he replied with a wide grin.

I stepped back and did a slow, sexy striptease, gyrating my hips slowly and pretending I was on stage like one of those video chicks. Dereon lowered onto the couch and leaned back with a grin.

Slowly, I removed the buttons on my shirt, one at a time, and allowed it to fall to the floor. Then I reached for the zipper of my slacks and slid the fabric over my hips. I swung around so that Dereon could see my behind in tight white boy shorts.

"Damn, look at all that ass!"

I giggled but tried to stay in character as I kicked my slacks away, standing there in nothing but panties and matching bra. I started rocking my hips again and reached behind me to unclasp my bra, letting it fall. The panties followed. I watched the way Dereon started to squirm on the chair.

"Baby, c'mere," he commanded.

I sashayed toward him and lowered onto his lap, straddling him. "Do you want something?" I cooed.

"Yeah … I do." His hand slipped to my mound, thumb searching for my clit. On contact, I flinched.

"You're not following the rules."

He swore. "I've never been good with rules."

Closing my eyes, I savored the sensation of his thumb stroking my most sensitive area. His index finger glided inside the crotch, across my slick opening, while his thumb continued the light pressure on my clit. Heat filled me, but I wasn't ready yet for what was dangling so close. I had other plans.

Moaning, I rose from his lap, leaned down and removed the knot in his tie and slipped it from around his neck. "Take off your shirt," I commanded.

While he unfastened the buttons, I dropped to my knees and slipped off his shoes and socks, then reached for his belt. When I lowered the zipper I heard Dereon's breathing hitch. His erection was front and center, peeking out of the top of his boxers.

"Stand up," I ordered.

Dereon rose and I pulled his slacks down his legs and tossed them aside. I remained kneeling, mouth watering, staring at his beautiful erection, while he stood long enough to shed his shirt and boxers. Finally, he flopped down in the chair and leaned back, erection jutting from the dark curls between his legs.

"C'mere, Christy."

My nipples tightened at the hunger in his voice. I rose and straddled him again. His penis was resting proudly against his stomach. Reaching up, he cupped my breasts, leaned forward and lifted one into his mouth and sucked the hard nipple. I gasped and clasped my hands behind his head, holding him close as he sucked and teased. My clit pulsed and I ached to have him inside me.

Suddenly remembering who was *supposed* to be in charge, I groaned and slid off his lap. I couldn't think straight around him. "Quit trying to take over! I said I'm running things." I wrapped my fingers around his hard length.

"Shit, baby, then let it do what it do." His fingers dug into the arms of the chair and he leaned back while my fingers glided up and down his erection. I stroked him harder, and when I noticed a few drops of precum on top, I swirled them around with my thumb. A moan escaped his lips and he pumped his hips. Leaning forward, I slipped the head between my lips.

"Shit, Christy." His voice sounded hoarse. I took him deeper down my throat, pausing long enough to suckle at the head. His hands cupped my head, coaxing me to increase the tempo. His hips pumped in rhythm with the up and down motion of my mouth. His abdomen tensed while his breathing grew heavier. "Christy, you have to stop," he groaned.

Feminine power surged within me. "Why?"

"You know why."

Ignoring his plea, I continued to suck and nibble, hearing his breathing growing labored and his thighs stiffening as he struggled for restraint.

"Either you get up here or I'm coming down there," he warned.

Gazing up at his heavy-lidded eyes, I licked my lips. "Do I get to choose?"

Dereon bit back a groan. "Yeah … you got five seconds."

"Hmmm," I replied, pretending to ponder a decision while I continued to lick the precum from the head.

"Yo … Christy … grab a condom from my wallet and get up here … Now!" he ordered.

Smiling triumphantly, I retrieved the foil packet and rolled it over his length while Dereon kissed my lips. As soon as it was on he lifted me up and I grabbed his penis, guiding it to where I desired it most. And when I finally slid down over his entire length, I exhaled. Dereon's hands flew up to mold my breasts, thumbs tweaking my nipples. My breath caught and desire swept over me. Biting my lips and closing my eyes, I rode him with a slow, steady tempo.

"You like that?" he asked.

I nodded, clit throbbing like crazy. "Yes, Dereon, I like that," I murmured.

He brought his hands to cup my ass, then raised his hips as I continued to ride him. His hips pumped, driving harder and deeper. "That's it, babe. Ride that dick," he whispered.

"Oooh, yesss," I moaned. The connection was fierce, strong, and downright amazing. I continued to bounce up and down on his lap, using the chair arms for leverage. Dereon slipped one hand between us to rub my swollen clit. He rubbed, and as my clit pulsed the walls contracted around his penis. "Dereon!" I cried and continued moving up and down.

"I'm right here, baby," he growled between his teeth. I could tell he was trying to hold on for me. He didn't have to wait long. A full body orgasm claimed me.

He pumped up hard, growling. His hips stiffened, and as we kissed, he came.

While he showered I slipped on my robe and lay in bed watching television and smiling to myself. I loved that man. I truly loved him. Dereon made my toes curl and my heart sing, and for the first time in my life I could truly say I knew what love felt like. No one, not Jeanna, not Portia, or anyone else was going to mess up my happiness.

Dereon's cell phone vibrated. I watched it bounce around the top of my night stand. When it stopped I leaned back and replayed the events of the last week. I didn't think I'd ever forget the look on Jeanna's face when Dereon announced he flipped houses. But I was proud of myself for finally standing up to my mother and making a decision that it was time to live my own life the way I wanted to live it.

I rolled onto my back, closed my eyes and released a deep sigh. Despite everything, Jeanna was still my mother, and in her own way she did mean well. I hadn't heard from her since the fallout and I actually missed her. If Portia could come around, then hopefully Jeanna would, too.

Dereon's phone vibrated again and this time it fell onto the floor. My eyes snapped opened and I rolled onto my side. Someone was seriously trying to reach him. I slid over to the edge of the bed and reached down for the phone. Rising, I headed toward the adjoining bathroom so I could hand it to him. On the way, however, I started wondering who it could be. I knew it was none of my business, yet I couldn't help it. Curiosity got the better of me.

I listened to make sure the water was still running, and when I knew he was still under the shower I tapped the screen.

I need to see you tonight.

I felt a pang of jealousy. Who in the world needed to see Dereon at nine o'clock at night, and why? I could think of a couple of reasons, but none of them were anything I wanted to dwell on for any amount of time. I grew angrier by the second and had to take a moment and ask myself, did I have a right to be mad?

Dereon and I hadn't said anything about a commitment or seeing other people, yet I had assumed … Okay, so maybe that was the problem. I had assumed since we were in a relationship and were in love that meant he and I against the world. I couldn't help but wonder if maybe I was making more of our relationship than it really was.

The water stopped. I returned the phone to the nightstand and lay back across the bed pretending I was watching *My Wife and Kids* when he padded out of the bathroom.

"Hey baby, you wanna order a pizza or something?"

I glanced over at Dereon and started licking my lips. He was wrapped in a burgundy bath towel with water all over his beautiful pecs and biceps. I watched water sliding across his neck, down over his tight abs and disappearing down inside the towel. I swallowed hard. There was no way in hell I was sharing that with anyone.

I forced a smile. "Sure, a pizza sounds wonderful. What kind you want? I'll order." I rolled over and reached in the bottom of the nightstand and removed the phonebook.

"A meat lover's sounds good." He leaned over and kissed my lips, then pulled back, grinning down at me. I felt my stomach quiver when he removed the towel and started drying off. I just sat there, staring at his magnificent body. I was ready to beg him to come back to bed when his cell phone vibrated again. I watched him walk around to his phone, glance down at the screen and freeze, his expression hardening. I pretended not to notice while I grabbed my house phone and ordered a large pizza and chipotle wings. By the time I had gotten off the phone, Dereon was stepping into his jeans.

"They should be here in about thirty minutes."

Dereon gave a heavy sigh and looked over at me. "Baby, something came up I gotta take care of."

"Something or someone?"As soon as the words were out of my mouth I wished I could take them back. There was no way I wanted him to think I was jealous.

"It ain't nothing like that."

"Then what is it?" I asked impatiently.

He hesitated. "It's business."

What kind of business could he have at nine o'clock? I wanted so badly to tell him I'd seen the text and knew he was meeting someone, but then he would know I had been snooping. Instead, I sat there, arms crossed, pretending to watch television but really pouting. Once

Dereon got dressed, he walked around to my side of the bed and took a seat beside me, placing a gentle hand on my knee.

"Baby, I'll call you tomorrow."

I rolled my eyes. "Whatever."

Grinning, he wrapped an arm across my shoulders. "Baby, why you gotta be like that? If I didn't have to leave I wouldn't, but there's something important I gotta do."

I pushed him away. "And what's that?"

He rose and rubbed a hand across his head. "I need to meet with my realtor. That piece of property I put a bid on, well, the owner accepted my offer. I need to sign some documents and meet with potential investors."

I glared up at him. "Congratulations. But why do I get the feeling there's more to it than that?"

"There ain't. Like I said, it's commercial property that I'll take you to see next week. But I've just gotta take care of things first." Reaching inside his pocket, Dereon removed several bills and set them on the nightstand. "Here. This is for the food. Now walk your man to the door."

I rose in a huff. "*Are* you my man?"

He gave me an amused smile. "Hell yeah, I'm your man. And don't you forget it." Dereon pressed his lips to mine, and within seconds I was moaning and my body was tingling. "Trust me, baby. I'm just trying to handle my business."

I took his hand and led him down to the door. Once there he planted a kiss on my lips, then left. I walked over to the couch and took a seat. Long after Dereon was gone the scent of his skin continued tormenting me. For the first time I realized how my mother must have felt when my father used to leave her to return home to his fiancée. There was one thing Jeanna had told me that rang true.

Love had no guarantees.

TWENTY-SIX

Claudia danced into my office, holding her coffee in one hand and swinging a piece of paper in the other. "The menu for the dinner cruise has *finally* been approved! I just got the signed confirmation off the fax."

I sat up on the chair, glad for something good to be happening. "About damn time. The event is next weekend." I shook my head. "That is the pickiest group of folks. How many times have they changed the menu? Twice? So the blown sugar display of the American flag is a go?"

Her champagne-colored eyes danced with excitement. "Yes, ma'am! I can't wait to get started." She flopped down in the seat across from me. "They didn't cross off one item from the last menu we sent them. Here, see for yourself." She swung her hips over to my desk and handed over the fax. "We're going to spend the evening onboard a fabulous yacht, bumping elbows with some of the most distinguished people in the state. I think that says a lot for *Cater to You*." She beamed with pride, and despite how miserable as I was feeling, I couldn't resist a grin of my own.

I was pleased that no changes had been made to the final menu. I laid the fax on my desk as Claudia took one of the chairs across from my desk. "It's going to be an amazing night. We need to make sure we have plenty of business cards in our pockets."

"Absolutely, because once they taste your ambrosia chocolate torte, they'll be banging down our door," she complimented between sips.

My cheeks reddened at the praise, which Claudia gave so generously. "Thanks, I just want the night to be a success." You would think now that Dereon had pretty much abandoned me I would be grateful for the time to focus on Saturday's big event instead of sitting around feeling sorry for myself.

Since the text message two nights ago, I hadn't seen Dereon. Instead, he'd called with one reason after another why he wasn't available. He was meeting with investors. He was busy working on his property that he needed to have back on the market by the end of the month. Apparently, the electrician he had hired had wired the house wrong and he needed to be around to supervise the rest of the project, but in my heart I knew it had something to do with that text message, not the house or the commercial property. I just didn't want to accuse him of something unless I had proof.

"What's going on with you?" Claudia studied me, trying to figure out what was going on in my head. "I know … you say it's nothing, but I'm not buying that. This is the second day in a row you've ruined a catering order. That is not like you, Christy."

I should have known I wouldn't be able to get anything past her. I guess a burnt carrot cake hadn't helped. "I'm starting to wonder if my relationship with Dereon is going anywhere."

Claudia crossed her legs. "I didn't know you wanted it to go anywhere."

I released a heavy breath, then leaned back against my chair. "Things have changed."

"What things?" she asked.

I met her intense gaze and confessed, "I'm in love with him."

She started squealing and bouncing in the chair and almost spilled coffee all over her bronze suit. Good thing Mia had a dentist appointment first thing this morning, otherwise she would have scared the girl to death. "That's wonderful!" she exclaimed and placed the cup down on the edge of my desk, then shuffled around and hugged me close until my nose was smashed against her massive breasts. "It's about damn time."

I struggled free. "Goodness, Claudia. What're you trying to do, suffocate me?"

She released me and fluffed her curls as she came back around and returned to her seat. "Sorry. I got a little carried away, but I'm *so* excited for you."

I shrugged half-heartedly. "Thanks."

Claudia gave me a strange look. "Now I'm confused. If you're in love, why the long face?"

"My mother hates him and Portia thinks it's a shame I'm settling for less. I've gone to battle with both of them, but it would help if I knew where our relationship was going." I leaned against the desk and told her about dinner at Jeanna's and the heated visit at Portia's.

"Have you told Dereon you loved him?"

"Yes, and he loves me, too, but there's something missing in our relationship. I'm just not sure yet what it is." I didn't have the heart to tell her about the text message.

"Maybe you're making more of it than it really is. Just enjoy the ride and everything will fall into place eventually."

I wanted so badly to believe that, but until I had some answers I was going to be leery.

"I just can't believe you're finally admitting you love this man."

"I finally had to stop lying to myself. He opened my eyes to a world I'd chosen to ignore. At first I thought I was just fascinated, but the more time I spent with him the more time I had to take a look at myself and the way my mother and Portia acted, and I realized I didn't want to be like them, I'm ashamed to admit that I was."

Shaking her head, Claudia reached for her coffee again. "My little girl is growing up."

"I guess I am." We shared a laugh, then I heard the bell over the main door ring. Before either of us could rise from our chairs, Mia appeared and stood in the doorframe with a long face.

"Good morning. Any cavities?" I asked.

"Just one. Listen, I've got something to tell you." She walked over and took the other seat across from my desk, looking suspiciously nervous.

"What's wrong?" I asked, urging her along.

Mia swallowed hard and folded her hands in her lap. "Well … see … last night my sister Kimberly and I went to this karaoke bar off Lucas and Hunt. Anyway, we were sitting there drinking Cosmopolitans and checking out the eye candy when this man jumped onto the stage and started singing James Brown's, 'I Feel Good.' *Girrrrrl*, he had a table cloth across his shoulder like a cape and everyone was dancing in their seats! Anyway, my sister thought he was sexy, so we moved up to get a closer look and … it was Dereon."

"What?" Claudia gasped, eyes large.

I tried to keep all emotion from my face and act like it was no big deal, but it was. How come he hadn't invited me to karaoke? "Really?" I replied and congratulated myself on sounding vaguely interested. "I would love to have seen that." I then gave a lackluster laugh.

"Yeah, I bet you that was a sight to see," Claudia chimed in.

Only Mia wasn't laughing. "Uh … you know I'm not one to gossip … "

Really? Since when?

"… But when Dereon left the stage I figured I'd introduce him to my sister, since you said there wasn't anything going on between the two of you. Anyway, I got up to follow when I saw him sit down at the table with this beautiful woman."

Claudia leaned forward on the chair, clearly intrigued. "What's she look like?"

"Long black hair, flawless skin, beautiful … Hispanic." She rattled off from memory.

I just sat there speechless, because I didn't know what to say. The person she had just described sounded like Milagros, the woman at the movie theater. How stupid could I be? I knew something was going on between the two of them. I had felt it in my gut when we had run into her at the theater, and again when Dereon had rushed off after receiving those repeated text messages.

"Maybe she's a friend or something," Claudia suggested, trying to soften the blow.

Mia bunched up her face. "Uh-uh, not the way she was all over him, rubbing his hand and smiling all up in his face." Quickly, she grabbed her phone from the side of her purse, pressed a few buttons, paused, then held it out to me. "Here … see for yourself."

I was shaking so hard I couldn't get my hand to move, so Claudia took it. As soon as she gazed down at the photos Mia had taken on her cell phone she started mumbling under her breath. "Yep, it's definitely him," she finally said, then leaned across the desk, holding the phone in my face so I could see. I glanced at it briefly, and the second I saw the two hugged up together I shook my head. I wasn't sure how much I could take.

"Well, good for him. And her. Anyway we've got better things to do than talk about Dereon. We've been hired to cater his parents' anniversary dinner, *not* keep track of his personal life." I didn't mean to snap, but I was pissed off. I should have followed my gut. And to think I had just confessed to Claudia how much I loved that dude. I was beyond embarrassed.

I reached for a pen and started scribbling on a yellow notepad when I noticed neither of them had moved. "What?"

"That's not all," Mia began, and that worried look was in her eyes again.

"What are you talking about?" Thank goodness it was Claudia who asked, because I didn't have the heart.

Mia waited until her phone was tucked back in her purse before continuing. "Well … you know my sister is one of those ride or die chicks with one ear always down on the ground."

Yes, I knew. That's why I'd had to ban her from dropping by the office with her weekly drama.

"Well, Kim recognized the woman he was with. Said she's Milagros Hernandez, the real estate agent."

As soon as she said her name aloud it made the betrayal all too real. Just as I suspected, he had been out with Milagros, the woman he'd said was no big deal. The one he'd said was from his past. And I had been stupid enough to have given him the benefit of the doubt. She was also the real estate agent he'd been working with. How come he couldn't tell me that?

Claudia's brow bunched. "Hernandez? Why does that name sound so familiar?" Then she snapped her fingers. "Ooh! She has that big billboard off of 170."

Mia nodded her head, then started talking and gesturing with her hands. "Rumor has it that she's into some kinda house flipping scam. Getting people to buy houses at one price and reselling them for more than they're worth."

I waved my hand in the air. "Hold up! That's illegal."

"Right. Only no one's been able to prove it. All I know is she's the baddest agent in the real estate game. She has the largest listings and properties all around town worth millions. Anyway, like I said, that's the word on the street … nobody knows for sure, but my sister says it's true. so you know I believe anything she says."

Goodness. Dereon was flipping houses. Was he part of her scam? I couldn't even bear to think about him doing something that illegal.

Unable to resist a second longer, I reached under my desk for the yellow pages and turned to the real estate section. Sure enough, Milagros had a two-page advertisement displaying a smiling face and plenty of cleavage.

"Yep, that's her," Mia said, pointing at the picture.

Claudia came around for a closer look, then nodded. "Yep, I've seen her ads."

"This is too much drama for me for one day," I said, and made of show of waving my hands in the air.

Mia slowly rose from the chair. "I just figured you had a right to know, considering we're doing business with him. The last thing you want is to be connected to anything illegal."

Oh, God. I could just see my mother catching wind of that. If Dereon was in any way connected, I would never live it down. But in my heart I knew there was no way Dereon would do anything like that, right? He took too much pride in his work, not to mention he was a good and honest man.

Thank goodness the phone rang and Mia rushed off to retrieve it. As soon as she was gone, Claudia lowered her butt on the edge of my desk and gazed at me for several seconds. "Are you okay?"

I scowled. "Why wouldn't I be? Like you said, it's alleged real estate fraud."

She shook her head. "No, I mean about him being with that woman."

I sat there a moment pondering her question before I finally spat, "Hell, no." With that I sprung from my seat. "Let's go."

"Where are we going?" she asked, flabbergasted.

I reached down for my purse and headed toward the door. "If Dereon won't tell me what's going on, then I'm going to find out myself." I couldn't believe what I was saying, but it felt right. He'd been keeping something from me and I wanted answers. Dammit, I was *supposed* to be his woman, therefore I deserved to know the truth.

I stormed through the receptionist area.

"Christina, you have a call from—"

"Take a message. I'll be out for the rest of the afternoon," I said, not breaking stride as I clicked my heels toward the door.

"And so will I," Claudia relayed as she hurried out of my office. "Wait! Let me grab my purse and I'll meet you in the parking lot."

* * *

"Are you sure you want to do this?" Claudia asked for the umpteenth time.

"Yes, now turn right at the corner." I slumped down on the seat with my Versace sunglasses covering my eyes, the same way I had done when Dereon had shown up at my townhouse in his Monte Carlo. It was amazing how much things had changed over time. During our last date I had even gotten behind the wheels and driven the vehicle.

There were so many emotions going through my head I didn't know what to think, except that Dereon had lied me.

"I don't see anything," Claudia muttered.

"Then turn left at the end of the street. If Dereon said he was rehabbing a house in Kirkwood that backed to the country club, then dammit, that house should be here somewhere!" I didn't mean to yell, but if I didn't find him soon I was going to freak out.

Claudia glanced over with concern. "Sweetie, you're starting to scare me."

I was starting to scare myself. If I didn't find that house, then everything he had ever told me would have been a lie, including his love for me. And that's what frightened me.

"Look!" I cried, pointing frantically. "Look over there at that house … with those men working out front!"

"Calm down, I see it."

While Claudia slowed the car to a crawl I peered out the window and scanned the area. Dereon's SUV was out front, as well as several other vehicles, including a white truck with RDH Construction airbrushed on the side. There was a man on the roof and another on the ladder.

"Park across the street."

Sighing heavily, Claudia wheeled her Acura TL over to the curb. I swung around on the seat and stared out the window at the lovely brick two-story Colonial with a double-car garage. Smaller than Portia's house, but definitely twice the size of my condo. It reminded me of a miniature doll house.

"Do you see him?"

I'd almost forgotten Claudia was in the car with me. "No, not yet."

I stopped admiring the house and scanned the yard looking for someone who resembled Dereon. Two other men came out from inside the house. I was ready to give up when I spotted him.

Dereon was the one on the ladder, sliding a window in place. I don't know how long I sat there staring at that nice tight ass in khaki shorts with my tongue hanging out of my mouth. The brown t-shirt he was wearing was drenched and his back was covered in sweat. He looked sexy as all get-out. Goodness. My sex clenched at the sight of him.

Claudia swung around and peered out the window with me. "Is that Dereon on the ladder?" she whispered.

"Yes," I had to take a deep breath. "That's him."

"*Lord have mercy*!" she cried. "Look at all five of them dripping in sweat. I could sit and watch them all day."

I had to agree, although my eyes were fixed on one man in particular.

Claudia lowered the window, leaned her head out and whistled. Before I could stop her she did it again. All five heads turned our way.

"Why did you do that?" I mumbled.

"You came down here to talk, didn't you?" she retorted with her eyes fixed on the view in front of us.

"Well … yeah."

"Then let's go talk." Claudia slid back over onto the driver's side long enough to grab her keys, and climb out.

Oh, my goodness! Was my best friend crazy? I climbed out of her car and hurried to catch up with her long-legged strides. "They're staring at us."

"Good," she said smiling and swaying her hips seductively as she crossed the street and stepped onto the sidewalk. I watched Dereon as he slowly came down the ladder. My heart was pounding like crazy. He was going to think I was some kind of stalker.

As the two of us drew closer we were met by a chorus of male voices and whistling. I guess it's not often that two beautiful professional women come strolling down the sidewalk in the middle of the day.

"Damn," murmured a chocolate dream.

"Hello, beautiful," cooed a cutie in overalls.

"Hello, yourself," Claudia purred, and at the end of the yard she stopped and struck a pose. Oh, boy. I rolled my eyes toward the heavens, praying for the strength to get through this embarrassing situation.

I stepped across the yard, hoping I wouldn't get grass stains on my white slacks. Unfortunately, the walkway to the porch was covered with materials. I finally found the guts to look over in

Dereon's direction, but instead of the frown I had expected he wore a big irresistible grin.

"Well, well, well, so you decided to come and check on your man."

"I-I'm not checking on you. I just thought … " Hell, I didn't know what I thought.

"C'mon, you missed Big Daddy and needed to see him. I'm so glad you did." He lifted me up off my toes and seared me with a nipple-puckering kiss that I felt all the way to my French-tipped toenails.

I know I was supposed to be mad at him, but my body had a mind of its own. Somehow my arms ended up wrapped around his neck and my tongue was dancing slowly against his. Okay, so sue me, but there was something about this man I couldn't resist. Like I said before, he's at the top of my list of addictions.

"Thanks, I needed that," he said as he lowered me back onto my feet.

"Glad I could be of service," I began, then cleared my throat, trying to regain focus. "Actually, we were in the area and I thought I'd check out this house you've been talking about."

A smile tipped one corner of his mouth. "I'm glad you did. I should have brought you out here myself, but I've been so busy."

Yes, you have been.

Dereon swung around. "But first let me introduce you to my crew."

"Yes, Lawd," I heard Claudia say under her breath.

"This over here is my homeboy, Reggie Hodges, and the owner of RDH Construction."

I glanced over at the tall, dark-skinned brotha with straight back cornrows and a sexy goatee. He had large sepia eyes and the deepest dimples when he smiled. "Whassup, ladies?" he said in a low masculine voice. When he held out a hand I noticed the gold band on his left hand. It appeared at least one member of the group had been taken off the market.

I shook his hand. "Nice meeting you."

Claudia nodded. "Same here."

Reggie pointed to the others. "This here is my crew, Trey, Braxton, and standing over near the circular saw is Maximilian."

I waved and exchanged greetings with the men. Each of the black men was handsome in his own right. They were physically fit and ranged from gorgeous to smoking hot. It was no wonder Claudia started batting eyes and moved in close. It was obvious she liked what she saw. I couldn't blame her. It wasn't often you found five sexy men in one spot.

Dereon moved up beside me and placed a hand to my arm. "C'mon in and let me show you around. Just watch your step. I hate to have to take your pretty little behind to the emergency room for getting a nail through the bottom of your foot."

Before I could object he'd scooped me into his arms and led me up the stairs. I glanced back at Claudia, who seemed to be doing just fine surrounded by four men who were clearly intrigued with her. In other words, she was in good hands.

Dereon stepped into the foyer, and after another searing kiss he lowered me slowly to my feet. Goodness, he was making this difficult.

Holding hands, he gave me the grand tour. There was a sweeping staircase, gleaming new mahogany flooring, and a fireplace surrounded by built-in bookcases. But what made me stop was the beautifully updated granite kitchen. It had forty-two inch cabinets, a large island, chocolate granite, and plenty of room to cook.

"Wow!" was the only word I could come up with as I swept an awed glance around the large room.

"I was hoping you'd like it," he said standing to the side with his hands behind his back.

"Like it? I love it." It wasn't as big as Portia's, but it didn't matter. As far as I was concerned, it was perfect. "Did you do all this yourself?"

He smiled softly. "Yep, with Reggie's help. He's the building contractor, not me. I couldn't flip houses if it weren't for my boy and his crew."

I peered out the large picture window in the living room. I guess the best man had won because, Reggie, Trey and Braxton had gone back to work while Maximilian was standing behind Claudia, showing her how to use a circular saw. He was whispering so close to her ear that all she had to do was turn her head slightly to the left and they'd be lip locking. My curiosity piqued. "Is Maximilian single?"

"Yeah. Reggie's the only one who's married. Why?"

I swung around, grinning. "Just asking."

Humor tugged at Dereon's mouth as he signaled for me to follow him upstairs. Together we strolled through the top floor of the house, laughing and talking, and it wasn't until we returned to the kitchen that I remembered I was supposed to be angry. Like I said before, Dereon had a way of making a girl lose her train of thought.

"I was hoping you would have dropped by last night."

Dereon cleared his throat and diverted his gaze out the window. "Yeah, we got kinda busy painting the rooms upstairs. Once we got started it ran late."

My heart sank at the lie. Not to mention Dereon had done it without batting a lush eyelash. "Really? That's your story and you're sticking to it?"

He looked confused. "Yeah, why wouldn't I?"

I was so mad I was certain there was smoke blowing out of my ears. I pointed a finger in the air. "Hold that thought." I then turned away, reached inside my purse and hit the speed dial. As soon as that chirpy voice came onto the line, I barked. "Mia, you know that picture you showed me earlier? Well, text it to me, ASAP!"

CLAUDIA

When my college sweetheart decided he'd rather be a missionary than spend the rest of his life married to me, I should have known then I was doomed for a life of relationship disappointments. Yet instead of recognizing the warning signs, I subjected myself to more years of dating fiascos. It wasn't until after wasting the last six months of my life with a man I was convinced was the one, I was finally ready to accept that what I'd read in those romance novels was simply make-believe. Love at first sight and that instant attraction crap only happened in the movies.

That was before I saw the gorgeous man standing in front of me. In fact, he was so sexy I had to wipe my chin just to make sure I wasn't drooling.

He had removed a black wifebeater. I wasn't sure if he'd done it for my personal viewing pleasure or because he was hot and sweaty, but whatever the reason, jolts of awareness ricochet through my entire body.

Slowly, my eyes wandered over his wide football shoulders and sculpted chest that tapered down to a flat ripped stomach and narrow hips. Maximilian James, or Max, as his friends called him, was shoveling tan pea pebbles and pouring them into a trench that would eventually be the sidewalk in front of the house. Muscles that were here … there … and everywhere flexed with every move. Goodness, a girl could get dizzy looking at him.

I decided I must have been standing out in the sun too long, and with a trembling breath I tried to shake off the effects. So what if he had muscles? Men did, after all. I didn't need this distraction. After my devastating break-up with Josh, I was through with men. Or at least that's what I was trying to tell myself.

"You wanna help?" Max asked, and leaned against the shovel. I tried to look away from him and found instead that my gaze had somehow slipped to watch a bead of sweat drip from his luscious neck down across a massive brown pectoral. Shocked by my own behavior I tried to drag my gaze away, when what I really wanted to do was run my tongue across his chest just to see if he tasted like sugar.

"No," I finally replied. "Showing me how to use a circular saw is one thing, but I think I'll pass on the shoveling."

He grinned, then winked, and I was aware that he was clearly flirting. "Then how about passing me a bottle of water?" he asked, pointing to the red cooler under the tree behind me.

"Uhhh … sure thing." I spun on the heels of my Manolos, knees wobbling slightly, glad for a chance to conceal the effect he had on me as I swayed my hips over to the tree.

"Damn! I hate to see you go, but I definitely enjoy watching you leave." That line was so tired, but from Max's lips it sounded as fresh as a pan of cinnamon rolls straight out of the oven.

I leaned over, fully aware Max was staring at my ass. My skin prickled with excitement and confusion as I tried to figure out what was happening. I couldn't believe how out of control my heart was pounding. I tried to rationalize that it had to be some kind of reaction to my break-up with Josh, because I'd never behaved like this, and was stunned that I had. Fingers trembling, I grabbed a bottle of ice-cold water, then took a deep breath, fighting for self-control, before carrying it over to him. "Here you go."

"Thanks." Maximilian took the bottle, but instead of screwing off the cap he pressed it against his cheek and dragged it slowly along his face, neck, and chest. "Man, it's hot," he moaned.

I swallowed hard, trying to maintain a control that was clearly slipping away faster than sand in an hourglass. Seriously. I couldn't even think straight. With Maximilian, I felt like a teenager with a girlish crush, and believe me when I tell you I couldn't remember the last time my body felt this alive.

Shifting nervously from one foot to the other, I watched sweat from the bottle drip onto his chiseled chest, trickling down a flat abdomen that was the true definition of a six-pack, before disappearing inside a pair of dark jeans that hung low on his trimmed waist.

Maximilian James was the epitome of drop-dead gorgeous. At six-three he had smooth nutty brown skin and eyes that were dark as midnight. And then there was his short-cropped curly hair and a perfectly trimmed goatee that surrounded a pair of the softest … juiciest lips I had ever seen. As I watched him finally twist off the cap and bring the bottle to his mouth and drink, my stomach quivered at the thought of those lips sucking my—

"Claudia."

The sound of his masculine voice knocked me out of my trance. Blinking hard, I tried pushing away the erotic feelings that seemed to be flowing straight down to the region of my body that yearned to feel those lips most. "I'm sorry. Did you say something?"

He smiled, showing off beautiful pearly white teeth. A diamond earring was in his left earlobe and a dimple on the right. Damn! His profile was sexy from either side. "I asked, what kinda work you do?"

In an attempt to regain the control I'd lost, I tilted my chin and replied, "I'm a confectionist."

He looked clearly intrigued. "You're talking about candy, right?"

"Uh-hmmm." *Just like you.* Mr. Eye Candy.

"Now that's whassup," Reggie chimed in as he walked over to the toolbox and removed what looked like a crowbar. "My wife loves truffles."

"I make delicious truffles," I said, pleased for the distraction.

Max groaned. "Yo, don't tell him that! He'll be calling you tomorrow to make him a batch. Anything for *Berlin*," he teased. And the other two men joined in on the laughter.

Reggie looked amused. "I see you got jokes. Just remember y'all fools are going home alone while I'll be arriving to a home cooked meal and a beautiful woman."

Trey shook his head and explained. "They're getting ready to have their first baby, so this brotha is sprung."

"Congratulations." A handsome and devoted husband, why couldn't I be so lucky?

"Thanks," Reggie replied as he playfully shoved Trey aside. "All jokes aside, I would love for you to make my wife some truffles."

I nodded. "No problem. Just get the number from Dereon and give me a call."

"No doubt." Reggie nodded. "C'mon Trey, help me get this last window in."

The two walked back toward the side of the house. I swirled around to find Max staring at me with hunger in his eyes. And my stomach did a series of back flips.

"You make truffles and still manage to look this good? Damn!" His lazy gaze took a leisurely tour of my body. I could feel the heat scorching my skin along its quest.

"Thanks," I replied in a shaky voice. It was hard to concentrate with him standing so close. His masculinity was so potent it nearly reached out and grabbed me.

"My bad," Max chuckled. "I don't mean to stare. It just isn't often that a gorgeous woman shows up on the job. Has anyone ever told you you look like Kimora Lee Simmons?"

Under the receiving end of his dark gaze, my thoughts got all jumbled in my head. I took a deep breath to steady myself. "Yes, I've heard it most of my life. My father met my mother while working in Japan, and three years later I was born," I explained.

"And what a lucky day that was," Max replied, licking lips I could imagine mine parting beneath, granting him entrance into my mouth. "You are *definitely* sweet." He stood there shaking his head and I smiled, and when he wagged his left brow while wearing an animated smirk the two of us started laughing, easing some of the sexual tension. "Sorry, but speaking of sweet, what other kinds of candy do you make?"

He seemed genuinely interested in my work. "Blown sugar displays are my specialty."

His thick brow rose. "Is that like ice sculptures except with sugar?"

"Exactly." Just talking with him like this made my nipples tingle.

"I'd love to see that." I saw a glint of something dangerous in his eyes before they traveled down along my sleeveless suit, pausing to admire my 36C's. A tightening sensation wound through my midsection and I nearly moaned out loud. It was obvious he liked what he saw, and as much as I wanted to pretend it didn't matter, inside my heart slammed merrily against my ribcage. To my relief, he finally looked away. I exhaled and realized I had been holding my breath.

Max finished the bottle in one final swig and shot it like a basketball over to a trash receptacle at the end of the lawn. He missed.

"You have no game," I laughed, then trotted over and retrieved the water bottle and carried it back to where he was standing. "Now watch this." I held it over my left shoulder, aimed, then shot it straight into the container.

"Day-umm!" Max chuckled. "A woman after my own heart."The low seductive timbre of his voice sent electric pulses through my bloodstream.

Max suddenly moved in close enough for my brain cells to go on strike. How could one man radiate so much raw masculine energy? So much sex appeal?

"You like seafood?" he asked, dark eyes sparkling.

Pulse thumping, I nodded. "Yes. Why?"

"I want you to have dinner with me." It wasn't a question. Thank goodness, because I was trembling too hard to answer.

He smiled, pleased that I hadn't objected. "How's seven o'clock sound?" he asked. His warm breath brushed my nose and made my stomach drop to my feet.

I realized I was leaning toward him, lips parted as if in invitation, my eyes drifting closed …

Before I could respond, one of the other guys—I think it was Trey—called from the ladder. "Yo, Max … here comes drama!"

Drama? My lids snapped open and I jerked away as if I'd been burned.

Max's head whipped to the right and mine followed just as a black Sonata came rolling down the street and pulled to a halt in front of the house.

"Oh, shit!" I heard Reggie chuckle as a woman stepped out from behind the wheel and glared over the hood of her car in my direction with eyes narrowed dangerously.

"Oh, okay, I see what's going on! You can't answer your damn phone because you got this hoochie over here all up in your face!"

Hoochie? "Who the hell she calling a hoochie?" I mumbled and was a second away from taking off my dangling earring and kicking off my Manolos.

"I bet you didn't tell her you had a baby on the way, did you Max?" she demanded to know.

Baby?

She walked around the vehicle with a hand at her hip and her stomach sticking out so far I was afraid she was going to fall over. She was like Humpty Dumpty.

"Excuse me," Max mumbled apologetically, then dropped the shovel and rushed across the lawn to talk to her while I stood there dumfounded. This had to be some kind of joke. Since I hadn't spotted a blinking camera light anywhere, I drew in a deep breath and pulled my jaw up off the ground. There was no way this was happening. *Baby mama drama.* I should have known Max was too good to be true, but that was the story of my life. And for an idiotic moment there I had found myself caught up under his spell.

Tires screeched and I blinked in time to see the Sonata peel away from the curb and zip down the street. As soon as the car hit the corner and made a right, Max jogged back over to where I was standing, wearing an apologetic grin.

"Sorry about that. I'll explain over dinner." He chuckled.

What? … for real? I shook my head. "Sorry Max, but I don't do baby mama drama."

He quirked a dark eyebrow at me. "What? Trust me, there's no drama."

My mouth hardened in a grim line as I returned, "Are you saying that's not *your* baby she's carrying?"

He hesitated. "No, I'm a suspect … and trust me, there's others."

I was standing directly in front of him, arms crossed. "Then why'd she say it's yours?"

Max dragged a frustrated hand across the back of his neck. "Because I was drinking that night. But I'm ninety-eight percent it's not mine."

"Well, it's the two percent that's ending this before it gets started." I retrieved my keys from my pocket. "Let Christina know I'll be waiting in the car."

No matter how sexy he was there was no way I could allow myself to get involved. I walked away feeling slightly disappointed that Maximilian James and I would never have a chance to see where this deep aching in my chest could have gone.

I guess like with every other man in my life, it just wasn't meant to be.

TWENTY-SEVEN

It took thirty seconds before my cell chirped, indicating I had a text message. The second I downloaded the photograph, I swung around and faced Dereon, who was leaning against the wall in the living room, waiting patiently for me to continue.

"Are you ready yet to talk?" He gave a nervous chuckle. Guess what? He had every reason to be nervous.

I moved closer to him as I spoke. "That depends on if you're ready to start telling me the truth or not."

"What are—"

I pressed a finger against his lips. "Think very carefully before you answer the question I'm about to ask you."

He had the audacity to look amused. "Okay … What's the question?"

"I'm going to ask you again … What did you say again that you did last night?" I held up the photo of him and Milagros so there was no question of where I was going with this conversation. "Because for some reason this picture looks like you were out singing karaoke with Milagros!" I couldn't believe the way I lashed out, sounding like a jealous wife, but hey, he started it by lying.

"I …" His voice trailed off. *Straight busted!*

I stood there, hands planted at my waist, tapping my designer shoe against the floor."What's wrong? Cat got your tongue?"

Dereon stepped away and swept a hand across his bald head. "Look … it's not what you think," he assured me.

"And how do you know what I'm thinking?" I retorted. I don't know why everyone thinks they know me. Hell, I don't even know myself half the time.

"Yo … She and I are not dating, if that's what you're thinking."

"Then what is it? Because that's what it looks like to me." He forgets I'm a woman, so I know what it means to smile up at a man with that hungry look in my eyes. That chick wanted something that I *thought* was exclusively all mine. I didn't mean to act possessive, but dammit, I never believed in sharing. If that were the case, I would have stayed with Logan and tried to get everything I could have gotten out of him.

I folded my arms and stared back defiantly. "The problem with this situation, Dereon, is that I *have* been patient with you. I asked you what you did for a living, you didn't want to tell me. I had to ask for you to invite me to your place. We're at the movies and I asked who that woman was . You said no one important. Then I find out that not only is she important enough to get all *snuggly* with at the club, she's also your real estate agent! What I can't seem to figure out is what the hell are you hiding?"

He stared at me for so long I was ready to scream. "Dammit, say something!"

When he took my hands into his and stared down at me I couldn't even look at him I was so mad.

"Christy, trust me when I tell you there's nothing going on. It's business, baby, nothing else. In a few days our business dealings will be over, and I'll explain everything."

"Excuse me, but that's not good enough. I have too much on the line for you to suddenly decide you no longer want this. I defended you to my mother and sister, so dammit, I deserve an explanation!"

He released my hands and started pacing around the room. "Oh, okay. So that's what this is really all about … You saving face? No way is Christina gonna be left looking like a damn fool by a man who clearly ain't even in her league."

I threw my hands in the air. "That's not what I meant."

Dereon frowned. "I think it is. C'mon, let's be honest. You've been looking for an excuse since the beginning."

"I have not!" I retorted.

"Yeah, sweetheart, I'm afraid you have. You don't like burgers. You refused to go out with me. You're ashamed to introduce me to your mother because she would never understand. Then you asked me to go with you to meet your father, and if you hadn't blurted it out at your mother's I'd have never known you'd already gone to see him."

I stared into his eyes and saw the hurt. Is that how he felt? I guess I had never thought about how he would have interpreted the situation. I just figured Dereon had agreed to go with me to see my father because I had asked him to, not because meeting Carlos was really important to him.

But as I thought about it I could see how he would have come to that conclusion. As excited as he had been when I told him my father was the owner of Boone Beer, I guess he had probably been looking forward to meeting him as much as I was looking forward to meeting his parents.

"Sorry, I guess I wasn't thinking. I just thought that after all these years it was best that I talk to him alone."

He nodded. "I can understand that, but you *never* even mentioned to me that you saw your father. I can't help but think that maybe you're ashamed of me."

Silence lapsed between us, stretching out uncomfortably. I took a deep breath and walked over to the large window and stared out at the charming street in front of me.

"Baby, talk to me." I heard him say.

There was another brief pause before I swung around and stared up at him. "Rumor has it Milagros is into some illegal real estate practices. You wouldn't know anything about that, would you?"

Before he could speak I could see it in his eyes.

He knew.

Nervously, I chewed on my bottom lip. "Please tell me you're not doing anything illegal."

Dereon came towards me slowly, his gaze latched onto mine. "No, I'm not." But there was more, so much more, that he wasn't saying. I could see in his eyes he was hiding something. "Sweetheart, just trust me on this. There's nothing going on between us. As soon as I close on this commercial property then our dealings are over. I promise," he whispered against my lips. Then he cupped my face between his hands and brushed my mouth tenderly with his. I wanted to believe him, but something in my gut made that impossible. I'd seen the picture of the two of them that screamed there was more than friendship going on between them.

Dereon's cell phone started vibrating and I glanced down at his pocket, then back up at his face. When he removed it from his pocket and looked down at the screen I could tell by his expression it was her.

"Sorry, but I don't believe in sharing," I said with as much composure as I could muster, then with a final glance I turned on my heels and walked out of the house.

TWENTY-EIGHT

"Here you go, all polished and pretty just like you asked," Tamara sang merrily as she handed me Grandma Celeste's locket. Then she plopped down on the couch beside me.

I gazed down at it with tears in my eyes as I looked inside at the picture of her and Grandpa. It was timeless. "Finally," I whispered. The family heirloom meant more to me than any pair of designer shoes in my closet.

She grinned at me. "Hey, we had a deal and you earned it. Although I'd planned on giving it to you anyway for Christmas."

"What?" I gasped incredulously.

She roared with laughter. "I'm serious. Hell, you love that thing more than you love me."

"I do not," I quickly denied with a chuckle.

"Yes, you do. And I know the locket should have gone to you all along, but I figured if that was a way to get you to open up your eyes, then I'd milk it for all it was worth." She planted a hand on her stomach and caressed it lovingly.

"Thanks. I do appreciate your making me see outside the box. If it hadn't been for you I'd never have given Dereon a chance," I said as I rubbed my fingers across the antique locket. I undid the clasp and within seconds it was hanging on my neck. Closing my eyes, I took a deep breath, and as crazy as it sounded I suddenly felt the warmth of my grandmother's arms surrounding me.

"Why do you look so sad?"

My eyelids fluttered open. "Do I?" At her nod, I shrugged. "I don't know. I guess the relationship was doomed from the beginning. We're just two different people."

"You're not as different as you think," Tamara pointed out. "Goodness, I still haven't met this gorgeous man, but he's definitely stirring up enough to have Aunt Jeanna call Daddy and ask him to call and talk some sense in you."

That figured. "And what did he say?"

"He told her you were just as pig-headed as I was. Hell, he couldn't do anything to stop me, so what made her think he could talk some sense into you?"

I shook my head, although I was not at all surprised by my mother's behavior. She just didn't get it. But to tell you the truth, I wasn't that much better. I no longer could blame her for the mistakes in my life. The only one responsible for my actions was me.

I drew my knees to my chest and told Tamara about what had happened the last few weeks with Jeanna and Portia. She shook her head and interrupted a few times, but wasn't all that surprised. Then I talked about finally seeing my daddy and our willingness to both start fresh. Finally, I swallowed my pride and told her about Dereon, the man, the mystery, and the woman in the photo.

After a moment Tamara blew out a long breath. "I'll admit having a little mystery is what made the man so sexy, but I guess that *is* taking it a bit too far."

Thank goodness she agreed. For a second I thought maybe I was overreacting. "I just don't get it."

Tamara leaned in close for a moment and looked serious. "Do you think he might be doing something illegal?"When she said the word out loud her eyes grew round.

I immediately shook my head. "I don't think so." Even though I had no idea why he was spending time with Milagros, in my heart I knew he wasn't involved in any house flipping scheme. So what wasn't he telling me?

Amber eyes probed me. "Have you talked to him since you confronted him?"

Shaking my head, I replied, "No. He's been calling, but I've been blowing him off. I just need some time to think. I can't understand why he won't just be honest with me."

Tamara held my gaze for a long moment. "If you love him then you're supposed to trust him."

I was starting to think that maybe I didn't love him enough. "I better get out of here. We've got a big event this weekend and I've still got a million things to do if I'm going to be ready."

She gave a dismissive wave. "It'll be a piece of cake for you. Ha! No pun intended."

I rose and gave her a big kiss, then headed out to my car. Reaching into my purse I retrieved my phone and saw I'd had another missed call from Dereon. I missed him and wanted so badly to talk to him, but not yet. Next weekend was his parents' party, and that would be soon enough.

TWENTY-NINE

"I think tonight's a hit."

I looked up from the table and gazed over at Claudia and grinned, even though my heart wasn't in it. "Yes, I think we did a magnificent job."

I surveyed the crowd on the main deck. Employees and invited guests in beautiful gowns and tuxedoes were laughing and drinking. Piano music was being performed down below by a wonderful up-and-coming artist who reminded me so much of John Legend. The servers we'd hired glided through the crowd with trays of sweet decadents and tall flutes filled with dessert wine.

It was a joyous occasion. The awards ceremony had been beautiful. The mayor gave a beautiful speech , personally recognizing ten local heroes for their selfless acts of heroism. By the time he'd shared the story of the bus driver who'd risked his own life by rushing out into the street to save a toddler who had run out in the middle of rush hour traffic, there wasn't a dry eye onboard.

"Tonight we've rubbed elbows with the crème de la crème," Claudia commented as her eyes traveled through the crowd. "I've gotten several compliments on my sugar display and I've handed out every last one of my business card to some of the most prominent members of the community."

That meant more business for us. One couldn't be anything but happy about that, except I was miserable without Dereon.

"How much longer before we leave the dock?" I asked.

"Claudia glanced down at the slim watch on her arm. "Thirty minutes and counting," she said with a dreamy smile. The yacht was schedule for a one-hour cruise along the Mississippi River, scheduled for after dessert. The honey brown beauty sighed dramatically. "All I need is a date and this night would be perfect."

"Why don't you give Maximilian a call? I'm sure he'd love to take you out," I teased.

"That man can't take my temperature!" she fumed. "I still can't believe he was trying to ask me out when he has a baby on the way. Bastard," she said, and mumbled some other choice words under her breath. Ever since that afternoon she had been ranting and raving nonstop about his baby mama drama. Even though I hadn't had a chance to talk to him personally, there was no mistaking the chemistry between the two of them from the window.

"Maybe it isn't Max's baby," I said with an innocent shrug.

"And maybe Dereon *really* isn't involved with that real estate agent."

"Some days I hate you," I retorted with a playful pout. Claudia and I exchanged laughter and then she floated through the crowd to check on the staff.

With everything appearing to be under control, I moved over to the railing and stared out into the water. It was a beautiful moonlit night and the temperature outside was perfect. I closed my eyes and inhaled the fresh clean air, hoping to clear my mind.

Ever since I'd confronted Dereon, things had been very different between us. After I had left Tamara's house on Thursday, I'd finally answered the phone, but something was missing. As much as I loved him, I knew I deserved more. So much more. Which was why I hadn't accepted any of his calls since then. Unless Dereon trusted me enough to be honest, I had every intention of ending the relationship.

"Now why is my little girl looking so sad?"

My head whipped around to see my father walking toward me. "Daddy!" I exclaimed "What are you doing here? I-I thought you went back to Miami." I was stunned and surprised, yet I hurried over and wrapped my arms around his neck and planted a quick kiss to his prickly cheek.

"I did go home, but I flew in tonight so I could see my little girl at work. Sorry I'm late. My plane was delayed."

We'd had dinner on Wednesday and when I had told him about the contract and the five-hundred dollar tickets to the event, I had never expected him to show up. He looked so handsome standing there in a tuxedo. "I'm so glad you came." I was so overwhelmed by emotion I didn't even bother wiping away the tears spilling from my eyes.

Smiling, he touched my face and brushed the tears away. "Seeing you makes this the best five hundred dollars I've ever spent."

I brushed my problems aside and focused on the man standing right in front of me. My father.

I took him down to the galley where there was dinner still left. He sampled every single dish Claudia and I had created, and with every *hmmm* and *ahhh*, pride pulsed through my veins. While he ate we talked and laughed, and for awhile I forgot all about my broken heart.

By the time we made it back on the main deck so I could check on things, the yacht was slowly pulling away from the dock and most of the guests were already dancing. Claudia was in the corner handing the staff trays of coffee to be served. As I watched Claudia in her element I heaved a deep sigh. This was supposed to be the most important night of our career, yet as much as I tried I was unable to bask in the glow of our success. Instead, I enviously watched the couples dancing and wished I too was an invited guest with a date for the evening. What could be more romantic than being wrapped in the arms of the man you loved?

"Okay, Chris. Tell me what's bothering you."

I startled, then blinked. I was so caught up in my pity party I had almost forgotten my father beside me. "I've got man problems," I replied, and we began strolling around the deck.

Carlos nodded, wearing a sympathetic smile. "Well, why don't you tell your old man all about it? I've been told I'm a good listener."

Smiling, I crossed my arms against my white ruffled blouse and heaved a shaky breath. "He's special … or at least I thought he was. He's different, ordinary yet extraordinary, and Jeanna hates him."

"Then I like him already," Carlos replied, and for the first time in days I had my first real laugh. "Come on." He pointed toward the dessert table. "Show me which of those delicious-looking goodies you're responsible for, then I'll get us both a seat and we can talk."

"I'd like that." It felt good having a man I could talk to. What was even better was knowing I had my father in my life.

DEREON

I made a right turn at the next corner and took my eyes off the road long enough to reach down for my cell phone and hit number one on my speed dial.

"C'mon Christy … pick up," I muttered under my breath and I hoped by some chance she'd take pity on a brotha and finally answer the phone. But by the time her voicemail picked up and I heard the soft sultry voice telling me to leave a message at the beep, I knew it wasn't happening.

"Damn!" I ended the call and tossed the phone onto the passenger seat. Christina was royally pissed at me.

Not that I blamed her.

After two days of refusing my calls and rejecting me when I showed up at her doorstep, it was obvious I had a lot of sucking up to do. And as much as I wanted to toss that woman over my shoulder and lock her in my bedroom and make love to her until she was screaming my name, straightening out our relationship would have to wait until after I'd finalized the closing of the commercial property and I had a beautiful check in my hand.

I glanced over in time to see *The Law Offices of Parker and Stephenson* to my right. I slammed on my brakes and quickly pulled into the small parking lot before a gray Altima rear-ended my ass. "Damn, Dee. Stay focused," I said aloud. I was too close to succeeding to start screwing up now.

I parked at the far end of the lot, then killed the engine and leaned my head back against the headrest and closed my eyes. As soon as I did, all I could think about was Christina's sexy ass. That chick was like no one I'd ever had the pleasure of being with. She was fine, feisty as hell and had a mind of her own, and I fell in love with every bougie hair on her body. The second I'd stepped inside her business she nearly brought a brotha to his knees. I knew I wasn't going to let anything stand in the way of me having her in my life, but I just hadn't realized how much work I had cut out for me.

The first task had been bringing Ms. *High Maintenance* down a few pegs so we'd be on an even playing field. I had always loved a challenge, and she had been my biggest yet. It had been worth every agonizing moment. I fell in love with her hard and fast. My boys might call me soft and a punk, but I didn't care. I knew she was the one I wanted to spend the rest of my life with. I just needed her to trust me and believe that what we had was real.

But she seemed to have a problem with that. That was partly my fault. Christina had been right. I hadn't been completely honest with her about what I was doing or who I really was.

Special Agent Dereon Sanders.

During my seven-year tenure with the FBI, I'd gone undercover numerous times and had been instrumental in putting away several high-profile criminals, including drug dealers, tax evaders and money launderers. But my most recent case had been different.

The feds wanted to bring down Alan Harrison, a mortgage fraudster and the mastermind of one of the biggest house flipping schemes to hit the Midwest. For years he'd been submitting phony mortgage loan applications and sales contracts that had included fake bank statements, fake tax returns, and a false name as owner of the property.

The way it worked was a person would buy a home at a true price then resell it at a price much higher than the property was really worth. False documents were filed convincing the bank to loan money for the higher amount without revealing the first sale at the lower price. The same lawyer oversaw both closings, then split the difference among all the players: the mortgage broker who prepared the fake loan paperwork, the appraiser who inflated the property's worth, the real estate agent who recruited investors, and the lawyer who drew up the illegal documents.

The group was involved in more than twelve million dollars in loans on more than two hundred properties, and the U.S. Attorney's office was determined to bring Alan Harrison in. But in order to do that we had to first uncover all the players involved, with the hopes of bringing down the entire operation. Since I was already flipping houses on the side, I was the perfect agent to send undercover.

For the last six months I'd been tracking Milagros Hernandez. She had been my agent on the house in Kirkwood and on two previous locations that were quick sales. Her signature had been on several of the phony contracts that had been uncovered, and since she was the only woman involved in the scheme I figured there was nothing wrong with using my good looks and charm to my advantage. I slowly gained her trust by wining and dining her and faking interest in taking our relationship to the next level. Two months ago, over drinks, she had hinted to me of a way e to make even more money flipping houses. It didn't take me long to understand that it was her job to recruit buyers for the scheme.

Before meeting Christina I'd had no problem keeping my personal and professional life separate. While undercover my disguise had to be that I was single and available, especially for someone who was possessive like Milagros. Even though she and I had never been intimate, the last thing I wanted was to cause suspicion. However, I found I couldn't think straight around Christina. She was my heaven, and there wasn't an inch of her body I hadn't kissed or caressed in my determination to stake my claim. I couldn't keep my distance and needed to see and be with her so much I'd started to lose focus. I'd had no choice but to pull back slightly. I wanted so badly to tell her who I was and what I was doing, but I couldn't take the chance of Milagros finding out. When she'd spotted the two of us at the movie theater, I'd feared she would back out of the deal. So I had to make myself more accessible to Milagros because I knew it would soon be all over.

I opened my eyes long enough to glance down at my wristwatch. Six-fifty. Ten minutes before show time. Yesterday I had closed on a large piece of commercial property appraised at a quarter of a million dollars that—with the help of false documentation—had been resold a couple of hours ago for more than three-hundred-and-seventy-five thousand. Milagros, Alan and several others would be inside the law office, ready to pop open the champagne. Little did they know that the second I stepped out of the office with check in hand, FBI agents would storm the building, while other agents would be sent to pick up the other players involved.

As soon as the entire ring was behind bars, I'd climb into my SUV and go over to claim what was mine. No was not even an option. Christina belonged to me and there wasn't a damn thing she could do about it.

Christy, I'm coming for you.

I pulled the key out of the ignition and climbed out of the car, then headed toward the front of the dark brick building. My eyes swept both directions in the street. There were agents posted at every corner just waiting for the signal from me.

As I moved through the double doors of the building I caught movement out of the corner of my left eye.

"Hey, Dereon."

I turned with a greeting on my tongue and found a Glock pointing in my direction. "What the …?" Before I could react a sharp pain ripped through me and everything went black.

THIRTY

I pulled a breakfast casserole out of the oven and a slow smile curved my mouth. "Perfect."

"It smells heavenly," Claudia commented without looking up from the table where she was icing two dozen homemade cinnamon rolls.

"It better be, because we definitely don't have enough time for me to bake another." The way I'd been messing up orders lately, it was a wonder we hadn't lost any of our clients.

I carried the casserole layered with plenty of sausage and mushrooms over to the island and lowered it inside the cardboard box alongside the other, then glanced around, making sure I wasn't forgetting something. "You about ready to go?" I asked.

"Just about. Why don't you finish boxing the muffins?"

"Got it."

I moved over to the end of the table where there were two dozen assorted fresh baked muffins: blueberry, bran and apple cinnamon. I reached for a medium box with a lid and started filling it with the delicious treats. They were one of Claudia's specialties, sinfully rich and gourmet. By the time I had packed the last one, I heard a tap at the kitchen door. Looking up, I found Mia standing there.

"We have a visitor," she sang, then stepped aside so our mystery guest could enter. As soon as Maximilian stepped into the kitchen Claudia almost dropped the pan of cinnamon rolls onto the floor.

"Max," I announced, clearly surprised to see him.

Claudia heaved a bored sigh. "What do you want?"

He gave her a half smile, then drew in a deep shaky breath as he started toward us. "I need to talk to Christina."

Max had a look that said something was heavy on his mind. I suddenly had an uneasy feeling. "Max … w-what's wrong?"

Silently he walked across the kitchen to where we were standing and loomed over us, making the room feel smaller.

"Don't just stand there. Talk!" Claudia commanded, with a hand planted to her waist.

Max raised a brow at her and then his eyes traveled to mine. The second I met his intense gaze a chill swept over me.

"Christina, have you talked to Dereon?" he asked.

I gave a pained frown. I'd spent the last few days ignoring his calls. "No, not in a few days, why?"

He hesitated a second before saying, "He's been shot."

"Shot!" I gasped.

"Oh, my goodness!" Claudia cried in horror.

"So he really was doing illegal shit!" Mia exclaimed.

Max's head whipped around and he looked a little confused. "Illegal? What the hell gave you that idea?"

"Please, everyone be quiet!" I cried, waving my hands frantically. "Max, what happened? How … ?" I swallowed, blinking back tears. There were so many things going through my head, but I didn't want to hear anything but the truth.

He took a deep breath. "Christina, Dee's FBI."

"FBI!" the three of us said in unison.

Max nodded. "He's been undercover for months, working on something he couldn't talk about."

"FBI?" I started trembling, because nothing made sense. I didn't want to think the worst, but if … if I didn't get a chance to talk to him, I wouldn't ever forgive myself. "How is he? W-What happened?"

"His mother called me this morning and told me he was brought into the emergency room last night and immediately went into surgery. He was moved from the ICU this morning and onto one of the medical floors. Mama Sanders assured me he gonna be just fine."

"Oh, thank god!" Tears well in my eyes. I shook my head free of all of the terrible thoughts invading my head.

"I'm on my way to the hospital to see him. You wanna ride with me?"

Quickly, I removed my apron. "Yes, I … Oh, no! Wait! We have to deliver these boxes and I—"

Claudia planted a gentle hand to my shoulder. "Don't you worry about that. Mia can come and help me."

"Absolutely," she chimed in. "We can handle it."

My best friend wrapped her arms around me and squeezed tight as she whispered, "Look, I got this. You just go and be with your man."

Tears were running down my cheeks when I pulled back and mouthed, "Thank you."

Claudia released me, then swung around and glared in Max's direction. "You make sure you take care of my girl."

Max raised one thick brow in amused challenged. "If I do, will you let me take you to dinner?"

Her cheeks became flushed before she grumbled, "Whatever," and brushed past him. "Come on, Mia, help me load my car."

Our assistant looked confused as she grabbed one of the two boxes and followed Claudia out of the kitchen. I turned and noticed the direction of Max's eyes as he watched the sway of Claudia's hips with lazy indulgence. If I hadn't been so worried about Dereon I would have teased him about his obvious attraction. But all I wanted to do was get to him as fast as possible. There was so much I still needed to know about Dereon, yet I loved him more knowing there was so much more to that complex man who had stolen my heart. That more being … there was an explanation for his weird behavior and his alleged involvement with Milagros. If he was undercover then that explained why he had been acting so mysteriously. My heart constricted. If only I had listened and had had faith in him and our relationship. Now I just needed to get to him as fast as I could and let him know how much he meant to me before it was too late.

* * *

As soon as the clerk at the information desk in the main lobby told us which room Dereon was in, I hurried down the hall toward the elevator, walking a few steps ahead of Max.

"Slow down before you have an accident," he chuckled low and soft.

"Sorry," I replied and slowed my steps as I stepped over the cord of a large piece of equipment in the middle of the hallway. I waited until Max was walking beside me before I glanced up at him and said, "Thank you so much for coming by to tell me."

He pushed the button for the elevator. "Hey, you're all Dee talks about. The second his mama called to tell me he was in the hospital, I figured he'd want you here."

My heart sang, hearing he had been talking about me. But I felt so guilty. Dereon had been calling me and I'd refused to answer the phone. Was he calling to finally tell me what was going on? I guess if I had taken the call I would have known the answer. Now I could only hope he would forgive me for not being there when he needed me most.

I stood there staring at the elevator, thinking how ridiculous I had been. I knew all along he was a good man, which was why I defended him against my family, yet I had taken one look at that picture of him and Milagros and assumed the worse. *What's wrong with me?* Dereon was right. From the start I was prepared to accept the worse.

We stepped inside the empty car and I pushed the button. I glanced over at Maximilian and admired his chiseled body and boyish grin. No wonder Claudia couldn't stop talking about him, even it was nothing worth repeating.

"Claudia tells me you have a baby on the way. Congratulations."

I didn't miss the scowl on his face. "I told your girl that's *not* my baby. My ex just wants it to be mine so she can hold onto me. That ain't happening," he hissed bitterly.

"Meaning … "

"Meaning, she'd been messing around on me since day one. I was just too stupid to realize it. However, I don't care how drunk I was, I *always* wrap it up." He winked and I couldn't help grinning as we stepped off the elevator. Maybe there was hope for Max and Claudia after all.

We moved down the hall and the smell of antiseptics and sickness plagued my gut. All that equipment beeping and call buttons going off were enough to make me want to turn and run. I'd never liked hospitals. When we reached 4W13, my feet froze and I halted outside the door.

"Are you okay?" Max asked, placing a gentle hand to my forearm.

I took several deep breaths, then nodded. "Yes, I think so."

"C'mon, it'll be fine." Still holding onto my arm, he led me inside the room. I guess he was afraid I might faint or something. The white curtain was drawn. Max peeped behind it then pulled it back so we could step inside.

Dereon was lying in the bed, eyes closed, with a big bandage over his left shoulder. An elderly couple was standing by the side of his bed. I gasped at the sight of his lifeless body.

"Is he okay?" I asked.

The woman turned and smiled, eyes crinkling. "Yes, they gave him something for pain so he's been drifting in and out." I released a heavy sigh of relief and moved closer and took his hand in mine. "Lucky for him the bullet went straight through the shoulder," she quickly reassured me.

Staring down at his helpless face, tears filled my eyes again. Leaning close to his ear, I whispered raggedly, "Dereon, please forgive me for not trusting you."

"Max, which one of your girlfriends is this?" I heard the man asked. I looked up and gave a shy smile.

"Why it gotta be like that?" Max said with a chuckle, and shook his head. "Sorry, but this one belongs to your son."

Blinking, I glanced from one to the other. "Oh, I'm so sorry. I didn't know you were his parents. Pleasure meeting you both." I reached over and offered each of them my hand. Mrs. Sanders pulled me against her bosom.

"Chile, we hug in this family," she replied, then released me. "And you must be Christina. We've heard so much about you."

"Thank you."

"Well, you sure are pretty," Mr. Sanders complimented, his golden eyes twinkling. "My boy says you're one helluva cook."

I giggled. "I try."

Smiling, he steepled his fingers atop his round abdomen. "Well we're looking forward to grubbing next weekend at this shindig Dee insists on giving us." I heard the quiet pride in his voice.

"You know you can't wait to shake a leg on the dance floor!" Max chuckled. "Christina, you have to watch that one. He used to be in a singing group back in the day."

I don't know why I hadn't recognized the resemblance before. Mr. Sanders was tall with a medium build and a head full of salt-and-pepper curls. They had identical eyes. His mother must have felt the same way when she first laid eyes on her husband as I had when I first saw her son. She was a beautiful petite woman with large brown eyes. If it hadn't been for the small wrinkles around her eyes, I would never had guessed she had a thirty-year-old son. A short tapered cut fit her smooth mahogany face perfectly.

I took a seat on the side of the bed and stroked Dereon's hand, while his father started reminiscing about his nightclub performing days. His wife cut in several times to correct him. I chuckled at the two. It was clear they were truly in love.

"Can you keep it down? I'm tryna sleep," Dereon grumbled and stirred slightly.

Mrs. Sanders clapped her hands together merrily. "Looks like my baby is waking up."

I squeezed his hand and shifted on the bed so he could see me. "Dereon."

"Hey, baby," he replied in a sleepy voice. I released a heavy sigh of relief and pressed my lips to his and said a silent prayer. That was something I didn't do enough of but definitely needed to start considering doing more.

Max took the subtle hint. "Why don't we give these two a few moments alone?" he suggested, and Dereon's parents agreed.

"We're going down to the cafeteria," Mrs. Sanders said. She met my gaze, smiled and fluttered her fingers in a wave.

When we were alone, I pushed out a long exasperated breath and leveled Dereon with a stern look. "Dereon, what's going on? Max said you're with the FBI. Why is it I didn't find out until after you'd been shot?"

"Luckily the bullet didn't hit anything important." He reached up and removed the top of his gown so I could get a closer look at the bandage at his shoulder. "See? Nothing to get excited about."

"What do you mean nothing to get excited about? You've been lying to me all this time. I thought you flipped houses."

"I do. On the side. But I'm also a special agent for the FBI. Six months ago I went undercover to bring down a local real estate scam."

I got comfortable on the bed beside him and listened to him tell me everything that wasn't classified information, clearing up every doubt I'd had in my mind about us. All those text messages and racing off was because he'd been working on the case. "I was going to collect my cut for the scam when the mortgage broker caught me from behind and shot me."

I shook my head in disbelief. It was so unreal. "But why?"

"Why else? He had a million-dollar business he wasn't ready to give up," he explained. "I guess he found out I was undercover."

"Oh, thank goodness you're okay! All this time I was thinking the worst, that you were involved in the scam or were married or you were some kind of drug dealer."

"You watch too many movies," he chuckled and then flinched with pain. "Ouch!"

"Ha! That's what you get for laughing at me," I teased.

Dereon grinned sheepishly. "C'mere and give your man a kiss."

My heart thudded at the deep timbre of his voice. I leaned down and pressed my lips to his and sighed when we made contact. "I'm so sorry for not trusting you."

"You know I love you, right?" A devilish grin I was dying to devour played on his lips.

"I do now."

"Then that's all that matters," he said. His expression sobered. "You just don't know how many times I wanted to tell you what I was doing, but I couldn't."

I placed my hand on his chest. I could feel the steady heartbeat, the lift of his hardened chest with every breath. "I understand that now. Just don't ever scare me like that again."

"I'll try not to." I kissed him again and stared into those golden eyes. "I love you," I whispered against his nose.

"Say my name, Christy." His voice dipped low, and there was no mistaking the flare of hungry in his golden eyes. "I love when you say my name."

My belly quivered. "I love you, Dereon Sanders."

"And I love you, Christina Holloway."

THIRTY-ONE

I glanced around the banquet room that had been beautifully decorated with gold streamers and photos of the happy couple over the years. They had been blown up to poster size and were on easels throughout the room. Tables were decorated with fine linen, and vases with candles inside were the centerpieces. Dereon said he wanted something classy and that's exactly what he got.

The women were elegantly dressed in long formal gowns and the men wore tuxedos. It was a wonderful night, and I was glad to be there. Dereon had insisted that we hire enough workers so Claudia and I could enjoy the party. Of course, how could I not work when it was my food being served?

"What are you doing?"

I jumped and swung around to find Dereon staring down at me. My pulse hammered at the base of my throat. "I was just checking to see if we needed to bring out another pan of potatoes," I explained.

He frowned. "I think the staff is doing just fine without your help."

"But—"

"No buts." His voice was a deep husky rumble. He practically dragged me out onto the dance floor. Giggling, I followed his lead. Once there I gingerly draped my arms around his neck. He looked amazing in an expensive black suit with a crisp white shirt and blue-and-black tie. That man definitely knew how to make anything look good.

"How are you feeling?" I asked, concerned.

"Horny. Ready to take you home and make love to you," he growled, eyes gleaming with barely restrained lust.

"Your doctor said—"

"To hell with what the doctor said. Nothing's stopping me from making love to you tonight. So get ready to take them panties off."

Framing my face between his hands, he pressed his lips to my forehead, cheek and nose before possessively claiming my lips. I was trembling at the tenderness in his touch. I flung my arms around him and returned his kiss hungrily, seeking the heat and the taste of champagne on his breath. He slipped inside, his tongue exploring my mouth with skill and finesse. As he deepened the kiss, Dereon's hand caressed my curves, traveling down my waist and round my hips, finally settling at my ass, where he squeezed and drew me closer, making sure I knew he was aroused. A moan escaped my lips. My breasts throbbed and there was a deep ache between my thighs. I rose on tiptoe and leaned in until my apex was cradling his rock-hard bulge. My libido was raging. I had been too long without this man.

"Get a room!" someone yelled from across the room.

I tore my mouth away, giggling bashfully. For a moment I'd forgotten where we were. Dereon winked and pulled me back into his arms and I swayed my hips again to the beat of the music. He kept one hand at my back and the other low at my waist. I closed my eyes and enjoyed being held in the circle of his strong arms.

"This is really nice," I said.

"Yeah, it is, and my parents really seem to be having a ball," he murmured, his cheek resting on top of my head. "Babe, thanks for not tripping when my cousin Henrietta snuck in that pot of collard greens."

I muffled a smile against him. "You're welcome."

Dereon pulled me even closer until our thighs brushed and I rested my head at his shoulder. I sighed deeply.

"Jeanna called. She invited us to dinner next weekend. I wouldn't blame you if you didn't want to go. But I think it's her way of apologizing."

He chuckled. "I wouldn't miss it for the world."

Dereon was such a good man. How did I get to be so lucky? I don't know, but I had every intention of showing him how much I appreciated having him in my life.

"Fifty years is a *long* time to be with one man."

"I know. I couldn't imagine wasting all that time with *one* woman."

My head snapped up and I saw the laughter burning in his eyes. "You're pushing your luck."

Dereon tossed his head back with hearty laughter, then kissed my lips. "How about this for starters?" He reached inside his breast pocket and held up a key.

My brown eyes probed his. "What's that for?"

He winked. "The house in Kirkwood. Since you loved it so much I decided not to flip it, but keep it … for us."

My heart thundered beneath my breasts. Did he say *us*?

Dereon held my gaze for a long, charged moment. "Tell me you love me and someday you want to celebrate fifty years with me."

I stared at him, my insides tingling with excitement. "I don't know. That's a long time to spend with one man," I teased. "Maybe we should try living together first."

"I don't want a woman to live with. I want a woman I can't live without."

His warm smile wrapped around me like a cozy blanket. "Anyone ever tell you you have a way with words?"

Dereon gazed deep into my eyes and whispered, "Yeah, but I don't mind hearing it again."

Crushing my mouth to his, I savored the moment. There was no question in my mind. I knew where I belonged—right here in his arms.

"Man, I was serious. The two of you need to get a room."

My eyes snapped open just as an attractive man punched Dereon playfully on the arm and walked away.

"Who was that?" I asked curiously.

"That's my cousin, Deion."

I nodded. Then his words registered and I suddenly stopped dancing. "Deion? Deion?" He nodded and my head whipped to the right in time to get a closer look at the hall of famer. "Oh, my God. You're sure that's the same Deion I'm thinking about?"

He chuckled. "Yeah, we get that all the time. C'mon, let me introduce you." Dereon draped an arm loosely around my waist and steered me off the dance floor. "Just think. You can tell Jeanna *all* about him at dinner and give her something to brag about."

I started giggled. He seemed to already have my mother figured out. "Oh, yeah. This just might get you invited back for Thanksgiving dinner."

Dereon roared with laughter. Life together was going to be quite interesting. And I wouldn't have it any other way.

Other Books by Angie Daniels

DAFINA/KENSINGTON PUBLISHING

When It Rains
Love Uncovered
When I First Saw You
In the Company of My Sistahs
Trouble Loves Company
Careful of the Company You Keep
Feinin' (Big Spankable Asses Anthology)

GENESIS PRESS

Intimate Intentions
Hart & Soul
Time is of the Essence
A Will to Love

HARLEQUIN/KIMANI ROMANCE

Endless Enchantment
Destiny In Disguise
The Second Time Around
The Playboy's Proposition
The Player's Proposal
For You I Do
Before I Let You Go

CARAMEL KISSES PUBLISHING

In Her Neighbor's Bed
Tease
Show Me
Say My Name
Every Second Counts

ABOUT THE AUTHOR

Angie Daniels has released over two dozen novels. She has won numerous awards including a Romantic Times *Reviewers' Choice* Award for *When it Rains*, and an Emma Award in the category of Best Steamy Romance, for *A Delight Before Christmas*. She began her road to publication in 2001 when she was offered a four-book deal with Genesis Press. In 2002, she signed with BET/ Arabesque which was purchased by Harlequin/Kimani Romance in 2005. Angie joined Kensington Publishing in 2003. She has a bachelor's degree in Business Administration from Columbia College, and a Master's in Human Resources Management. For more information about upcoming releases, and to connect with Angie on facebook, please visit her website at www.angiedaniels.com.

Made in the USA
Lexington, KY
27 November 2012